P9-CFJ-247

WEST GA REG LIB SYS
Neva Lomason
Memorial Library

DREAM
A LITTLE
DREAM

TOR BOOKS BY PIERS ANTHONY
Alien Plot
Anthonology
But What of Earth?
Demons Don't Dream
Faun & Games
Geis of the Gargoyle
Ghost
Harpy Thyme
Hasan
Hope of Earth
Isle of Woman
Letters to Jenny
Prostho Plus
Race Against Time
Roc and a Hard Place
Shade of the Tree
Shame of Man
Steppe
Triple Detente
Yon Ill Wind
Zombie Lover

WITH ROBERT E. MARGROFF:
Dragon's Gold
Serpent's Silver
Chimaera's Copper
Mouvar's Magic
Orc's Opal
The E.S.P. Worm
The Ring

WITH FRANCES HALL:
Pretender

WITH RICHARD GILLIAM:
Tales from the Great Turtle (Anthology)

WITH ALFRED TELLA:
The Willing Spirit

WITH JAMES RICHEY AND ALAN RIGGS:
Quest for the Fallen Star

WITH JULIE BRADY:
Dream a Little Dream

DREAM A LITTLE DREAM

Piers Anthony
&
Julie Brady

A Tom Doherty Associates Book/New York

This is a work of fiction. All the characters and events portrayed in this novel are either fictitious or are used fictitiously.

DREAM A LITTLE DREAM

Copyright © 1999 by Piers Anthony Jacob and Julie Brady

All rights reserved, including the right to reproduce this book, or portions thereof, in any form.

This book is printed on acid-free paper.

A Tor Book
Published by Tom Doherty Associates, Inc.
175 Fifth Avenue
New York, NY 10010

Tor Books on the World Wide Web:
http://www.tor.com

Tor® is a registered trademark of Tom Doherty Associates, Inc.

Book design by Jennifer Ann Daddio

Library of Congress Cataloging-in-Publication Data

Anthony, Piers.
    Dream a little dream / Piers Anthony & Julie Brady.—1st ed.
        p.   cm.
    ISBN 0-312-86466-3 (alk. paper)
    I. Brady, Julie.   II. Title.
PS3551.N73D74   1999
813'.54—dc21   98-46147
                                                      CIP

First Edition: January 1999

Printed in the United States of America

0 9 8 7 6 5 4 3 2 1

To the true dreamers and Ligeias
who hang on to life by a thread.
Please don't give up your dreams.
You may one day find a reason for hanging on.

CONTENTS

DREAM
A LITTLE
DREAM

1

NOLA

Nola lay facedown on her bed, staring at the knife in her hand. Its steel blade shone in her face. She had honed its edge every night, for the past year and a half, until she could use it to shave the fuzz from the back of her hand. She knew it would cut her flesh like butter.

Her eyes were filled with stinging tears and her throat still throbbed. This was the second time that John had choked her until she had blacked out.

He had come home four hours late, as usual, and complained that she had not kept his dinner warm. This being their second year as a couple, she had decided to make a special meal for him and decorate the apartment with candles. He had promised to be home on time for her surprise.

Nine o'clock came and went. Nola turned down the oven and sat at the table. She straightened the napkins and blew out the candles. She had hoped that just once he would surprise her by coming home on time and give her a big hug and kiss and say "I love you." But the only time he kissed her anymore was when they were going to make love.

Nola choked on the thought, *make love*. They never made love anymore. That had stopped the middle of the first year. They didn't even have sex. To her, it was a chore. Something that had to be done, but not enjoyed. If she didn't agree to do it, she was forced to, and that often led to injury and doctor bills—and worse, guilt and anger. He had loved her once; she was sure of that. Somewhere deep inside, she was always hoping that he would change, that if she loved him enough her love would make him realize that he loved her still. She had seen this happen to the women on TV. She remembered wondering why these women would stay with abusive men. The women knew that they could be seriously injured or killed, yet they remained. Why?

Now she knew. It was something that just couldn't be explained. It was like living in a prison that she had built herself, yet leaving the security of the prison meant death. She could never quite bring herself to leave.

Now, she was at a point of despair. It was rare when John came home at all at night. She suspected he was sleeping with someone else, but she could never confront him about it. That would surely cause him to beat her. Again.

She had spent a day at the doctor's last week, being treated for an infection that she was sure John had given her. She often found pieces of paper in his pockets with girls' numbers on them.

This night he had come home not just hours late for her surprise; he was drunk and crazy as well. He threw his food on the floor and screamed at her. She told him that she was worried because he had promised to be home on time and he was late. She realized that when she said she was worried, he would take that to mean she was accusing him of cheating.

He got that look. That look of evil that burned into her memory and would remain there forever. He lunged at her, his huge hands grasping her neck. He squeezed tightly, staring at her all the while with angry, dead eyes. She clawed his wrists, unable to draw breath, until she became asphyxiated and passed out. He wouldn't come home for a week now. She always had to track him down and bring him home. He always told her he ran away because he felt guilty about hurting her. She knew in her heart that this was a lie. He ran away, hoping that he had succeeded in killing her, and he didn't want to be found at the scene of her death.

Well, maybe this time she would oblige him. Nola sat up, putting the tip of the knife to her wrist. She pushed down until she felt the pain of slight penetration and dragged the blade across. The cut was not deep and did not bleed much, but she liked to watch it ooze. She squeezed her fist and relaxed, drawing more blood to the cut.

Death fascinated her. She thought constantly about being dead. What bliss it must be! To have no thoughts, to have no pain or heartache. Death would finally let her have the peace she craved so much.

There was only one thing that kept her from cutting deeply. The thing that would often cross her mind when things were at their worst.

If she died, she would lose the one thing in her life that she loved more than anything else: her dreams. Not her ambition-type dreams, but the dreams she experienced when she slept. The wonderful escape from reality, her one tie to sanity and to life. Dead people didn't dream. She couldn't quite bring herself to lose those dreams, though she could no longer face life.

It would soon be time to make a decision. Should she continue to try to live, even though all of her attempts to do so were bound to fail, or should she let herself go and lose her dreams forever in the process?

She thought of Esprit. His real name was Spirit, but she affectionately called him Esprit. He was as much a part of her as was her soul. *Esprit* meant "spirit" in Latin, but meant "vivacious" in English, and that pretty much described him.

He was her best friend, a piece of her. A huge black creature, half unicorn, half Pegasus or winged horse. He was all black, except for his green eyes. He loved her and took care of her in her dreams.

When she'd have a nightmare about John, Spirit would come flying down from the clouds and come crashing through the window. She'd get on his back and he'd fly her away. She'd look back and see John's disappointed and amazed expression. It filled her with longing.

Most times, he'd fly her to a castle, wherein lived her dream man, Michael. Mich was always glad to see her and he'd comfort her in his warm embrace. He was the only man she could trust with her love. He loved her more than anything in the world. If she killed herself, the dream, and the love, would die with her.

But that was all just dreams. She knew that things were not that way in life. Though her dreams comforted her in the night, she always awoke to a cruel reality, one of abuse and death wishes.

She was faced with the question again. Live or die? Was it time to cut her losses? She wondered what Esprit would want. She thought he would want her to hang on. If she died, so would he, because there would be no one to dream of him then. But it was more than that. They shared everything best friends would share. He was a part of her. He could read her thoughts, emotions, and her pain as sharply as if they were his own, yet he was stronger than she. He would tell her to cheer up. He'd tell her that she had the ability to make her life all that she wished, if she could only discover how.

Nola put the knife aside and went into the bathroom, where she washed the drying blood from her wrist. As she dressed it, she made a decision.

Spirit was right. She had to try; she had to try to do something, to go somewhere. But she was trapped here. She had no other place to go. What could she do? She decided the closest thing to leaving was to take a short vacation. The beach was only a few hours away. She could stay there for a few days. Yes, that would be heaven.

First, she had better go after John.

Nola walked across the street to Chris's apartment. Chris was John's marijuana source. They were good friends.

Chris looked at her. "John hasn't been to see me today."

That was odd. It didn't follow the pattern.

She tried to call him at his home. His mother answered. Nola could hear the disapproval in the woman's voice: she thought Nola was a bad influence on John. She had not heard from him either.

This was downright unusual. She usually found him hiding there. He always felt safest there. Was something wrong, by his twisted definition? No, he must just have found a new hiding place.

Well, she had tried. What more could her conscience ask of her? Her rational mind informed her that she owed John nothing. Too bad she wasn't rational.

She made a call to a hotel that sat right on the beach and had a wonderful view of the waves. She called the bus station and booked a seat.

She had saved some money, by taking bits of the grocery money that John gave her and hiding it away. She would use that for a bus ticket and a night's stay at the beach. She riffled through John's closet looking for the credit card he kept for emergencies. She found it jammed into a coat pocket.

She clutched the card a moment and shivered. John would certainly give her a few more bruises if he found out that she took it. Well, she would just have to make sure he didn't. Good thing she was always home before him. She could easily intercept and dispose of the credit card statement when it came.

Her cat, Kudo, sauntered into the closet and rubbed against her leg. Nola picked her up and kissed her head. "It would be so nice to be you!" she said, putting her down again. "What a life. No one to beat you up, no worries about cooking the food just right. You just eat, sleep and be loved."

She went into the living room and called her friend Lori, asking her to watch Kudo for her. Lori promised she would take good care of her while Nola was away.

Her mother knew nothing of her life and her suicide attempts. Nola preferred never to tell her. It would hurt her too much, and she would never understand why Nola stayed with John. *Nola* didn't really understand that, either.

After the phone call, Nola climbed into bed, with Kudo nestled at her feet. She fell into the welcome arms of her dreams. She didn't know that the world she so wished were real was in dire jeopardy.

In another city, Tina stirred, aware of something. It had bothered her at odd moments in the past few days. Not exactly déjà vu, but an urge that wasn't of the body. There was somewhere she wanted to go, something she wanted to do. Something nice. A friend she wanted to meet, maybe. But she had no idea who, what, or where. Who would want her for a friend, anyway?

Then she saw a car slow, as if its driver was looking for something. There was a prospect. Her fleeting fond awareness faded as she walked toward the car. Another day, another dollar.

2

MICH

King Erik Edward sat on his gold throne wondering what he should do about the new crisis. His crown sat askew on his head, and the way he let his dull brown beard grow made him look like Father Time. His brow was etched with deep furrows as he worried over the problem of the Fren.

The Fren lived north of the Shattered-Glass Glade, near the River of Thought. They lived in an ominous place called the Fren Cliffs. The cliffs were a new addition to the Kafkian landscape, and an unwelcome one. The cliffs were rough and ugly and they marred Kafka's appearance like a great wart on the nose of a goddess.

The Fren were cruel and evil creatures with no positive emotions whatsoever. They cared little for anyone except themselves. Their king, Reility, was crueler than all his minions put together. He had some strange power that Edward was not yet sure of. But he knew Reility was using it for evil.

Reility would send his motley, vicious armies into the wilds of Kafka to crush villages and do what they pleased with those who were unlucky enough to survive his attacks.

Now King Edward had an even bigger problem. The River of Thought was receding from its banks, and Edward knew that Reility was behind it. He also knew that if something wasn't done soon the river would dry up, and that could spell big trouble for Kafka and its neighbor, Earth.

He had never seen Earth, nor had he known anyone else who had. His sorceress, Madrid, knew of it. She had a big picture book with paintings of it. The creatures that lived on it were somehow connected to Kafka, and he knew that if one realm was destroyed, the other would also go.

Edward reached down to stroke his son's pet basilisk, Snort, who raised his scaly chin in response. He stretched his leathery wings and exhaled a little puff of steam. Most basilisks in Kafka could kill with a glance, but Snort had been tamed by his son as a baby and he was as lovable as any grass dragon. In Kafka the distinction between dragons and other reptilian creatures could become fuzzy, and Snort was a good, if ugly, example.

Edward looked across to the entry hall where his guards stood holding their swords.

"Guard!" he called. "Has my son returned yet?"

"I will check, Sire."

One of the guards stepped out of the throne room and called to someone down the hall. Another guard came in, followed by a young man. Snort half crawled, half slithered over to Edward's son and insisted that he be petted. The young man obliged with a vigorous scratch behind an ugly ear.

Edward brushed back the loose folds of his robe and stood up. "Mich," he said, "have you been able to find out anything useful?"

Mich smiled. "Yes. More than I'd hoped. The river isn't drying up. It's being dammed."

"I suspected as much. Is anything being done about it?"

"There is nothing we can do, Father. It's being dammed at its source."

King Edward scratched his beard. At its source? This could be very bad news indeed. No one had ever been to the source or even knew where it was. The river splayed into many different streams in the glade, but no one knew where the water came from. No one, except—

"That's not all," Mich went on. "It is rumored that the dam is being built of dreamstone."

"Dreamstone?" The hairs on King Edward's chin stood on end. "How have the Fren gotten their claws on dreamstone? I have men guarding every deposit in Kafka!" He paused a moment, then doubled his panic attack. "Unless there is a deposit in the cliffs! What'll we do if the Fren are controlling a dreamstone deposit?"

Mich smiled in that unconsciously patronizing way he had. "Don't get so excited, Father; it's only a rumor."

The king regained his composure and cleared his throat. "That may be, but you know how easily rumors turn into fact around here." He sat back down on his throne and smoothed his robes. "The dam must be destroyed."

"But how? We don't know where the source is and even if we did find it, it is impossible for us to destroy, if the rumor is true."

"Impossible for us, yes, but for them, no."

"Them who?"

"Earthling humans."

"Father, what are you saying? That we get an Earthling to destroy it?"

Edward nodded gravely.

Mich looked his father in the eye and squared his jaw. "Yes, Father," he said sarcastically, "that would work. Just let me know when you find out how to reach one."

King Edward rubbed his ear. He loved his son, but from time to time the lad needed to be taken down a peg. "I know how you can find out for yourself."

Mich backed away a few steps and his face became pale. "No, Father, please don't say what I think you're going to say."

Edward smiled. "You can ask—"

"Don't say it!"

"Madrid."

Mich kneeled on the floor and clasped his hands in a dramatic pose. "Please don't send me there! She hates me!"

The king's smile deepened. "Oh, I wouldn't say that, son."

"You know what I mean. She'll try to—to kiss me!"

"Get up, son! It's not that bad! Actually, she's kind of pretty . . ."

Mich gave his father a you've-got-to-be-kidding look.

" . . . if your eyes are closed!" the king finished with a laugh.

Mich knew how his father liked to tease him about Madrid. She was a sorceress who lived in the Mountains of Mangor. She had a very old body, but a vivacious spirit. She also had a thing for young princes, especially Mich. She was a very good person at heart, but one would not know it if one had just met her. She was rude and had a very foul mouth. However, the land of Kafka depended on her advice and help, and therefore always treated her with respect. In order for King Edward to maintain good relations with her, he often sent Mich to visit, and Mich hated every second.

"Son, you know if there was another way to do this, I would gladly do it, but she is the only one in this world who can help us find an Earth person and she is the only one who may have seen the source of the river."

"But, Father, you know she will ask that I keep her company through the night, as payment for her help."

"Yes, I know. But she never harms you and she would never do anything you don't want her to."

"That doesn't stop her from trying," Mich grumbled.

"It is a long way. It would be best if you got a good night's sleep and began your visit to Mangor in the morning."

With that, the conversation ended. Mich hugged his father good night. Snort followed him through the corridor and up the winding stairway to his room.

The next morning, Mich bathed and prepared himself. He bid farewell to his friends and set out on his steed, Heat. He brought with him a three-day ration of food, a lightweight steel sword, and Snort for protection. "You may come in handy if the sorceress tries to go too far," he said.

Snort snorted a ferocious jet of fire, looking outraged. Mich laughed.

Mich urged Heat to go faster and they broke into a trot. The palace stables fell behind. It wasn't until he was some distance from it that he could get the whole castle in view.

It was a large castle in the most extreme way. He, his father, the palace scribe, three cooks, the gardener, the guards, Misty the resident friendly ghost and a few assorted pets were its only inhabitants. They had no choice about its size. It had been built beside the River of Thought, out of dreamstone, at the time he was born, and it had never deteriorated.

The dreamstone walls were of a brownish hue, and they gleamed as if made of glass. Mich knew that dreamstone could be any color. Dreamstone could not be destroyed by any normal means. It was magically hard and could not be crushed, broken or shaped. It was mined from deep beneath the ground in various places. The dreamstone that made this castle had just appeared one day and had been here ever since, forming the perfect fortress.

They rode through the orchards that surrounded the castle. Then they entered the Forest of Imagination, where all sorts of strange creatures lived and worked. It was normally filled with the joyous sounds of birds singing and tree creatures squeaking and chattering. This day, the forest seemed empty and quiet.

As Heat trotted beneath a low-hanging branch, a small bird dropped something on Mich. Luckily, it was a cluster of burrs instead of a dropping. He tried to work them out of his long black hair, but ended up pulling out a few strands.

He looked back, but the bird was gone. He heard a faint sound, something like the babbling or cooing of a baby. He heard some rustling in the brush. Suddenly, Heat reared, slightly opening his wings, and Snort shot a small flame into the air.

"What is it, friend?" Mich asked, patting his steed to calm him down.

I'm not sure. I saw nothing, but I am cut, thought Heat.

Mich looked down. Sure enough, there was a small, blood-streaked wound on Heat's foreleg.

"Do you need any healing spice?"

Of course not! The wound is merely a scratch. I believe I can survive.

Mich reminded himself of how proud an animal Heat was. He had to constantly watch what he said, lest he insult his friend.

Heat could read Mich's mind and feel everything that he felt, and vice versa. Their relationship was one of true friendship. Mich did not think of him as a beast of burden, but as an equal. The only reason Heat let Mich ride on him was because it was logical. They would get to their destination much faster this way than if they were slowed down by his having to walk.

They rode through the morning until Mich and Heat both started to get hungry. Heat drew to a halt at the edge of the Forest of Imagination, where they had lunch. Snort, who had been keeping pace by whomping along behind, slunk off into a thicket to flush out a few creatures. He snapped them up as they ran in his direction. Heat cropped the dry grasses and chewed distastefully.

After a short rest, Mich remounted Heat and they moved on into the forest. Mich hoped the trip would be uneventful. There were many creatures in the forest, some of which could be dangerous.

The forest is quiet. I'm worried, Heat thought to Mich's mind.

"Yes, it is. I'm sure it has something to do with the river. It's been like this ever since the villagers reported the drop in the water level."

If the river runs dry we could all be forgotten. Heat shook his silken mane disdainfully.

It was kind of scary. To be Forgotten was to be dead. No one had ever told Mich what the river had to do with life in Kafka, but he knew that they were somehow connected. If the river went, so would Kafka.

The small group traveled on for two days. Just before nightfall, on the third day, they set up camp at the base of the Mangor Mountains.

The Mangors were a forbidding place. Their charcoal slopes were rough and rugged, as well as steep. It was as if they suddenly shot straight into the air. They would be impossible for any ordinary creature to climb. That is why Madrid lived there: she enjoyed the solitude.

Mich took the last of his food from the bag tied around Heat's neck. He sat on a clump of grass next to Snort, who was already resting. Gentle curls of steam rose from his nostrils as he exhaled.

He put the lucream pastry into his mouth. A loud noise caused him to squish out all the luberries, which splattered onto Snort's nose. Heat reared up, his bright silver hooves flashing red in the sunset.

"What is it?" Mich whispered.

Trolls! Wood Trolls!

Snort sat upright and curled back his lips, showing his dangerous, needle-sharp teeth. Mich stood on guard.

The trolls soon emerged from the surrounding brush. They were about five feet tall. They were stout creatures that hadn't a whit of beauty about them. Their faces were the color and texture of squashed green caterpillars.

There were twelve of the little anal-retentive creatures and the closer they came, the worse the odor. They each carried a torch and a little dagger or a club. At last they stood close to the group, forming a semicircle.

Mich got to his feet. One of the trolls stepped forward and focused his beady black eyes on him. "What are you doing out here, brothher?" it asked.

"Yesss, what?" hissed another troll.

Mich decided to be more polite than these creatures deserved. "None of your business, you putrid ilk, and I am not your brother." Foul language was the only dialect some creatures understood, and wood trolls had the foulest mouths in the forest.

"Oooh, he sspeaks harsshhly to me! What have I done to you to desserve thiss, brother? We only need a favor," the first one said, kneading his hands. The other trolls were crowding in to hear the dialogue better.

"Why would I do you a favor, you vile creature? I wouldn't give you the pleasure of urinating on you, much less helping you."

The troll was undaunted. It looked Mich over from head to toe and did the same to his companions. "Look at thiss, brotherss! A stareless bassilisssk! He'ss no threat!"

The trolls cheered and took turns walking up to Snort and staring him in the face. The basilisk was angered terribly by this treatment. He was very sensitive about his handicap of not being able to kill with a glance. It was the price of being tame. He did have fire, but he knew that if he fired on the ugly green trolls, they would only explode into a noxious gas cloud and the remaining pieces would reconstruct into twice as many new trolls. This was an ability more than one type of creature had.

At last the trolls became bored with this game. They moved on to more entertaining things. "Give usss that sssword, bassstard mann child," one troll said courteously.

"Yesss, you two-legged grub. Givve!" another echoed.

"We neeed a fine weaponn like thhat."

"Nooo!" another troll cried. "Take the flying mucilage factory and do away with the lizzzard!"

Mich grew annoyed. He'd had just about enough. He unsheathed his saber and brought it to bear on the throat of the first troll. "Touch either, and you will die." When that didn't faze them, he added: "Slowly." The trolls knew what would happen if Mich tried to cut them, but nevertheless they did feel pain and did not enjoy being cut to ribbons. Slow death meant that their reconstitution and revenge would be agonizingly delayed. They especially hated being threatened, believing that that should be a one-way process.

One of the trolls pounced on him, knocking his sword away, while another screamed, "Get the lizzard!"

All at once, the trolls pounced on the little basilisk and began stabbing at him with their daggers. Snort's resilient scales protected his body from the knives, but didn't help much with the heavy clubs that pounded his head and tender nose. Snort felt a troll sink his teeth into his floppy bat-wing ear. He howled with pain.

Mich tried to shake off the trolls so he could help his friend, but the disgusting little creatures were strong for their size, and with three of them holding on to him he could not shake himself free.

Snort was bleeding now and was getting agitated. One of the trolls made the mistake of biting his tender tail tip. Snort couldn't help it. He bawled with pain and exhaled a stream of white-hot fire. He melted the offending troll into green glop and used a hind foot to scrape dirt into the mess so that it was unable to reconstruct right away.

The other trolls backed off, because they did not appreciate effective resistance. They joined the attack on Mich. Snort could not fire at them for fear of burning Mich as well.

Mich could not move. He screamed as one of the monsters slashed his face with his own sword. He realized belatedly that he had been a fool to underestimate the little monsters. He had been contemptuous of them, and that was about to get him killed.

The next thing he knew, all the trolls were gone. In their place was a putrid smell, fading as a breeze wafted it clear. What had happened? Had they suddenly dived for cover?

Mich blinked his eyes, peering around. There was no sign of the rancid beasts. Just the white unisus standing there. Then he understood.

Heat had dissolved the trolls into nothing by pointing his dangerous, ridged horn at them. The unisus had delayed as long as he could before acting. Although his friend needed his help, Heat still did not enjoy killing the trolls. They couldn't help it if they were part of the lowest rung of the ladder of society.

"Thank you, friend," Mich said, recovering his wits and his sword.

You're welcome, Heat thought regretfully.

Once a year, Heat was able to generate a laser that could vaporize almost anything in an instant. The good thing was that his laser was selective. He could use it to kill whomever he wished and however many he wished, all at once. It built up slowly in his body, and after it was used, it took another full year to recharge. It was quite possible for Heat to destroy the whole world. He was not an evil creature, fortunately, and used his powers only when the need was dire. He hated to destroy lives, even those of trolls. He also regretted expending his charge on something relatively insignificant, instead of saving it for a truly impressive feat. Suppose the next attack was by ten large dragons, or there was a massive avalanche threatening them, and Heat was unable to help?

Mich was grateful that Heat had used his power to save him once again, but guilty for not being able to handle the situation himself. Had he had the sense to tackle the trolls rationally, he would have kept his sword out of their reach and used it to cut off their toes, fingers, noses, eyeballs, and ears. That would have distracted them, because such small appendages couldn't reconstitute into anything dangerous, while handicapping the trolls so that they would not be able to fight effectively. They would have had to pick them up and put them back on, and might have quarreled over which was whose. By the time the trolls got their digits and things sorted out, Mich and his party would have been gone. Instead he had acted rashly and bungled it. His father would have frowned with disapproval, had he witnessed the encounter.

After Mich bandaged Snort's tail and ear, they settled down to rest. Mich leaned against Heat's flank and was kept very warm. Snort didn't need much respite so he kept watch in case more trolls should show up. They had been unforgivably careless to be caught by surprise; that would not happen again. Snort felt a personal responsibility there.

Mich had trouble relaxing. He thought about how Heat always managed to save him from likely doom. Sometimes he felt like a coward and other times he was glad that Heat was always there for him. When he sprang from the waters of the River of Thought, Heat had been there to protect him and teach him about friendship, loyalty and honor.

Heat was a unisus and Mich's best friend. He had once belonged to a huge herd of unisi that lived in the sky, above the clouds. They were all the colors of the rainbow and all shades in between.

All except for two: Heat and Spirit. Heat was the color of purest snow, leaning toward silver, while Spirit was the color of a starless night, leaning toward a black hole. All the unisi could fly on strong, feathered wings, and each had a single magical aspect. They could purify water, or cure illness with a touch of the horn, or do something similar. When they ran through the sky, each colored creature would leave a streak of light behind that matched his own color. So when the whole herd flew, a beautiful rainbow formed.

Eventually, Heat was abandoned by the group. He could leave only a white streak and white was not an appropriate color, so he could not help with the rainbows. White was the combination of all colors; therefore he was not considered an individual. Instead of curing sickness with his horn, he destroyed things by making them disappear forever, so was considered evil and dangerous. Soon after that, Spirit was abandoned too and was never seen again. No one really knew what strange power he had, except for Heat, who never mentioned it and ignored inquiries. Apparently Spirit and Heat had been good friends and Heat preferred not to remember.

Mich wished he could find this black maverick unisus and bring him home, if he still lived. It would be the perfect way to repay Heat for all his years of protection and friendship.

Mich let his mind wander back to the first time they met, relaxing, and finally fell into repose. Such thoughts always cheered and relaxed him.

3

MADRID

Early the next morning, they ate and prepared for the ordeal ahead. Snort wrinkled his snout. He didn't speak in words, of course, but his expression conveyed his attitude clearly: Did he really have to go there?

Mich knew why. The sorceress liked basilisks almost as well as she liked young men. She would ruffle Snort's scales affectionately. That might not seem like a bad thing, except that the scales were hard to unruffle, and for hours thereafter would smell of sweet perfume. It was quite unbecoming for a basilisk. If trolls spied Snort at such a time, they would fall into an ugly pile, laughing. That was why Snort had breathed fire when Mich teased him about protecting Mich from Madrid: Snort was as vulnerable himself.

"I think we can manage without you on this particular mission," Mich said dryly. "If you're quite sure you wouldn't rather go in my stead."

Snort shook his head so vigorously that wisps of fire puffed out of his mouth. He would remain in the valley while Mich and Heat flew up to Madrid's cottage.

Mich wished that Heat didn't become tired so easily. It would save so much trouble. But poor Heat's wings were too small for traveling great distances, though they were powerfully effective and quick for short distances. This was why he flew only in emergencies, and he was always very tired after a flight.

Heat spread his wings. Though small, they were still large enough to create a dust storm from the downdraft. In a few strokes, his hooves lifted off the ground. It was more difficult flying straight up than it was flying up at an angle, but even with a passenger he managed it. Mich hated to make his friend work so hard, but he loved the experience of flying, and regretted that he hadn't come into existence with a set of wings of his own. There was so much to see from on high, as the realm of Kafka appeared below. The Forest of Imagination spread out like a rich and variegated carpet across the land, keeping it magically warm. Beyond—who could guess what he might see, if he could only fly high enough, long enough?

Near the summit, nestled among the evergreens, was a well-camouflaged house. It was made of mud and pine branches. It was almost covered over with fallen pine needles. If it weren't for the smoke curling up from the chimney, it would look just like a hill covered with dead twigs and needles.

A small woman appeared in a hidden doorway. "Ah, Mich!" Madrid exclaimed. "At last you've come! You sure took your damn time getting here."

As she stepped through the doorway, a little shower of pine needles decided to take refuge in her curly red Afro. She walked toward them with a slight limp and looked her guests over.

"Well?" she said, placing her hands on her somewhat gnarled hips.

"I came to ask you—" Mich began.

"How can you find an Earthling who can destroy the dam made of dreamstone?" she finished. Her expression became droll. "I know why you're here. Come inside and make yourself at home. I'll escort Heat to his stall and make sure he is comfortable."

Mich cast a worried glance at Heat. His friend looked unconcerned, so he entered the house. The unisus was not the one who would be receiving the brunt of the sorceress's attention, and the food in the stall was bound to be excellent.

Inside, it was warm and cozy. A fire crackled in the fireplace and cast dancing shadows on the mud walls. A kettle hung over the fire, and he could smell the delicious soup simmering in it. There was no doubt that the sorceress had nice accommodations. If it weren't for Madrid herself, they would be perfect.

Mich walked over to the fireplace and sat down among the many fat cushions. In a corner of the hut was a high shelf with many books. In front of the shelf was a desk with a huge text sitting on top. His eyes traveled around the hut he had been in so many times before.

Madrid always had a chore for him to do when his father needed a certain spell. She would usually try her hardest to seduce him, and never got even as far as a kiss. But it was clear that this was idle play for her; Mich dreaded the time she might get serious. Her powers were such that she could have him by magical force, if she chose. But she preferred to make it a game. She wanted him to truly want her.

He heard the door open and shut as Madrid returned. "Heat is settled now. He really likes the grass that grows up here. He told me there was no grass sweeter than Mangor's." She paused and shut the door. "Do you know why?"

Mich shrugged, trying to avoid being drawn into her game. Anything he said could be turned around to seem suggestive. For example, if he said that the grass was well fertilized, she might reply that that was because lovers had slept on it, and it was time to add to the effect.

She waited a moment for a reply that she knew wasn't going to come. Then she said, "Because the leaping cows crap on it!" Madrid doubled over with laughter, knowing she had faked him out with a crudity instead of an endearment. Her ploys with words were end-less. She didn't stop at words, however; they were merely the warm-up exercise.

After the euphoria wore off, she wiped away a tear of mirth and sat down beside him. Mich shook his head, silently pitying her on one level while fearing her on another. He almost wished he could find her as attractive as she evidently found him.

She put her spindly, callused hand on his. Mich wished he hadn't come here. She took his chin in her hand and turned his face toward hers.

Oh, no, here it comes. Mich got ready to pull away, as politely as possible, but she shocked him by not trying to kiss him. She only studied him.

"I know you have no personal interest in me, you dear boy," she said. "I'm tired of trying to trick you."

Mich sat back on the cushions and breathed a sigh of relief. "You're a nice person. Just a bit—mature for me." He hoped that would please her instead of annoying her.

"I do know why you have come here. Kafka needs your help more than you know. So I will have to help you, though one aspect of it sorely grieves me. My dear boy, you are about to discover ro-mance, and not with me."

That was not entirely reassuring. "I don't know where to find a human, let alone a human who has the ability to destroy dream-stone," Mich said. "And I don't know anything about romance."

"That's obvious. Do you know your Creator?" Madrid's eyes were sharp and piercing.

"Of course! The River of Thought. Everyone comes from there."

"Yes, that's true. But where does it flow from?"

"That's what I'm here to find out."

She sighed. "Well, I suppose I'll have to start at the beginning."

She positioned herself better on the cushions and folded her hands in her lap. "In the earliest years, the land surrounding the River of Thought was quite normal, with trees, grass, rocks, birds and sky. One day, a great dragon appeared. His name was Kafka. He was an immortal creature.

"He was the son of a greater dragon, along with his brother. Kafka's father was cruel to him. His father had absolute power over his family, and Kafka often felt low and cowardly in the presence of his father. He lived like a slave under his father's cruel hand. Kafka had always searched for something to make him happy. He never found happiness in his life, yet he found it in his imagination.

"As the years passed, he became bored with his situation and more and more curious about his growing world. He longed for escape. Kafka had a special power apart from his family. His imagination, coupled with his ability to write, was so strong that when he wished it, his stories became real. So, he invented Kafka. A place of dreams rather than nightmares. An escape from the nightmares he suffered. He gifted his new world to its neighbor, Earth. Earth was facing self-destruction, and without escape for its people, Earth would die. He understood this need and provided the cure, so long as Earth's people had faith.

"He was the ruler of Kafka for many years. And with each year, the land of the river grew larger. He explored every new border and every new territory. He is gone now, killed by the Fren that pollute the land, but he left behind Kafka, the land of dragons and dreams."

Mich was perplexed. "What does this have to do with humans?"

"I'm getting to that!" she snapped, as if annoyed by his shallowness. "Now, Kafka himself sprang from the river. The river was always there. It was there before the land and sky. The river is, indeed, a river of thought. However, these are sleeping thoughts; dreams, if you will. Human dreams."

Mich's confusion grew. What was she getting at?

"Sometimes there are births. When an Earthling human believes so strongly in a living, nonliving or otherwise fantastic creature that he sees in his dreams, that creature is born from the river. These Earthlings are called Creators. If the Creator of the creature ceases to believe or forgets, then the creature will no longer exist and it will be as if he had never been." Madrid took a deep breath.

"So the humans are the source of the river!"

"Yes and no. They provide its waters, but exactly where the waters flow into Kafka is unknown. Now, there are very few humans who can create or destroy dreamstone. Your Creator is one of them. If you can find the human, and get to where the physical river flows into Kafka, to find the dam, then we will have a fighting chance."

"Where is the source and where can I find him?"

She spread her hands. "No one knows how to locate the source. Not even me, and it's her, not him. I will tell you how to find her in a moment." She got up and poured a little more stock into the simmering pot. Then she walked over to the desk. "Come here, Mich, I want to show you something."

She ran one long, red, curled fingernail along the contents page of the huge text on the desk. She flipped through the quill-written pages. "There," she said.

Mich's eyes followed the bony finger to the nail tip, which was gouged into a painting on the page. "That's her," Madrid said.

Mich couldn't believe his eyes. She was more beautiful than anything he had ever seen. She looked to be three or four years younger than he. She had long red hair and intense, slate-blue eyes.

"She's my Creator?" he asked.

"Yes. Her name is Nola Rollins."

"She's so striking," Mich said, half to himself.

Madrid ignored his drooling. "When you find her, she may not be so eager to cooperate with you." She closed the book and walked over to the simmering kettle to stir it.

"But if she believes in me so much, why would she even hesitate?" he asked.

"Because, though she is one of the few true dreamers left, she still lives in a world of reality and she may not believe that you are really who you say you are."

Mich heard a noise, and turned around to see the shape of a unisus standing outside the open door. That was odd, because he hadn't summoned his friend. Was something wrong?

The sorceress nodded, evidently aware of something he didn't know about. "You must convince her, and not just because you will love her. So, to help you with that, all you have to do is show her this."

Madrid gestured to the door, and as Mich approached, he could see that the unisus wasn't Heat. It was Spirit.

He was a huge beast. He was not taller than Heat, but he was broader and definitely more muscular. His wings were each two lengths his own body size. It looked very awkward and unbalanced, but he stood as if his wings weighed nothing.

He reminded Mich a little of himself. Spirit's eyes were the exact shade of green as his own and his hide was glossy black, the same as Mich's hair. There was an air about him, something intangible but powerful. Around his neck was a thin strap of leather bearing a silver crosslet with a tiny pallid, blue dreamstone. The pendant was lightly engraved with a crosshatch pattern and was over an inch in diameter. It was a meager speck of glitter against the great black chest.

"That is what you must show her," Madrid said.

"You mean the pendant?"

"No, idiot! I mean the unisus." She paused, then added: "But that's not a bad idea. Take him with you."

"But how can we survive in her world if we are only dreams to her?"

"Oh, all these petty problems! Must I do everything myself?"

"But—"

"Oh, very well!" Madrid flicked her fingers and mumbled some indecipherable phrases. "There, now you will be protected from her reality for the period of one week. That is the most any Kafkian can survive there, even with magic. I must warn you, stay longer and you will cease to exist, no matter how much she believes in you. In her world, you can die and you cannot be brought back." She flashed a grim smile. "Please take care that you do not exceed that week."

Mich had no idea about death, or what it was like to die, but he knew that he didn't want it to happen to him. It was probably worse than being Forgotten.

"Now it's time for dinner," Madrid said briskly. Mich realized with a shock that much of the day had passed, in what had seemed like half an hour.

He was hungry, and the soup was very good. There was a certain magical ambience about it. The more of it he ate, the less repulsive the sorceress looked, and the more pleasant her words sounded. At another time he might have wondered about that.

It was getting dark outside when their conversation dwindled, and Mich began to long for a good night's rest. Madrid did insist that he spend the night, and after stuffing him full of soup, she left him to rest on the cushions.

"I thought you would try to get me into your bed," he remarked dazedly. She now looked young, slender and lovely.

"You may never appreciate how great a sacrifice I am making for the good of Kafka," she murmured sadly. "I must leave you chaste, lest your Creator be repulsed. But if there is ever another time, be assured I will show you this." She opened her gown to reveal a truly stunning bosom.

Truly stunned, Mich knew no more.

In the morning, her beauty faded, Madrid told him how to reach the world of the Creators and the nonphysical source of the River of

Thought. He had only to lie down in the shallows of the river and fall asleep.

"That seems too easy," he said.

"Neither dreams nor reality care what is easy or hard," she said. "Only what is appropriate. Remember that."

She took the cross off Spirit's neck and wrapped it in a swatch of black silk and gave it to Mich. He tied it tightly to his belt so that it wouldn't be lost.

Then he called Heat from the stable. The unisus whinnied with excitement when he saw Spirit and galloped over. The two unisi reared in a mock fighting match. It was obvious that they were happy to see each other. Apparently Spirit had not checked the stable the day before.

Mich turned to the sorceress. "Uh, thanks," he said awkwardly. He had never been good at such social requirements.

She grimaced. "I could think of a better way to express it than that. Don't you at least owe me a kiss?"

"I guess I do," he agreed reluctantly. He knew she was making it possible for him to try to save Kafka, so he shouldn't begrudge her that much in return.

She spread her arms. "Then do it, you handsome hunk."

Mich nerved himself and took her in his arms. Her body was surprisingly supple. Suddenly she looked exactly as she had the night before, the most exquisite creature he could imagine. It turned out to be easy to kiss her.

After a while she drew away. "I made myself an oath I wouldn't vamp you, this time," she murmured. "Go, before I forget it." Her hand touched the décolletage of her robe as if barely restrained from ripping it open. "At least now you suspect what you've been missing."

He did indeed. He turned away, afraid that if he didn't he would tear open that robe himself. She laughed, satisfied.

Mich, Heat and Spirit flew back down the mountain. Snort was waiting for them and they trotted eastward toward the river, just as if there had been nothing special during the past day and night. Snort even had the grace not to sniff too obviously at the scent of the sorceress's perfume, which clung to Mich.

"Where did you go after you were rejected by the group, Spirit?" Mich asked.

There was no response from the huge beast. He just kept pace with Heat and ignored any talk that was directed at him.

"I wonder what's up with that unisus," Mich muttered. "Is he deaf?" he thought privately to Heat.

I don't know, his mind is closed, but I can feel that he has some hostility toward us. Perhaps he is just nervous about the journey.

"I hope that's it." Mich decided he shouldn't push the issue. Spirit might be dangerous. He didn't try to talk to the black unisus again.

Meanwhile their journey continued. He hoped that they would arrive at the river before nightfall. The dangers of the night were worse than the dangers of the day.

4

KUDO

Nola had just finished her household chores and was ready to go to the beach, when Kudo knocked over one of her favorite plants. Clods of moist dirt spilled over onto the carpet. Nola's face reddened. "Bad cat! Bad, bad, bad!" she yelled. The cat scooted under the sofa and cowered while Nola vacuumed up the mess. She loved that cat, but sometimes Kudo got on her last nerve. If John decided to come home and found the mess, he would throw Kudo out the window and probably slap Nola for it.

She thought about her trip today. She wondered what had possessed her to go to the beach anyway. She never liked to go alone, so she never went anywhere. She had no friends. Except for Lori. Nola had known her for three years. She was the kind of person one wouldn't want to associate with on the first meeting, but she did have her points. Nola had not been to see her in several weeks. Oh, well; it was not as if Lori would miss her. No one would.

Nola's mother lived in the apartment building down the block from hers, but she could never get her mother to do anything with her. Nola just turned into a blob of flesh after doing the chores.

Most often she would go right to sleep. She loved to sleep because sleep brought dreams. That was another reason she wished to die. She could sleep and never wake up. She could live in her dreams forever, except that as far as she knew, dead people didn't dream. Every-

one had strange dreams but Nola knew that hers were really unusual.

Her dreams were different each night, but she dreamed of Spirit
and Mich every time she closed her eyes. Mich was her true love. He
would slay demons for her and she would make him happy, in her
fashion, in return.

Every now and then Mich would be astride a nightmare that
looked just like Spirit in every way except color. This other stallion
was purest white, and instead of green, its eyes were like two huge
silver ball bearings. When they were side by side, they looked like
light and shadow.

Kudo crawled from under the sofa and didn't even glance at Nola.
She trotted over to the window and jumped into the sill. Nola walked
over and patted her.

"Well, Kudo, I hope for your sake that our apartment isn't torn up
when I get home. I'm going to the beach now." She paused, then
added, "Come to think of it, I hope *I* don't get torn up when I get
home. Well, John's never come home on his own before, so why
would he now?" She scratched Kudo between the ears and Kudo
turned her head, hissed and bit at her.

Nola knew that Kudo was not by any stretch an affectionate cat,
but Kudo would never intentionally hurt her. She had come to accept
Kudo's strange way of acknowledging her love. A nibble and scratch
meant "I love you" and a hiss meant "please pet me."

At one-thirty Nola was ready, and left for the bus station. It was
a long walk and the trip was costing her, but she wanted so much to
go. Even alone.

Once on the bus, she sat and stared morosely out the window,
watching the trees and houses go by. She tried to convince herself
that she would have the best time ever. She would shop, swim, relax
and eat, but most of all, sleep and have fun.

Nola's mind's eye did a double take. This is fun? she thought.

What was she doing? It would be fun if she was with two or three friends, but she wasn't.

Then she got that funny feeling again, thanks to Esprit, that everything would be great. Esprit would want her to go. He'd say that everything would be great.

The first thing Nola did after the four-hour bus ride was check into a hotel and eat. After dinner, she figured she'd have just enough time for a swim and then she could watch the sunset. She grabbed her beach bag and sketch pad and headed off to the beach.

Tina woke from a dream of horror. She was shivering and sweating simultaneously. Probably she needed another fix. But the dream seemed like something else.

She tried to focus on it, but it was already fading. All she caught was something about a monstrous worm. A gigantic underground worm named Kras.

Did that make any sense at all? She doubted it, yet the dream had seemed so real.

But what was the point in thinking about a stupid dream? It was her life she had to be concerned about, though that was collapsing. In fact there didn't seem to be much point in waking or dreaming.

5

RIVER

Mich and his friends reached the River of Thought at sunset. This was the fourth time that Mich had visited the river and it looked more lovely each time he saw it.

The river looked like a liquid rainbow that had been slightly stirred. There were so many colors, and yet there were none. If he looked too closely for too long, the water would run clear in the spot at which he was staring, then recolor itself as his eyes moved to another spot. It was quite possible for one to sit for days at a time just watching the river, but Mich had no time for that now. He stepped forward, leading Spirit.

"Halt, obtrude!" cried a frail voice. A mermaid floated to the surface of the river, astride a hippocampus. She brushed back her wet blond hair with one hand and threatened with her trident in the other. Once her face was clear of hair and water she opened her eyes and stared. The fish-tailed horse bobbed up and down with the motion of his hooves and tail.

"Obtrude?" Mich asked, admiring her bare upper torso. "Do you mean 'intruder'? In any event, I hope I'm not one."

"Oh, my!" she gasped, putting her hand across her lips. Her gills fluttered nervously. "Please, Prince, you must forgive me!"

Mich saw how embarrassed she was. He tried to make her feel at ease. "It's all right; you were only doing your job."

"I'm sorry, Your Excellency. I did not know it was you. My side of the river was attacked not too long ago by the evil Fren. Reility put a potion in the water that forces my comrades and me to breathe air. I thought we could ambush him if we pretended that his pollution trick didn't work and we hid under water, but we become weak if we stay under too long." She was crying now. Mich could see others coming to the surface and gasping for breath.

The mermaids were commissioned to guard the river, and they were very well equipped for the job. Unless their power to breathe water was taken away.

"It's okay," he said. "I'll try to find a cure for the spell if you will let me lie in the water."

"Your Highness, you know we cannot let you touch the water. We are immune to its intoxication but it can be very dangerous for you." She looked distraught. She held her trident pointed at him.

"My father sent me. My mission is too important to let you stall me. Madrid of Mangor instructed me to lie down in the river and I must do it. Snort!" he called. "Help the mermaids to back off."

Snort moved forward, licking his teeth.

The mermaid dropped her trident and threw up her hands to cover her face. "No! Do not harm me, good basilisk. I am sorry, Your Highness. I was only doing the job I was told to do, but I cannot harm you. You may lie in the water."

"I couldn't hurt you either." Mich smiled and stepped out into the gentle current.

"Thank you," he said, and bid the mermaids and his friends farewell.

Return soon, Michael, Heat thought, nervously stamping a foot.

We must bring Nola here and return her to her home safely, Spirit thought.

This was the first time Mich had felt Spirit's voice in his mind. Spirit's thought was forceful and demanding, yet there was a wonderful fondness in his deep voice when he thought her name.

Mich bowed his head to the mermaids and knelt in the water. Heat and Snort walked into the forest.

Mich felt the strangeness of the water as he leaned back into it. The liquid was tepid and soothed his body. He could feel the water as it slowly sucked away his conscious mind. He was suddenly surrounded by every hope and dream he could imagine. Never seeing them, only feeling them in different degrees of urgency, like different temperatures and textures. Then he could feel nothing at all. There was only a peaceful ambience. Similar to when he rested at night, only much deeper, as if his soul had slipped away for a moment.

Something changed.

When he opened his eyes again, he could see nothing but silver and blue. He started to take a breath, but discovered his mouth filling with a salty fluid. His face was now under water and he couldn't breathe. The soft, rounded stones that were supporting his body in the shallow water of the riverbank were no longer there. He felt himself sinking.

He kicked his powerful legs and moved his arms frantically, trying to swim. His face broke the surface and he quickly inhaled, sucking in some of the briny water. He continued to struggle, and managed to get another breath.

This wasn't at all what he thought would happen. He thought that he would have a dream. No Kafkian ever slept deeply enough to dream. Maybe this was a nightmare, but it sure didn't feel like one. It was way too physical.

His lungs started to ache for oxygen and he could feel panic sweep through his body. He tried to calm himself, but that was almost impossible while drowning.

On his third attempt to breathe, he missed the surface and swallowed another pint of salt water. He was unable even to choke.

This was no nightmare. He was going to die.

6

BELIEF

The beach wasn't very crowded, and Nola was glad of it. No one would disturb her daydreaming.

She opened her sketch pad and started drawing her favorite subjects. She drew the young man she had seen so many times in her dreams, Mich. The one she made up from her imagination. She had tried so hard and waited so long to find someone to meet her ideals of what a man should be, but she never found him. So in desperation she decided she could have anyone she wanted, even though he could exist only in her mind.

Naturally she crafted him well. He was handsome and muscular with long, thick, black hair and grass-green eyes. He was a prince (of course) and enjoyed riding Heat, Spirit's white counterpart. He loved music. He had a pet dragon that he played with in much the same way she played with her cat. In fact, maybe Snort was based on Kudo, making him more of a basilisk. Animals could be ugly or bad tempered and still be loved. If only that were the case with people! In the dream land Mich loved her unconditionally, but to make him seem more real, she gave him human flaws.

Sometimes he had a corny sense of humor, and he tended to be overly dramatic when he was bored or bothered. He was inexperienced in certain things like grim adventure or romantic love, so tended to make foolish mistakes that got him into trouble on either front. Just like most men, he enjoyed a good white lie. But he would never lie to deceive or hurt her. For example, he might tell her she looked lovely, when she knew she did not. To Nola, he was just perfect, including his imperfections. It didn't matter that he lived only in her mind. The way she looked at it, it just made her love and long for him more each day. Deep down, she knew he wasn't real, but she didn't care. To think of him made her happy, and why not be happy if she could be?

She also drew a picture of her best friend, Esprit. His eyes were the same shade as Mich's. Nola could read his thoughts and emotions as well as he could read hers. She would often have imaginary conversations with him. She knew that it was silly do this sort of thing, but she didn't care. Her life had gotten so hard to live that this piece of fantasy was the only thing that helped her face reality. There were many other fantastic people and places she dreamed of, but Spirit and Mich were the first and they entered her mind most often.

She finished the picture in her usual way, by drawing a little cross in the bottom right corner. Each of its four arms were equal in length with arrow-shaped ends. She had made up the cross one day to symbolize her faith in God and the wonderful gift of imagination that he bestowed upon her, and she always drew it on her pictures as a thank you.

As she sketched it, she felt a jolt in her spine as if someone were trying to push her out of her beach chair.

That was not part of the usual way. What had happened? She was sure it meant something. Because the jolt really hadn't been physical, but emotional.

She poked her pencil into the sand and cast a glance across the waves. The water was fairly placid and pretty. Nothing unusual there. Or was there?

She peered more intently. About halfway between the horizon and the shore, she saw something sparkling. At first she thought it was a bird diving into the surf for a fish.

She squinted her eyes and shielded them from the sun. She saw that it was not a bird, but a person, and whoever it was seemed to be in trouble. She thought it was probably a kid playing a joke, so she just watched. But something about it compelled her attention; she felt what was, for want of a better term, a spiritual connection. Whatever was happening was important to her in some vital way.

The person went down once, then twice and did not come up a third time. That was no joke! She felt almost as if she were drawing herself: Nola threw down her sketch pad and ran toward the sea. She dived in with such speed and grace that she mirrored a leaping dolphin.

This was one thing she was proud of. She could outswim anyone she knew and could hold her breath for almost two minutes. She ducked below the surface and stroked with all her might, slowly expelling the spent air in her lungs as she swam. She could swim more quickly below the surface because she didn't have to deal with the waves splashing her face. She did not swim as quickly as she did when she was in a pool, but she reached the drowning victim as he was sinking below.

She slid her arm under one of his arms, across his chest, and pulled him to the surface. She tried to swim to shore. He seemed to have blacked out. This was a kind of blessing for Nola. She knew that if he were awake he could panic and make it very difficult for her to be heroic.

Though it was summer, the water was chilly and Nola's muscles and joints found it hard to work right. She didn't want to pause, because the man would need immediate attention, but it would do nobody any good if she wore herself out and went under too.

Just as she was about to stop and rest, her feet came down on sand and she managed to pull the stranger to shore. She lay him down on the sand. His long hair was plastered across his face. She was surprised to see that he looked very handsome and very familiar. But this was not the time to reflect on that. She hastily cleared her wandering thoughts and kneeled over him. His lips and eyelids were beginning to turn purple and his face was turning blue. She emptied his mouth of water and proceeded to give him mouth-to-mouth resuscitation. She pushed on his chest with her hands.

Finally, the stranger started vomiting copious amounts of salt water and coughing harshly. His face turned from blue to bright red. He sat up with his eyes squinted tightly shut and coughed for several minutes. Then he sat silent for a moment looking in his lap and wiping the water away from his face.

Nola pushed his straggled hair away from his eyes. "Are you okay?" she asked.

"Yes. Yes, I'm fine now." The stranger looked up at Nola with his big green eyes.

Nola's hand snapped from the stranger's head to her mouth and she gasped hard, sucking in air between her fingers, making a hissing sound. "Oohh, myyy God . . ."

"Is something wrong?" he asked.

Nola tried to hold back another hurricanelike gasp. Could this actually be happening? He looked so much like *him*. It was amazing! "No, it can't be," she mumbled.

"I'm sorry," he said. "I haven't thanked you for saving my life. You are——?"

"Nola," she replied with her mouth still covered.

The stranger stood up. "Oh, it's you! I wasn't sure, you're so much more beautiful than the pic——" He evidently realized he was rambling. "Please forgive me. Thank you so much for saving me." He extended his hand and Nola accepted it. "My name is Michael, but I am known by my friends as Mich. I knew I was supposed to arrive

near you, because the magic binds us to each other, but I didn't realize that you would have to rescue me from deep water!"

He paused, startled, as Nola fell into him. He caught her and held
her in his lap while he tried to revive her. There wasn't much else he
could do.

A few moments later she opened her eyes and looked up. She
startled him again by suddenly bolting up and away from him.

"I am sorry," he called after her. "I did not mean to affront
you. You fell into me, and I—I apologize. You saved me from the
water, and—"

Realizing that the last thing she wanted was a public scene, she
composed herself quickly. "Excuse me," she said, dusting herself
off. "You are very welcome for the help, but I have to go now. I
would suggest that you see a doctor before you go home." Nola
walked over to her beach chair and began gathering her things.

"A doctor? What's that?"

Nola began to walk off. She knew she had to get out of here before succumbing to this craziness. It was just a silly coincidence of
names and appearance. It had to be.

"Don't you recognize me, Nola?"

"Of course not! I've never met you before! How could I recognize you?" She stuffed her towel into her bag and folded her chair.

Where was Spirit? Mich prayed he hadn't drowned. Right now,
he had to convince her before she fled. How could he do that, when
she seemed determined to go?

He started to worry. This wasn't working out at all. How could
he satisfy her to who he was? She had already gathered up her be-
longings and was turning to go.

Then he remembered the cross on its leather strap, tied to his
belt. He walked over to her and gently took her arm. He put the
cross in her hand. "Then, do you recognize this?"

Nola looked at the cross. It was about one and a half inches wide and the same in length. It was silver and looked very old. Every detail from her drawings was there, down to the star sapphire in its center.

"Where did you get this?" she asked. There was a hint of anger in her voice.

He was startled by her snappishness. "It was a gift from a friend of mine, but it really belongs to you and your unisus," Mich replied.

Nola paused a moment and studied Mich's face. The faint light of recognition flickered behind her eyes. She looked back at the cross. "You mean that this is from—Spirit?" Nola felt suddenly sad and then terribly happy. Did she dare believe? Or was someone playing a really cruel prank on her? If so, they had certainly found a way to score. Her eyes started to blur with wetness.

"Yes," Mich said.

Nola clutched the cross in her fist and grabbed Mich's shoulder. "Where did you get this?" she asked in a savage tone. "Is this some kind of vicious joke? Who are you?"

Mich sighed. And tried to tell her again who he was.

Nola studied him, looking for proof. She avoided looking directly into his eyes again, for fear she would not want to look away. He just seemed too good to be true.

For she knew, through experience, that everything that seemed too good to be true was just that. Not once did she have something that made her happy forever. It was always a day or two, then it would disappear, crushing her inside. It took her a long time to learn her lesson, but she did learn. She trusted no one. Even though her heart begged her to believe, she knew that when she let her heart lead her, it led her into suicide.

"I'm sorry, but I just cannot accept all this. I must be going insane! I must be seeing things. I've got to get out of here."

Nola started to walk down the beach. Even though this man was calling her name in such a pleading tone as to be begging, she walked without looking back. She was very confused and didn't know what to do. Maybe she was just seeing things. In fact, she was sure that she was just tired and overworked. After a long nap, this would all be over.

Nola was about to turn onto the road when she heard a great commotion behind her. There was the sound of something heavy splashing in the water, then a sound similar to thunder. She closed her eyes, took a deep breath, turned around and opened her eyes again.

There, running toward her, was a huge black horse. He was galloping at such a great speed that he stirred up a sand storm in his wake. His tail flew behind him like a silk banner. His hide was deepest pitch and his gaze didn't waver from Nola. His eyes were black, but glowed like stars in the night sky. Then the huge beast stopped on a dime, his nose only a foot from her nose.

Nola felt no need to look twice at him. It really was her nightmare, minus the wings and horn, but she knew it was him. Her resistance to belief was crumbling. If this was insanity, then let it come!

Spirit arched his graceful black neck and gently rubbed the palm of her hand with his nose. She stroked his long muzzle and threw her arms around his neck.

"Where have you been?" she sobbed. "You're even more beautiful than I imagined!"

Mich approached cautiously. "He can't talk with you here; it's not our world," he explained. "He's just an ordinary horse here."

"Well, I want to talk to him. And what do you mean he's ordinary here?" Nola took hold of Esprit's mane and walked toward Mich. Spirit followed her and it seemed perfectly natural that they should be together. Mich wondered why she accepted Spirit so readily, yet did not accept him.

Now she noticed how strangely he was dressed. His clothes were very unusual. It looked as if some of them had been washed away. He wore a pair of dirty, tan-colored trousers that had been torn around the ankles. He also wore a belt and sheath with the hilt of a sword exposed. His bronze chest was partially covered by a dark blue shirt. The shirt was badly torn down the front, but looked as if it had once been held together by laces. He looked almost medieval.

This couldn't be happening! She pinched herself. "Ouch!" Then she got serious. "What happened to you?" she asked Mich. "Did you get in a fight or something?"

"No," he replied. "I'm trendsetting. You like it?" He did a sarcastic little half turn.

Nola smiled. There was that sense of humor. "As a matter of fact, it is very sexy," she teased. She could see that she had embarrassed him because his ears were turning red. That was typical of her dream man too.

Nola tried to make herself believe that this was not really Mich, but he resembled her dream in every way. She had no choice: it was Mich.

Yet if this really was Mich, then he should know everything about her; but he seemed to know very little. However, she could see a muted passion in his eyes when he looked at her. If this was all real, then all her dreams were real. What a wonderful thing that would be, if she could really believe it.

She had to accept it, at least for now. This was really happening; she was not dreaming. If she wasn't going crazy.

Despite the feeling she had welling up inside her right now, she remained highly nervous. After all this time, all this searching, and all this dreaming and wishing . . .

Mich told Nola why he had come and how she was the only one who could help save Kafka from being destroyed by the Fren. Nola listened, but remained unsure. She wished she could believe he was telling the truth. How wonderful it would be to live in a world where her dreams were reality. But this was utter foolishness. There would never be such a place. It was a fantasy and nothing more. But she would humor him and herself for a while. After all, how could she resist the man who so resembled the love she longed for?

"We should start right away," he concluded. "Is there anything you need to bring?"

She laughed, accepting it for the moment. "Nothing but you and Esprit."

"Who is Esprit?"

"Oh, that's just a little nickname I gave Spirit here. He likes it."

Mich's brow wrinkled. He glanced at the horse, who nodded. "One question."

"Yes?" This suspension of disbelief was fun, as long as she didn't take it too seriously.

"Why is it that you accept Spirit without question, yet you have so much trouble believing in me?"

Nola was afraid she had hurt his feelings. She tried to explain without doing so again. "Spirit isn't human. It's not in his power to cause me pain. I've never met a horse I didn't like. I've met many humans with blacker hearts than Spirit's coat. Do you understand? It's nothing against you."

He did not seem quite satisfied. "If you wouldn't mind, please tell me what happened to cause you so much distrust of people."

"I can't. I barely know you! Don't take it the wrong way. I am very grateful to you for bringing me my dream, but I'd like to leave my sordid life out of this. At least for now."

Mich suddenly felt guilty for pressing her. "Of course. I can respect that."

"Well, let's go. I can't wait to see Kafka!" Nola hesitated. "Just one thing, though. How do we get there?"

"You know, I'm not quite sure, but legend says that there are portholes from your world to ours called beds," he said with one cute eyebrow raised.

As a come-on, this was too clumsy to be believed. He figured on a transporting experience in bed with her? "What do you mean?"

"I have a spell that works when a person is in a sleeping place, like a bed or a couch."

Nola's suspicion returned. He *was* trying to get her into bed! "Are you hitting on me?"

Mich was baffled. "I would never hit you!"

She laughed, realizing that he didn't know the idiom. "You mean sleep, as in losing consciousness? Dreaming?"

"Yes, of course. Only we don't dream in Kafka. We know that phenomenon only by description. It must be interesting."

"And such sleep, with or without dreaming, along with your spell, will take us to Kafka? Just like that?"

"Yes, it's supposed to." He smiled. "All it takes is a little moonlight and a lot of faith."

Nola was beginning to like Mich despite herself. She still didn't believe a word he said, but she was curious about him. And the truth was, she wouldn't mind getting into bed with him, even if he was a fake. Since her true dream man couldn't exist, the next best thing was the image of her dream man. But she would make him work a bit harder before letting him score, on general principles. "Would you care to join me at the hotel for a bite to eat?"

"I'd love that. I'm starved. Will you be cooking?"

"No. We'll be eating at the restaurant."

"Rest room? You eat there?"

She laughed again. "Restaurant. It's a place where they serve food."

"Oh, a kitchen."

He was good! "Call it a dining room. You do have those, don't you?"

"Darn," he swore. "I was hoping to see you doing woman's work."

Nola shot him a dark stare.

He threw up his hands, smiling. "Just kidding! I'm sorry, that was in bad taste. I would never ask a Creator to be a mere woman."

"A what?" she asked sharply.

"A woman."

That had not been what she meant, but she decided to let it go for now. She had fashioned her dream man to have a certain quaint naivete, and so it was consistent for him not to understand what was objectionable about the qualification "mere." Nola forced a laugh. "You have a terrible sense of humor! Where'd you get it?" she asked, smiling wryly.

"I was created with it. It disgusts Snort, not to mention my father. They say the River of Thought must have been polluted when I emerged."

Nola studied him a moment, deciding not to challenge that. He would be stared at in the clothes he was wearing. She'd have to take him by one of the souvenir shops on the boardwalk and buy him something better to wear. It would force her to use the credit card, but that was okay. "First, I'd like to get you some clothes. People here don't dress that way."

Mich looked down at himself. His clothes were pretty ragged as it was. He could use some new ones. "Very well."

One problem remained. "But what'll I do with Esprit? They don't allow horses in my hotel."

"He can't talk to you," Mich said, "but he can understand you. Maybe you can tell him to stay here on the beach, if you think it's safe enough and if he stays out of sight."

Nola turned to her black friend. Before she could say a word, he tossed his head, turned tail and galloped off down the beach. He headed away from the hotels and streets.

"He read my thoughts!" Nola said, believing it just a little.

Mich took Nola's bag and chair from her hands and carried them for her. She led him for a whole mile down the beach before they were in sight of the boardwalk.

Mich was constantly stared at. Teenagers pointed and adults laughed. Nola was glad to see that it didn't affect him. He held his head high and ignored them. It was possible that he didn't even realize that he was the object of their ridicule.

They entered one of the stores. Nola found a pair of black swim trunks and a surfer T-shirt. "These look like your size," she said.

Mich stared at them. "Are you sure those are proper?"

"For the beach? Of course, but I wouldn't wear them in the city. Go ahead and try them on."

She directed him into a little stall with mirrors all over its walls. It was interesting, being able to see his backside, even the back of his head. He would have to suggest such a mirror chamber to his father. He closed the door and removed his torn clothing and dressed in the strange new clothes. He stepped out of the stall and faced Nola.

"Well," she said. "You look brighter! With that gorgeous black hair and five o'clock shadow, you look exactly like a surfer! All except for that sword. Well, that can't be helped."

Nola paid for the clothes with John's credit card, and they walked down the boardwalk to her hotel. It was quite small, compared with most of the others, but the room was nice, with two double beds and cable TV.

Nola made the mistake of turning on the TV. Mich was instantly hooked. "A magic mirror of a strange and marvelous new kind! But how does it answer questions?"

"You don't question it," she said wryly. "You just sit like a vegetable and watch it until your mind rots."

Mich covered his eyes. "Evil magic! I didn't know."

"Humor," she said quickly. "It won't hurt you immediately. That takes days or weeks."

Relieved, he watched for over an hour. Every ten seconds, he'd say, *"Wow,* look at this!" or "What is that?" When he was silent for a while, she got suspicious. Sure enough, it was a feature showing buxom young women in scant costumes. She had better do something about that.

He was horrified when she flipped to the news. She had to explain about guns, crime, war and poverty. He was morbidly fascinated by the images and concepts.

"Why is your world so destructive of itself? How can a man shoot another man and not care? How can a mother leave a newborn child in a garbage can? Why do people not share their food when they see someone who's starving? Why does your world need so many weapons that they could blow the whole thing up? Who would win a war like that?" he asked, his eyes glazing over as he stared at the television.

Nola just shook her head. "No one. I wish I knew why all these things happened. If you asked those who committed the atrocities, they would have a reason, but I don't think you'd understand it. *I* don't understand it, and I'm pretty low on the scale of human decency."

"But you're a Creator!" he protested.

There was that term again. She didn't trust it, so she didn't address it. "There are some good things about the real world. Unfortunately the process of growing up strips children of their innocence, until they become as bad as the rest. You're better off not understanding."

Mich looked at her with an almost hurt expression. "No, I wouldn't understand. There's no reason for stealing someone's life from them and there is no reason I would understand why a mother would abandon a helpless child. I don't mean to offend you, but I don't much like your world."

"Me either," Nola mumbled.

Mich heard her. "You were raised here. Did you ever witness anything like that yourself?"

"No, thank God."

"I don't see why you seem so sad all the time. Is it all this destruction? That would make me sad. Maybe if you never turned on the magic mirror, so as not to be assaulted by its horrors, you would be happier."

"I wish it were that easy." Nola had tried her best not to think of John, or of her family, while on her vacation, but Mich kept dredging up memories. Perhaps if she told him it would make her feel better. No. It was best to keep her hard-learned lesson in the forefront of her mind. Mich seemed too good to be true, therefore must be false. To trust him would be to invite disaster.

Instead, she forced a smile. "Let's go eat."

They sat in the restaurant and talked. When the food was served, Mich seemed a little reluctant to eat it. Nola found it difficult not to fall for his tricks. He acted as if he had never eaten in his life, and did it well. He liked the chicken, but not the green beans. He had a slab of cheesecake for dessert and ate every crumb. "This is a fine establishment," he remarked. "But how is it that we are permitted to enjoy it without being introduced to the lord of the house?"

She kept a straight face. "He's busy elsewhere right now, having many important matters to attend to. He told me it was all right to eat here during his absence, provided I behave discreetly."

Mich nodded, satisfied. She had spoken his language.

When they finished the meal, Mich questioned her about everything. Even why she handed the server a piece of green paper. She had a hard time trying to describe how money was transferred for services and products. She explained that each piece of paper was backed up by a promise of gold. He asked why gold wasn't used instead of paper. The best answer she could come up with was that gold was heavy and people preferred to carry the lighter bills. After all, even she didn't know everything.

Back in the room, they watched more TV. Mich started spinning stories of his childhood. He explained that he was only eighteen when he was born. Nola found that funny, but also found it to be a strange coincidence. Considering that she didn't begin dreaming of Mich until she was sixteen. She dreamed of Mich as being eighteen.

They fell asleep. Nola never thought to mention the magic spell that was supposed to enable them to visit Kafka. She had mixed feelings when he did not even try to make a move on her. He was peculiarly diffident, being both friendly and respectful. She didn't understand it, but found she liked it. Respect had never been large in her life.

Then, the next morning, Mich explained how the act of sleeping caused him a little discomfort. He insisted that he did not dream.

Nola loved dreams and knew a lot about them. It was a fact that all people experienced REM sleep, rapid eye movement, with the eyes closed. During REM, a person dreamed, whether or not she wanted to. Everyone dreamed. Maybe Mich just hadn't experienced REM. Perhaps he was just nervous. He would sleep tomorrow.

She had planned to go home today, but Mich's presence changed her plans. She also couldn't leave Spirit. So she did what she had to do, and used the borrowed credit card to extend her stay. How she would ever make good on the debt she was accumulating she didn't know; every time she borrowed the card before she kept a close eye on the credit balance and didn't run up more on the card than she could pay off within a month, so as not to incur the ruinous interest rate, not to mention incurring the wrath of her abusive boyfriend. But she had no choice now.

They spent the next three days together, talking. They went to the beach often to visit Spirit. Nola would bring him food and ride him for a while. That was a glorious experience. She and Mich would race him on foot down the beach, only to trip and fall in the water, laughing.

The fifth day, they went back to the beach. Spirit was there, waiting for them. He knelt in the sand and tossed his head, indicating that Nola should get on his back. She grabbed a handful of his mane and pulled herself up.

She looked down at Mich. He was staring up at her, smiling broadly. She noticed that he looked rather pale.

She had a flashback from one of her dreams. She suddenly discovered a way to settle her indecision about Mich. In her dreams, Nola would often see people who admired Spirit and would try to steal him or would ask for a ride. Every time she offered a ride, Spirit would buck and kick and sometimes bite them. Once, she remembered, she was on Spirit's back while he flew below a cliff. A friend of hers had jumped from it, trying to commit suicide. Nola turned him around and tried to maneuver beneath her falling friend. Spirit turned away at the last moment and her friend fell to her death. The only person who could ride Spirit, besides herself, was Mich. Spirit would often fly Nola to his bedroom window in the castle and always let Mich ride.

"Why didn't I think of this before?" she blurted out.

Spirit stiffened beneath her. That was not a good sign. She stretched a hand toward Mich and gestured for him to mount up behind her.

"I don't think—"

"Come on. You want me to believe you, don't you? This'll prove it. If you are really who you claim to be, then he will not hurt you."

"What assurance do I have of that? I don't know him!"

"You trust me, don't you? If you are not lying, then he won't hurt you, I promise."

"Of course I trust you!" He reached up to take her hand.

Spirit flared his nostrils and tossed his head, but Mich did not let go. He pulled himself up and sat behind Nola. Nola sat still a moment, waiting for a response. There was none. Then, Spirit took off down the beach. Mich threw his arms around Nola to keep from falling off. They galloped on and on, until the beach came dangerously close to a housing area. Then they returned to the private part of the beach and dismounted.

Later that night, Nola discussed what had happened with Mich. Mich was disappointed to learn that Nola still had strong doubts. While they rode Spirit, she seemed very happy and sure. But as they walked home, she seemed more and more distant.

Sometime in the middle of the night, Mich awoke in an ice-cold sweat. He complained that he was terribly tired and he couldn't get comfortable in bed. He got out of bed, shaking and walking back and forth.

Nola finally believed him in one thing: he had not been sleeping. Not the way she did. And he still hadn't come on to her. He never tried to join her in bed in the night. What was with him?

"Please, Nola, come back to Kafka with me. I will not leave without you! If I stay here, I'll die. Let me use the spell now."

Nola felt very sorry for him. Even though he was crazy, he was in real pain. What harm would it do to humor him?

"Okay. Use it. Take me with you."

"Oh, thank you, Nola!"

"Don't mention it. Say, don't you have to be in bed with me?" Maybe now he would make his play.

"No, I'm a Kafkian. The spell will find both me and Spirit. Only you need to be on the bed. Here is the spell."

He handed her a globe about the size of a baseball. She wasn't sure where he had hidden it all this time. It looked as if it was made of glass. It was warm to the touch and there was light coming from it.

"What do I do with it?"

"Just think of your dreams, that only you can dream, and wish you were in them. That's it."

That seemed easy enough. Nola loved thinking about her dreams. That was her problem: her dreams were so much better than the dismal real world she endured.

Suddenly, there was light everywhere. Then a hole appeared over her and another hole over Mich. They hung in the air like a black piece of paper suspended by a string.

"Reach up to it!" he said. "Climb in!"

She did. Then she believed.

7

KAFKA

Meanwhile, in Kafka, Heat and Snort waited. They waited all day, then through the next day as well. They waited and waited. They waited by the river for five days, growing more and more worried. If Prince Michael didn't return on the next day, all would be lost. And there was nothing they could do to help.

On the sixth day, they were joined by one of the palace guardsmen. He explained to Heat that King Edward had sent him to find his son. It had been ten days since his departure from the castle and Mich should have returned on the sixth day. Strange things were going on at the castle and everyone was worried about Mich. But Heat had no answer. He feared the worst.

They waited all through the morning. At noon the guard sent Snort downriver to do some fishing in the rapids. He brought back three large fish and cooked them for himself and the guard. Heat cropped the dry grasses. He didn't enjoy it, but he was hungry and there wasn't much else here to eat.

Then the long vigil abruptly ended. Three figures emerged from the water, just before sundown, striding to the bank. Mich had arrived with Spirit and a young girl. Heat knew immediately that she was the Creator despite her ordinary appearance, while Snort was doubtful.

Mich made introductions. Nola was afraid of Snort at first, but her curiosity overcame her fear and it seemed that they would get along quite well. Heat was very friendly toward her. She was his Creator also; that was why he had recognized her. Yet she was also a new girl who seemed very glassy-eyed and did not speak much at first.

They spent the night camped well inside the Forest of Imagination, away from troll territory. Mich went into more detail about the Fren and Reility. He had no idea why the Fren would dam off the River of Thought, but they had to be stopped. And, gradually, Nola came to feel, if not at home, at least present in Kafka. At first she had seemed, even to herself, to be not quite real here, but now that was changing.

Nola tried her best to understand and comprehend what Mich was telling her, but she still felt as if this weren't really happening to her. It wasn't until very late that evening that her belief strengthened enough to eliminate her sensation of disorientation. She had thought Mich was crazy, or a clever impostor who had somehow learned of her secret dream; now she knew that he was her real dream man.

Nola was tired but could not fall asleep. She tossed and turned and even tried counting sheep, but nothing worked. She curled up next to Spirit and still could not drift off.

She was surprised to see Spirit in his dream form. He was so beautiful and noble-looking. Somehow in her initial confusion she had not picked up on that. He was no longer a beautiful horse, he was a unisus—a winged unicorn. A completely magical creature, now as real as she was, in this realm.

Is something wrong, my friend? thought Esprit in a deep resonate voice. *Your mind seems troubled.*

"I'm not sure; I just can't get to sleep," she whispered.

Spirit grinned in an obscure, humanlike way, bearing his large white teeth. *Of course not,* he thought, *it is impossible to truly sleep in*

Kafka, for that might lead to dreaming. Unless, of course, you are in the waters of the River of Thought. Even then you don't actually sleep. You merely relax and tune out consciousness for a time.

Nola wasn't certain of the distinction, but decided to stop worrying about sleep. "What is the River of Thought, exactly?"

It is the source of all life in Kafka. Its waters are formed by all the dreams of humankind. Every drop is a separate hope, wish or fantasy. It is composed mostly of children's dreams. Not many children are Creators. They are taught from the beginning that imaginary people and animals and monsters are not real. Nor will they ever be real. A child is taught that it is wrong to believe in fantasy and dreams. A child's dreams last only through childhood, then reality steps in and deals them a fatal blow. You, however, are a very special case. You continue to believe in me.

"I could never bring myself to stop believing in you. You are my friend and I love you." She put her hand on Spirit's neck and smiled. "But what about you and Mich and others like you who have been here a long time?"

There are some like us here, but we are few. We remain here because of the small handful of people like you, who retain their dreams throughout their lives.

"What happens to you when I die?"

We are not quite certain, but legend says that if you believe until the end, that your dreams are carried with you wherever you go and that you live within them for eternity.

"Why is it you never spoke to me before I came here?"

In your world, my body and mind are rendered null. I turn into an ordinary horse. That is the way of it for us unisi.

"Oh."

Dawn is coming up. You should prepare.

"Prepare for what?"

So many questions! To deal with the Fren, of course! Now I will

*help you to find something to tide you over until the other guards come
with new clothes and rations.*

They got up. Nola felt refreshed despite not actually sleeping.
But she resolved that the next night she spent here, she would tune
out consciousness and see if it wasn't actually pretty close to what she
called sleep. It might be just a matter of definition.

Esprit found a small luberry bush. It was covered with white
berries. Nola, hesitant, accepted Spirit's reassurance and ate half of
them. They were unlike any fruit she had ever eaten. They were
about the size and shape of large cherries. Their flavor was a mixture
of blueberries and peaches. The thin skins were very sweet while the
centers were very tart, and each contained a small, pale pink pit. She
picked some more and put them on a clump of grass next to Mich.

Mich was resting peacefully. He opened his eyes as she knelt
down. He saw Nola leaning over him. She was wiping a smudge
from his face.

He noticed she was still wearing her semi-translucent undergar-
ment that she had called a "nightie." Her pale skin looked as soft as
cream and her reddish-brown tresses fell forward, almost into his
face. He wished he could kiss her, but dared not. He wasn't sure if
she would react positively to that. He had been excruciatingly careful about that while in the real world, lest he offend her and lose
everything. She was, after all, not merely a pretty woman; she was his
Creator. He decided it would be better to play it cool for a while
longer. However, it was hard to be cool with Nola's half-naked body
so close to him.

"Good morning, Nola," he said, sitting up and stretching. "I
hope you weren't too cold last night." If only he could have warmed
her by wrapping his arms around her!

Until now Nola wasn't consciously aware that she was still wearing her little white nightie. She had been showing entirely too much

flesh where it was tight, and possibly even more where it wasn't tight. It was too late to even try to blush, so she ignored the embarrassment. "Spirit kept me warm last night. So, when do we get started?"

"Soon," Mich said, stretching and flexing his gorgeous muscles. Nola averted her stare. If only the big hunk had shown even a little urge to grab her! But he remained as indifferent as a brother to a sister. "First we must wait for my father's guards to bring us clothes and food."

Nola thought it best not to make any more inquiries on the subject. This was his world, and he knew its conventions far better than she did. Certainly she was scantily clothed.

"You are beautiful," he said, looking intently at her in the gentle dawning rays of the sun. "You are very brave to uproot your life and come to another world with me, a stranger. Beautiful not just on the outside."

Nola tried to run her hand through her hair, but it was hopelessly tangled. There was a white lie for sure! Regardless, she could not hold back her blush this time.

She was, however, able to come back with a brilliant retort. "Ditto," she said.

Mich looked blank.

Nola felt herself compelled to lean forward and kiss him. Then she met his gaze. Once again she found herself locked in Mich's sparkling eyes. She wanted to stay that way forever! But she somehow found the strength to turn away.

She stood up and walked over to Spirit, who was gingerly plucking the last of the luberries from the bush with his dexterous equine lips. Meanwhile, Mich gulped down the berries that Nola had left for him. It wasn't much, but it would do.

The group was startled by the sound of something running through the forest. It was one of the king's guards. He was waving a piece of parchment in the air.

"Sire! We have found you!" The guard tripped and fell at Mich's feet. Nola managed to stifle her giggle as Mich reached to help him up. "What's going on?" Mich asked. "Is my father okay?"

"No, sire, he's gone! We have searched since you left. We sent Misty up the mountain to see Madrid."

Mich held back his alarm and tried to settle himself. He thought he had seen Misty last night but couldn't figure out why the little graveyard ghost would be out in the forest, especially at night. Misty was terrified of the dark.

"Did Madrid know his whereabouts?" he asked, his voice cracking.

"No, sir. Madrid gave this to Misty and told her to give it to you. She was with us, but she disappeared only a few moments ago. Something is terribly wrong."

Mich took the paper from the guard. "It seems to be an instruction and a map. It says at the bottom here that by the time I get this she will be gone. What is going on here?"

At that moment, another guard came jogging through the woods. The guard stopped a few yards away and leaned against a tree. He was short, fat and sweaty, and he was panting roughly. Strapped across his shoulder was a large satchel.

"Why [pant] must you always [pant] run so fast [pant], Marcus?" he demanded.

"Come on, you dolt," Marcus retorted. "Bring the Prince's clothes!"

The guard stumbled forward and threw the satchel down. "That thing is heavier than that sow you were with last weekend! Hello, Derek!" he said, waving to the guard who arrived the night before.

Marcus turned and cuffed his friend on the side of the head. "Enough! I should have fired you long ago! Now unpack their things so they can get on with this."

Nola couldn't help but laugh. She didn't want to hurt their feelings so tried to cover up by helping them remove the clothing. Her hilarity turned to awe as she removed the dress that was meant for her. It was beautiful. It was made of red velvet and delicately embroidered with gold thread. The cuffs reminded her of the cuffs of a wedding gown, but were more intricate. There was a bright yellow sash that hung from each of the sleeves. Nola had never seen anything like it. She also found a hair brush and four golden hair combs.

"Forgive me for the dress, unsuitable as it is, but we were in quite a rush," the fat guard said. "Quickly now, Lady Nola, you must dress and be on your way."

Nola went behind a dense clump of saplings and dressed. She had a difficult time tying the bodice in the back. It was very tight and smashed her breasts almost flat, causing them to peek out over the top. She tried to loosen it but there was a gap in the back. She exhaled and tightened the strings. Now her breathing was labored, and every time she inhaled her breasts swelled dangerously above, not wanting to be bound. This was definitely not her notion of fit apparel for forest travel!

She brushed out her hair and piled it, piece by piece, on top of her head, fastening it with the combs. "Okay, I'm ready now," she said as she stepped from behind the tree. "Where do we go?"

The two guards guffawed and the fat one whistled. Marcus slapped the back of his friend's head again. "Don't be a jerk!"

Mich walked over to her and took her hand. "You look exquisite, Nola," he said, his eyes seeming to track her every breath. But perhaps that was just her fond imagination.

Nola was also stunned by Mich. His hair was now brushed and shone as brightly as Esprit's hide, his face was clean and his clothes were neat. He looked like the knights she had read about in her fairy tale novels. "So do you," she said, blushing.

"If you please, sir," Marcus said, "Kafka is falling as we speak."

"Uh, yes," Mich agreed, hauling his eyes from Nola's décolletage. "We better get going now. Madrid drew a little map on this paper that will lead us to the river's source." He looked up. "Do you know where my father went?"

"No, sir. It appears that he has been abducted, but there are no signs of violence."

Mich was highly disturbed about his father's disappearance but didn't let it show. He would have to be in command now. In his father's absence, he would be responsible for Kafka's welfare. He hated to admit it, but his father would have to wait. Kafka's survival was far more important. He hoped that his father had not been Forgotten.

"I'm sure he is fine," he said insincerely. "We will have to search for him later. Let's go. Thank you for your service, guards. Return to the castle, and if you find her, send Misty to inform me with news of my father upon his return."

"Will do, Highness!" Marcus said. His chubby friend was staring at Nola and seemed not to comprehend that they were to depart. Marcus pinched him, hard, on the shoulder. "Come on, you moron!" he said impatiently. They disappeared into the forest.

Nola allowed herself a faint smile. This corset bodice was a pain, literally, but it seemed to be doing wonders for her image. Now if only Mich would notice more than her labored breathing!

Spirit knelt down and Nola grabbed a handful of mane and tried to mount. The dress prevented her from spreading her legs wide enough. Spirit was a large animal. He had the size of a draft horse, but the build of a morgan. She loved it, but she just couldn't swing her leg over him unless she hiked up her skirt so far as to make it pointless. She was forced to ride in the fashion of ladies, sidesaddle. She thought the position was not only degrading to women, but dangerous at high speeds as well. She knew that an actual sidesaddle had stout bars and things to hold the legs firmly in place, but she was riding bareback. Still, she had no choice. She sat square with both her legs in front of his left wing, close together in the manner evidently required of ladies. She had to sit up by his withers to do this. When she tried to sit behind his wings, her legs ruffled his pretty feathers and got in the way. There were times when she wished it didn't matter so much just how far a woman spread her legs. Suppose she slid off and fell? Then she was likely to show more than her bare legs to the sky, while her face was in the muck.

Spirit rose up and started trotting southward toward what was Welton Town on the map. Snort half slithered and half galloped behind her. Mich mounted Heat, who caught up and took the lead.

Nola was still a little excited and confused by all of this. She was terribly happy, and yet she was also terribly afraid of what might happen to her precious dreams if she let Kafka down. She couldn't imagine going through life without being able to escape reality in her dreams. She hugged Esprit's neck, and he blew air through his nostrils in response. How could a simple girl like her possibly hope to save an entire world? She decided she had to try, for the sake of Mich and Esprit. She just *had* to do it!

Nola looked at Mich, who was riding ahead of her. He sat confidently on Heat's back. He bounced a little, as there was no saddle, but he rode well. His broad shoulders were squared and his hair flew about wildly in the wind. He was very comely. He turned and smiled back at her and she was reassured. Actually she seemed to be keeping her place on Spirit's back well enough; maybe there was some magic holding her there, because even if she had been an expert rider, she wouldn't be able to ride well bareback sidesaddle.

"We don't have much time left! Come on!" Mich yelled. He delicately squeezed Heat's ribs with his knees and Heat faltered, then lunged forward into a full run.

Nola figured this would be a laudable time for her to show off. Esprit already knew what she wanted. He too lunged forward, almost dislodging her despite the magic as he thrust his body ahead. She clung tightly to his thick mane as he galloped. His great black hooves beat thunderously beneath them, kicking up large rocks and clods of dirt. The hairs of his mane were so fine and silky, yet it seemed as if each one was made of steel wire.

It was only a moment before Esprit was in front of Heat, and he was still running strongly when Nola heard Mich call faintly for her to stop. He wasn't very far behind but it was difficult to hear over the pounding of hooves. Nola started to wonder if something was wrong. Esprit slowed to a trot and stopped, his sides heaving.

They had covered a lot of ground. Nola had dreamed that Esprit was fast, but this was incredible. She'd never experienced anything so pleasurable. She was pleased to read in Spirit's mind that he felt the same. They had left the Forest of Imagination behind and were within sight of the River of Thought, on their left, and Welton Town was also nearby, though out of sight.

"What's wrong, Mich?" she asked, panting for breath.

"Nothing," he said as he caught up. "It's just that we're almost to Welton Town and the townspeople wouldn't like it if we just came crashing in. Besides, we left poor Snort far behind. He can fly pretty fast, but he's not *that* fast."

She realized that she had been thoughtless, in her sheer delight of the ride. It had been fun to ride Spirit on the beach in the real world, but here in Kafka it was absolutely glorious. "Where is the town?"

"It's just over that rise in the meadow," he said, pointing. "The Welties don't like unisi. They are scared that their crops will get trampled."

"Welties?" Nola asked, perplexed.

"Their name implies their state. They are people like you and me, but their bodies are black and blue and covered with lumps and bumps, otherwise known as, you guessed it, welts." Mich looked up. "Here's Snort."

Nola looked up too. Snort was flying downward to them on his

nearly inadequate wings, leaving a trail of steam behind. He landed
with a thud on his short front legs and did a clumsy somersault. He
shook himself and looked toward Mich, annoyed.

"I'm sorry, little guy," Mich said, patting Snort's brown head.
"We just got a little excited. We won't leave you behind again. That
is, except for now. I don't think the Welties would appreciate you as
much as we do, so you will have to stay with Heat and Spirit and
travel to the southern fringe of Welton Town. We will meet you
there. Be careful; the Fren might be wandering about. We'll see you
soon." He patted Snort again.

"One question," Nola said. "Why do we have to go through here
at all? Can't we just go around?"

"We are going to need all the help we can get." With that, he dismounted and walked out into the meadow.

Nola followed uncertainly. These creatures sounded disgusting,
but if Mich thought that they could help, then they probably would.
After all, he was a prince here.

8

NYMPH

Welton Town was incredibly similar to a Virginia suburb. It consisted of a few town-type houses and some ramblers. Each had a beautifully manicured lawn, and flowers bloomed in backyard gardens. It was all surrounded by small plots of farmland.

On each plot was a specific kind of fruit or vegetable. On some plots, there were familiar livestock such as chickens, goats and pigs.

One of the town's inhabitants came out to greet them. It was a tall, slim woman. She was wearing a white tight-fitting minidress, a pair of sandals and a flowing black cowl. Her face was greenish blue and her lips were black. In contrast, her eyes were a sparkling gold color. She smiled, showing perfectly straight white teeth.

She bowed deeply to Mich. "Welcome, Your Highness, to Welton Town. My name is Greyden. The Welties have heard of your coming. I and my husband would be so honored if you and your lady friend would consent to stay at our inn during your brief visit."

Mich was forced to reply, as Nola was too disgusted by her beaten appearance to speak. It reminded her of an abused woman and dredged up thoughts she wished not to think. "We would be happy to," he said, nudging Nola.

"Yes, of course we would!" she agreed with feigned enthusiasm.

The woman smiled and led them through the paved streets to the inn. It was really a small motel. It looked like the kind one would end up staying in if one's car broke down in the middle of nowhere.

Nola was surprised at the inside, however. It was lavishly furnished with Oriental rugs and Victorian furniture. In the ceiling of the lobby was a massive crystal chandelier lit by flickering candles.

She led them down a narrow hallway and through a squeaky door. Inside was a small chamber. Bookshelves lined the walls. There was a desk with an elderly gentleman sitting behind it. The room was lit by a tiny window. A haze of dust floated along the rays of sunlight that sprang through the glass.

The old man looked up from his papers when he heard the squeak of the door.

The woman bowed to them. "I'll prepare a dinner if you'll be staying."

"We will stay for dinner, thank you," Mich said. He hadn't thought about dinner, and the guards had forgotten to bring them some food. It was kind of Greyden to offer, as the Welties were not normally so hospitable to strangers, even royal ones. Greyden bowed again and left the room.

"Greetings," the man said. "My name is Daree'. I am governor of the eastern territory." He put his paper aside and removed his spectacles. He stared at Nola with intensity. Nola, feeling uncomfortable under the weight of the stare, shifted her gown and averted her eyes. She was relieved when he turned his eyes to Mich.

"So, Prince Michael, it has come to my attention that you are in need of our help and I in need of yours." His staring dark eyes became slits and his voice was excited as he leaned forward so that his guests could hear him better. "The Fren have destroyed two of my villages and have repeatedly burned up our crops. With no food to export, our people cannot continue to produce and we will become too poor to feed our children."

Daree' leaned back and quieted himself; he was becoming angry

to the point of losing his dignity. "Therefore, I shall offer what little I have left to you. As you know, my people like to keep their distance from other humanoids, but in a dire case like this, exceptions
must be made, and in this circumstance," he looked again at Nola, "I
believe that I have nothing to fear."

Daree' stood up and put his spectacles back on. "My army will be
waiting for you at the Shattered-Glass Glade." He skirted the desk to
open the chamber door. He held the door open for them to pass
through it. Before they exited the chamber he said, "I will make the
arrangements tonight, but it will take some time. After dinner, you
must travel on with this woman." He gestured to Nola. "Get to the
Source and destroy the dam. Our world and hers depends on it."

"The palace thanks you for your help, Daree'," said Mich. He
bowed and left the old man to his reading.

Mich and Nola stayed almost until nightfall. They were served a
feast of piglets and luberry cake. Nola wasn't fond of the idea of
eating piglets, but she tried them and decided the taste wasn't too bad.
She just had to imagine them in some other way, lest she toss her
"cookies" and humiliate herself.

After dinner, Greyden suggested they get going before moonrise.
The Fren were diurnal creatures, so it would be safest that they travel
by night. At this hour, the Fren would be resting and it would not be
likely that they would run into them.

Snort, Heat, and Spirit were waiting anxiously for them just south
of the town, right where expected. Once together again, Mich looked
at the map and instructions that Madrid left him. They must continue
southward along the river. It would lead them past the newly estab-
lished Fren Cliffs and into the most dangerous place in Kafka, the
Forget Mists, where they were to meet someone who could help.

The group traveled most of the night unmolested along the river.
They reached the Fren Cliffs a few hours before dawn.

What a forbidding and ominous place it was! Mich and Nola were very nervous as they walked below the towering cliffs. They seemed to rise forever through the early morning mists. Their faces were covered with small dark caves. The area smelled awful. They walked close to the cliff walls and finally made it through to the meadow beyond.

Nola stopped and breathed, it seemed, for the first time. "Couldn't we just have flown over this region?" she inquired plaintively. "Or around it?"

"No. The cliffs rise forever and it is impossible to go around without being captured by guards."

Spirit suggested that they mount and ride from here to the sea and the Forget Mists.

"What a disgusting place!" Nola said, mounting Spirit.

Yes, it is, Spirit agreed.

"Who would have dreamed up a place like that?" she asked.

I don't think it is a dream, Spirit thought. *No one really knows who the Fren are, but I think that they are the leftovers of good dreams that were not forgotten, but destroyed. I felt nothing there but hate and regret.*

"Destroyed by whom?"

Probably just someone who doesn't care about whose dreams he has to step on to push his reality on others.

At that moment, Snort growled menacingly and blew some steam through his nostrils.

"What's wrong?" Mich asked.

Heat translated for him, *He said he smells something.*

"Is it a Wood Troll?"

No, it smells sweet and delicious.

Mich wondered if it was some kind of food. "Well? What is it, Snort?"

A nymph. More specifically, a Foliar Nymph.

Now Mich knew exactly what Snort had smelled. No wonder it

excited him so much. "It's just a foliar nymph," he relayed to the others.

"Oops!" Nola said.

Mich turned and looked at her. "Don't tell me!" He put his hand over his brow and shook his head. "You created the plant nymphs as well?"

Nola shrugged. She wondered how closely it would resemble her dream nymphs. In her dreams, they'd appear occasionally when she was lost. They helped her to find her way, though they were often unreliable and flighty. The strangest thing was that they spoke as if they knew everything about everything.

Spirit scuffed his hoof through the grass as a form appeared out of the dim morning light. It was a small woman, about four feet tall. There was no doubt she was a woman, for she was very well endowed. Her slender torso was scantily covered in blue flower petals. Her green hair grew down to her ankles and matched her pale green skin. Her tiny feet were covered in white blossoms that matched the color of her milky eyes. She resembled one of Nola's dream nymphs exactly.

She approached Spirit and looked up at Nola, who felt so small and delicate from atop Spirit's huge body.

"Creator," she said sweetly, "why are you going this way?"

"Madrid told us that we must," Nola replied, somehow not surprised to be recognized in this manner. Mich had known her immediately, on Earth, and Heat had recognized her nature in Kafka. Apparently there was something about her, and it wasn't the constrictive dress.

"But, Creator, there is no need."

"But the map says that we have to fly through the Forget Mists across the sea to some island where we are supposed to meet someone who can help us."

The little nymph laughed musically and her eyes shone bright with mirth. "Dear girl! I am the one who is to meet you. Don't you know you can never go into the mists? You would be Forgotten! If that happened," she spread her hands, "this wonderful world would be gone."

"Well, what do we do?" Nola asked, uncertain whether it was wise to go against the sorceress's instructions on the word of a stranger. Yet this was definitely a nymph of the type she had dreamed of. Maybe Mich had misunderstood the note.

The nymph stroked Snort's neck and looked thoughtful. "Madrid sent you to me because we know the ways of dreamstone. Our ancestors mined it from the land. However, we are not sure ourselves how to deal with such a problem."

Snort was enjoying her caresses and didn't hide it. The small dragon was now rolling onto his back like a kitten. Nola already knew that though Snort loved attention, he was choosy about whom it came from. The nymph must be all right.

"You understand," the nymph continued, "that dreamstone is indestructible."

Mich was becoming impatient. "Of course we know that! What do we do, then? Is there some other way we can let the river flow freely again?"

"There is a way, but it is so very difficult. The human girl must destroy the dam herself." The nymph turned her white eyes to look at Nola. "She must disbelieve the stone."

The group looked at one another. "But how?" Nola pleaded. "How can I disbelieve what plainly exists?"

"As I've said, it is difficult. There are others who dream of dreamstone and one type is even linked to the great dragon, Kafka himself, and cannot be destroyed by anyone, living or not. I believe you wear such a stone. We are doomed if the dam is made of this type. But if it is ordinary dreamstone, you can do it. You must simply not believe it exists. Or, even better, Forget it."

"Do you have an idea what type it is made of?" Mich asked.

"No one knows because no one has ever even seen it. It is located at the source. No one can find it, let alone destroy it."

"We will handle it," Nola said optimistically, though inside she was trying to digest a bolus of doubt. "Just tell us how to reach the source." Yet, paradoxically, she felt suddenly strong. She figured that she was responsible for the rescue of this vast world and she had better get some control of the situation.

"Just follow the river. There is one area, past the Shattered-Glass Glade, where you can reach the source by sleeping in the river. It is guarded by a winged hippocampus. Just utter my name before you enter the water and it will leave you alone."

"But you haven't told us your name," Nola protested.

"You did not ask."

Nola took a deep breath. "What is your name?"

The nymph smiled. "My name is Violet."

Then, for a moment, the little nymph had a look of confusion on her pretty face as if she was forgetting something. The moment passed and her face returned to its bright state. She curtsied and prepared to leave. But then paused. "By the way, in respect for Kafkian security, if or when you return to this side of Kafka, you will forget the location of the gateway to the source and you won't remember, even if you stumble into it again, unless I tell you where it is. I think that's the rule."

Again, she seemed to hesitate. She shrugged her shoulders and with that she turned and disappeared as quickly as she had appeared.

Nola stared after her. What a curious encounter!

Mich smiled at Nola. "I know you can do it," he said supportively. "You're the best. After all, you created me."

Nola laughed at his immodesty. She kicked her feet a little to alert Spirit, and he turned tail and leaped into the sky, following the river.

Mich followed beside her and Snort also took to the air, but was quickly left behind, again.

Nola hung on, reveling in the wonderful flight through the morning air. The landscape spread out below them like a richly variegated tapestry. She wished she could identify specific places, but she just wasn't familiar enough with this region to get properly oriented. Still, it was a phenomenal experience, no matter where they were.

They flew on for hours and covered much territory before Heat began to tire. He seemed to have gained strength now that his friend was with him once again. Spirit also was feeling strain in his wing muscles, though he could fly on if necessary.

The day was beginning to lose light. Esprit and Heat were both exhausted. They were strong animals, but both had limits. Nola realized with a start that this meant that they had been flying all day. It had seemed like only an hour or so to her.

They were still not yet in sight of the glade, but they landed to rest and wait for Snort to catch up. When the little dragon did, Snort galumphed over to Mich and snorted a puff of steam at him. He was angry for always being left behind.

Night had fallen and the unisi could no longer navigate by land. Unfortunately, the sky was overcast and dark. No hope there; they would have to camp, which was just as well.

They found a spot that was fairly clear of big rocks and sprinkled with soft grasses. Nola was still a bit shy around her dream man, but Spirit wanted to graze, so she was forced to choke back her shyness and lie down with Mich. The nights could be cold in Kafka, and Mich's strong body should help keep her warm and safe.

Nola was very tired. So much had happened. She wondered how her ornery cat was doing and hoped that Lori would stop by, as promised, and feed her. Since Snort was doing well enough, considering, she thought Kudo must be all right too.

Despite Mich's closeness, the chill air made Nola shiver next to him. Mich covered her with the blanket he was using in lieu of a saddle. It smelled of sweat and horsehair, but it was warm. He put his arm over her shoulder.

As Mich held Nola's small body, he knew it would be only a matter of time before he lost his senses and fell for her. The Sorceress Madrid had predicted it. He hoped he could complete his mission before thoughts of love clouded his mind. He was king now and he had to prevail, for the sake of his people and for his father.

Nola snuggled closer. His arms were strong and secure. He was so like the man in her dreams; how could she ever have thought he wasn't? She wished she could lose herself in those green eyes forever, but that was ridiculous. She barely knew him. Or did she?

Again she experienced the strange sensation of conscious sleep. Her body was relaxed and numbed while her mind wandered over the day's events, fully aware of the sounds and smells of the night.

Yet at the same time, it seemed like such a waste. Here she was with the whole night to pass away, unsleeping, in the arms of her dream man—and they were doing nothing but just lying here? She could think of a thousand things to make the time pass swiftly and pleasurably. Well, one thing, anyway. But until *he* thought of it, she wasn't about to suggest it. A girl just didn't in a situation like this.

9

WORM

In the morning, Mich got up early and picked fruit. He lay a large pile of it next to Nola. The fruit looked like oranges with green spots. These were more like it!

She tasted one. It was just like an orange. She ate two of them and discovered underneath a small pile of mushrooms. She ate those too, sure that Mich wouldn't pick poisonous ones. Wouldn't do to wipe out a Creator before the job was done, after all! They were sort of squishy and slimy, but they tasted okay.

Snort was busily crunching on some small animal that he had hunted down, and Heat was plucking leaves from the orange tree.

Spirit trotted over to where Nola was standing. *I smell something foul,* he thought urgently.

Nola, feeling his distress, conveyed the information to Mich.

"Heat smells it too. What is it, friend?" Mich asked, patting Heat's nose.

I can't place it. I haven't smelled anything this grotesque in ages, Heat replied.

Mich could smell it too now. The aroma of mud and rotting flesh. Every second the foul odor grew stronger. Then they heard a low, rumbling noise. Soon everyone was attuned to it. It was coming toward them.

"What is it?" Nola asked, alarmed.

"I'm not sure," Mich confessed. He glanced at the unisi, but they did not seem to recognize it either.

Mich and Nola stumbled as the ground moved beneath them with the force of a small quake. The stench burned their eyes, and the source of it appeared at their feet.

The rocky ground was cracked open and an enormous, wormlike head poked through the rubble.

Its breath was that of carrion that had been slightly cooked with sulfur gas. It was slimy pink and had thorny protrusions, sort of like a spiked collar, around a bulbous head. It had no visible eyes or nose. Inside the mouth was a tube. It was lined, all the way down the throat, with sharp, backward-pointing teeth.

It struck out at Nola, who reflexively tried to punch it. Her fist squashed into the thing's head and slurped as she pulled it back out. No damage showed on the creature, but Nola's hand was covered with putrid goo.

Heat dashed it with his chrome hooves and skewered it with his long horn, but they simply squashed through it with a sickly sound and the hole left by the horn immediately healed over. Without, however, abating the festering stink.

"Enough!" Mich cried. He valiantly unsheathed his sword and pointed it at the worm's head. The worm seemed unconcerned and did not even turn its head toward him.

Instead, it opened its mouth and stuck out a red tongue. The tongue was ropelike, and it wrapped about Nola's legs and pulled her down. Nola screamed and struggled uselessly. Some Creator she was! She was about to be eaten by a miasmic worm!

Mich brought down the sword and separated the worm's massive head from its neck. Purple slime spilled out. The body and severed head writhed and formed two new worms, each smaller but every bit as awful as the first. The second worm lashed another tongue around Nola's arms and waist and began pulling her into its tunnel.

Mich could do nothing but watch. The worms seemed to have the same power as the Wood Trolls. If he tried to cut the worm again, it would only form two more and that would just make it easier for them to drag her in. He felt more helpless now than ever. How could he leave her to creatures like that? She was too nice a girl to be killed by a giant worm. He had to rescue her! Quite apart from the fact that his mission and the salvation of Kafka depended on her. He couldn't afford to let it happen.

That helped get his inadequate mind operating. "Snort! Follow them! Scorch their tails!" he yelled.

The brave little basilisk slithered down the tunnel after the worms. Mich followed into the dark tunnel on his hands and knees, leaving Heat and Spirit outside. The hole was small, and crawling was difficult. The tunnel wound down steeply, and in a moment it was dark.

The tunnel ahead was lit momentarily as Snort scorched the worms' tails. More rancid fumes wafted toward Mich's nose. In the glow, he could see that Snort's fire did little to stop the worms. They didn't even seem to notice.

Farther in the tunnel, Mich could walk. The tunnel continued to wind into the ground, corkscrewlike. He followed Snort by holding on to his tail because it was too dark to see. The floor of the tunnel was slippery, probably from the slime of the worms. The smell was so awful that Mich could barely breathe. He could hear Nola's faint sobs and that gave him strength to withstand the smell and press on.

Abruptly, Snort halted. Mich wondered why his pet had stopped, as he could hear the worms slurping on down the tunnel. Too bad he couldn't talk to Snort the way he talked to Heat.

He tugged the tail gently. "What's going on? Give me a little light."

Snort lit the tunnel with a tiny flame, enough to see by but not enough to call attention to them.

Ahead, there was a huge cavern with alternating tunnels and round doors. He could see the worms dragging Nola through one of the doors and into a small room. They cast her down and nudged the door closed, making her a lone prisoner. It seemed they weren't going to eat her just yet; she would keep until they finished whatever other business they had.

When the worms had gone down another tunnel, Snort and Mich crept to the chamber that held Nola. There was a small round window he could look through, but no visible latch. Nola saw the light of Snort's flame and ran over to the door.

"Mich! Where are we? What are those things? I'm so afraid!" She collapsed next to the door.

Mich couldn't bear to see her so distraught. He drew his sword and was preparing to deal the door a fatal blow when the weapon was wrenched from his grasp by a red tongue. He stood for an instant, uncertain what to do.

Then Snort blasted the worm with fire. This toasted its skin and melted a little of its thorny collar into goo. It quickly healed itself, but Mich used the respite to take action. He grabbed on to the tongue and pulled it out of the worm's head. He recovered his sword while the worm was forming a new tongue.

Mich had his sword again, but in only a few seconds the tongue he still held in his other hand became another worm, and started wrestling with his hand. This was useless! How could he fight a creature like this? While he was trying to throw away the clinging tongue worm, the larger worm was shoving against him, trying to lasso his head with its new tongue. Mich tried to chop it with the sword, but it dropped down and caught his ankles while the rest of its body jammed against him. He couldn't step back because his feet were entangled. He crashed into the door with such force that the catch apparently broke.

He fell ignominiously into the chamber, landing on his back. The worm shoved Snort after him and closed the door, barring it somehow.

Nola sat up and threw her arms around Mich. "Oh, I was so scared! I thought that thing was going to eat you!" She released him. "I don't think I could survive in this place alone. Look!" She pointed behind her.

At this point, the source of the smell became apparent. Behind her in the chamber was a heap of rotting refuse. It looked to be composed of mud, manure and bodies of dead creatures. It was likely that this stuff was what the worms ate. They probably stored it here until it was sufficiently dead and rotten to be tasty. That explained why they hadn't eaten Nola immediately: she was too fresh.

"I wish I could tell you what this place is," Mich said, "but I have never seen anything like it, or those worm things."

He stood up and went to the door and felt along it. It felt hard and slick; there seemed to be no way to open it. He chopped at it with his sword and Snort fired a jet of flame at it, to no avail. The door was impervious to damage. The worm had done a good job of jamming it closed.

"This doesn't make sense," he muttered. "My sword is magic; it should cut through almost anything."

"Almost anything?" Nola asked. "What are the exceptions?"

"Well, dreamstone, mainly. But—" He paused. "Dreamstone! The worms must have found a lode and mined enough of it for their purposes. Who would have guessed? We can't make a dent on this stuff."

"But it opened right away for them," Nola pointed out.

"They must have some secret mechanism, or maybe they found out how to make it respond to them."

"Well, maybe we can find the key," Nola said. She faced the door. "Open sesame!" There was no response. "Well, I didn't really think that would work."

"Maybe if you screamed at it," Mich suggested, trying to be humorous.

Nola screamed, piercingly.

A worm creature slurped up to the door and poked its head through the window. Nola squirmed, thinking it was going to crawl in and consume them. That was why she had screamed. Instead, it spoke.

"Keep schilent, humanoid creature. You are schupposed to be schaved, but I will not heschitate to make a schnack of you right now!" It slurped its tongue around the orifice in the middle of its head.

The thing was surely bluffing, because Nola was nowhere close to being spoiled rotten, and would be hard for the worm to digest. But Mich, being a pampered prince, was not used to this kind of treatment. He didn't yet understand that his life could actually be at stake. So he did something stupid.

He poked the worm in the snoot with his sword, hard enough to make some goo well out. "Leave us alone, you refugee from a troll's dump, or I'll cut you into little pieces and stuff them into cracks in the floor."

The creature could of course heal itself long before he could make good on such a threat, but was evidently annoyed at this challenge. It opened the door so suddenly that it banged Mich's sword from his hand, pulled Mich up with its tongue and drew him toward its mouth. Mich knew better than to pull out the tongue again. That would just make it harder on him. What could he do? As a hero, he was failing miserably.

"Help me, Nola!" The words were out before he realized.

Nola was taken aback. What could she do? What could anyone do? But she had to try. Mich had risked his life to save her and had gotten captured himself. She could do no less. So she picked up the fallen sword and advanced on the monster, hoping that a two-handed slice would accomplish something. Snort moved with her, ready to toast any flesh she managed to cut off. Maybe they would be able to bother the worm enough to make it let Mich go. Of course it might then grab Nola. But she would try to deal with that problem when she came to it.

Just as she was about to stab the worm, the thing let go of Mich. Nola looked at the sword, wondering what could have cowed the worm so easily. The worms had shown no fear of the weapon when Mich had wielded it, and it should have been clear even to them that she was an utter novice at swordcraft.

The worm spoke again in its slurpy voice. "You schpeak the name Nola. Why?"

Mich looked shaken but retained his composure. "I am Prince Michael Edward of Kafka, son of King Erik Edward, and this is Nola Rollins of Earth, and Snort of Mangor," he said, indicating them in turn.

The worm leaned forward as if trying to get a closer look at Nola, though it had no eyes. "Sche doesch not schmell like a Kafkian."

"Sches not! I mean, she's not," Mich said indignantly.

"Why do you hold us?" Nola put in, realizing that dialogue was safer and a whole lot less messy than fighting. "Who are you?"

The worm swung its grotesque head to orient on Mich. "Thatch isch not for mech to schay. The king of Kafka chwill give you audiancech. Come with me."

Mich wondered what he meant by "king of Kafka." After all it was his father who was king, wasn't he? But he had come to a similar conclusion about fighting, and would happily talk with the worms as long as they cared to. He recovered his sword from Nola, and sheathed it.

They followed the worm through a side tunnel, with Snort illuminating the walls. The smell was not as bad as it had been because his nose was now numb to the odor, but the fumes still stung his eyes.

Soon they arrived at a great domed chamber. The room was absolutely huge. It was lit by a tiny dot of daylight, high in the ceiling of the dome. In its very center was a tall pedestal made of a silvery material, probably dreamstone. On that elevation coiled a huge worm. It was twice as large and twice as ugly as the ones they had seen thus far, and it had two gleaming red eyes. It wore a silver bowl, upside down, on its head. It was obviously the king.

"Approach me, you foul nothings," the worm called down. He spoke plainly, with no slurring accent. Rank evidently had its privilege.

Uncertain what the king intended, the three did as they were told, which was probably the best course.

"My guard informs me that you have among you a Creator. Is this so?"

Nola stepped forward, nervously. Mich could see that she was terrified.

"Yes, Your Highness!" Nola thought how literal that address was as she looked way up at him. "I am Nola." She had to speak loudly in order to be heard.

"You?" the worm roared. "You are such a pitiful creature! Hardly even worth notice and yet you claim high status! How can that be?" He looked at her more closely. "I see you wear a Creator's stigma around your neck. From whom did you steal it, cretin?"

Nola fingered the cross around her neck; she had forgotten that it was there. "I am what I am, sir! I was told I am a Creator. I am here to help save Kafka from the Fren." She was slightly offended.

"*You?*" he roared again. He laughed so hard that he loosened his coiled body and his hind end dropped over the side. "You? Protect Kafka from the Fren?"

"That is what I said," Nola said, quirking her lips and crossing her arms. Her fear was turning to annoyance.

"Look, you pitiful excuse for a humanoid, the Fren are far too powerful for the like of you. They would overwhelm your pitiful group in the blink of an eye! I do not believe you are a Creator. You are nothing to me." He blinked his red orbs.

The worm who had escorted them to the chamber was coming forward and sticking out his tongue. He wrapped it about Nola's arm and pulled on it.

"Wait!" Nola screamed. "I am! I am a Creator! If you kill me, many people will die, and if Kafka falls, so will you!"

This gave the worm king pause for thought. He certainly did not want the blame to fall on him if Kafka was destroyed. The guard released her.

"All right, then. Prove your status," the king said, re-coiling his fallen tail.

Nola looked at Mich, who just shrugged his shoulders. "How?" she asked.

The king's snout wrinkled. "Guard, bring Prince Chitie."

The guard worm left the chamber through a side tunnel and after a few moments was back, carrying a large iron cage. Inside the cage was a small, crumpled animal. It was black and looked like a deformed man. The guard put the cage down in front of Nola.

"This is my son, Prince Chitie. He was ensorcelled by Reility. He can no longer burrow and is therefore not fit to be heir to the throne. He is my only son and must take kingship. If he does not, my bloodline will end." The worm king looked almost sad as he blinked his red eyes. "If you are a Creator, you can change him back. If you do not, you will be promptly sprinkled with rot elixir so you can be consumed."

Mich, unable to control his anger further, stepped beneath the worm and shook his angry fist. "You can't do this, you pile of refuse! I am Prince Michael, son of King Edward! I command you to release us at once, or face the consequences!"

The worm king looked down. "You are in no position to command me or anyone else, twerp. I care snot for your human king. Below the surface, I rule." An eye swiveled to cover Nola. "Now, comply or die."

Nola rested her hand on Mich's shoulder. "It's okay. Don't get us killed before I have a chance to try."

Mich was slowly realizing their situation. These were creatures not to be taken lightly, and they could surely kill the captives if they felt the need. He hated to admit it, but for once, his status didn't matter. He was sufficiently daunted.

"How can I change him? I don't know how," said Nola, studying the transformed prince.

"That I cannot tell you. You say you are the Creator; do you not know how to Create?"

Nola noted the gleam in his eye and immediately covered her mistake. "Yes, of course I know how," she said, wringing her hands nervously.

"Then get on with it!" he snapped. His voice boomed through the chamber, making it sound more authoritative.

At that moment, Nola heard a noise like that of glass being broken. She looked up. High in the ceiling, the glass of the tiny window was tinkling down to the floor. The window was actually not small, but looked that way because it was so high up. Above, she could see hooves crushing the glass and the rock around it. The iron shoes made sparks as they struck the rock, dislodging huge chunks, which the group was careful to avoid.

"What is this?" the worm king demanded. "Guard, stop that creature!"

But as he spoke, Spirit broke through and jumped into the chamber. It was not large enough for him to fly down, but it was too high not to. So he half spread his enormous black wings and glided down, landing on the rock floor.

Spirit's eyes were showing white around the edges and his ears were flat against his skull. He stepped slowly toward the pedestal. His head just reached a quarter of the way up it. He bared his square teeth.

If you do not let my friend go, I will surely kill you, he thought in a calm voice. He pawed the floor, striking up more yellow sparks.

For once, the worm king seemed not sure of what to do. His head retracted into his coils and disappeared. The rest of his body followed. In a moment, the worm was gone.

Nola watched Esprit nervously, and Mich held up his sword. A small door opened up in the base of the pedestal and there was the worm king.

He approached Nola and dropped his head low. His crown tumbled off his head and spun like a top when it hit the floor. "I did not realize you were a friend of this wonderful creature. You *must* be a Creator. If you will stay and listen, I will tell you all I know of the Fren, and I will give you my warriors to help you defeat them," he said, picking up his crown with his tongue.

Mich was confused by this sudden change of heart and sheathed his sword. "Why did you abduct us?" he asked, still not trusting the worm.

"Because Nola ate some of our young."

"What?" Nola asked, disgusted. She imagined swallowing a small version of one of these things and her stomach roiled.

The worm king blinked at the guard, who brought forth a pile of mushrooms from a nook in the wall. "These are our eggs," he said, showing Nola.

Nola turned her head. She didn't feel so good and was afraid she might splatter the king with her vomit, which probably contained partially digested worm eggs.

"Oh, I'm sorry, I didn't realize," she said, covering her mouth to choke her stomach back down.

The king was gracious, accepting her apology. "It's no sin, my dear. You did not Create us, so you would not have known. Nevertheless, it irritated my minions."

"Why does a creature like you lay eggs, when all you have to do is have your body severed?" Mich asked, still suspicious.

"It is true that we can multiply this way, but it is a somewhat debilitating experience when repeated, and our clones may live only for a week or so at the most, while I am over two hundred years old." He gave the platter containing the worm eggs back to the guard. "Now follow me."

He led them to another chamber, apparently a study. He pulled down a small volume and opened it. The pages crumbled slightly as he turned them with his tongue.

"This, I'm afraid, is all we know about the Fren. They are what's left after a creature is disbelieved."

"You mean Forgotten?" Mich asked.

"No, to be Forgotten is to no longer exist. To be disbelieved is worse. It is to be transformed into living cruelty and evil, the product of a shattered dream. They are still there, but they are warped and badly deformed."

"That sounds right for Fren," Mich said. "What else can you tell us?"

"Just that no one has ever been able to defeat them." The worm king looked thoughtful for a moment. "At least, no one we know of."

"There is a first time for everything. We have the help of the Welties."

"Ah! Now, there is a fighting force! Even we have trouble when we fight with them. We have been at odds with them for many years, but we have become allies under the present situation. We try to be at peace with them. They have such lovely skins! It's too bad that they must ask now for help. The Fren should have been destroyed long ago. Where will you meet them?"

"At the Shattered-Glass Glade."

"Then you will definitely need our help to get there." He turned to look at Nola. "Accept my apology, Lady Nola, and some of my warriors." He nodded his head to her. "And one piece of advice; my source tells me that you spoke to a nymph and she told you to lie down in the river, is this so?"

"Yes, it is. Her name was Violet."

"You must understand that nymphs are largely ignorant of what is real and what is legend. As well as this liability, Kafka has cursed them with stupidity. They forget significant details of their lives. Reility may have sent her to intercept you. He knows who is able to help you and he is trying to destroy all chances for our salvation. Both the lying in the river to reach the source and the winged hippocampus are legend. Legends may be true, but often require special interpretation, and are best not taken literally. So I do not say that the nymph was trying to deceive you, but you must be cautious. I'm sure you will come to know more of them and you must beware of this. They are good at giving messages, but bad with personal information." Then he added, "Trust not the stupid. Do you trust me?"

"Of course!" She wondered if she should, but what choice did she have? Obviously, he wasn't stupid. Ugly, but not dim. She didn't know this land, and he did. She looked at Spirit, then back at the king. "But how is it you know Esprit?"

"He has been protecting our entrance tunnels from the hazards of the upper world for as long as I can remember. We have never done anything for him in return. We don't know why he does it. Once he saved my son from being eaten by a giant crow. We normally do not fear such a fate, but if one of us is consumed entire, it is very uncomfortable, and may result in awkwardness. So we are duly grateful."

Surely swallowing one of these things whole would nullify it, Nola thought. "And what about your son now?" she asked.

The worm king looked a little sad. "If it wouldn't be an imposition, Lady Nola, would you consent to break the spell on my son and change him back?"

Nola shook her head sadly. "I'm sorry, I may indeed have the power, but I don't know how."

The worm king lifted his head high and his eyes brightened. "I understand. Do not worry. You will find a way. I have faith in you." He looked at his guard and blinked, then looked at Mich. "Get on his back. He will carry you through the rock to the surface. My warriors will be waiting for you."

"Wait, what about Nola and Snort?" Mich asked as he mounted the slimy worm's back.

For answer, Nola mounted Esprit, who jumped up to the top of the pedestal, then up through the aperture in the ceiling. Snort followed, spiraling doggedly upward.

Mich dug into the worm's back with his hands. It was disgusting, but it was the only way he could hold on, and the worm didn't seem to mind it. The worm dived into a wall and proceeded up. It was a strange experience. The rock that touched him crumbled away into dust and sand and mostly disappeared. This was a powerful creature indeed!

Once on the surface, Mich was glad to be rejoined with Heat, but something was bothering him. He thought about the mermaids and the poison that had been cast into the water and of the worm king's son and he thought of the Welties and the nymphs. He worried that, maybe, the Fren would be more than they could handle.

What good would he be if he too were changed into a creature like that? He hoped Nola would be okay. She, being Earthborn, should not be affected by Reility's evil spells, but she could not prevent the doom of Kafka or Earth by herself. She was, after all, a gentle woman, with not much heart for violence.

The worm king was true to his word. They were met by a motley-looking group of five worms. They were each almost as large as the king himself. Their collars of spikes were deadly long and sharp, and their tubular mouths armed with glistening teeth. Mich hadn't fully appreciated those teeth before; these must be special warrior worms instead of household worms.

Nola was speaking with one of them. She seemed to get along with everyone she met. Her appearance was dulled by the dust and slime that had gotten on her during their trip underground, but even now she was lovely and her sheer spunkiness made her even more attractive. If only she had been a regular girl instead of a Creator!

She bounced over to him, smiling. "You were great in there! I thought we were history. It was so smart of you to say my name and save us."

Mich refrained from reminding her that his calling her name had been cowardice, not intelligence. He doubted himself even more now. What would she think if she knew that he was really more afraid than she was? But her praise in whatever form made him feel better, however foolishly.

"The worms say that once we arrive at the Shattered-Glass Glade, they will lose their power of burrowing," Nola said.

"Did they say why?"

"Yeah, they don't know why, because they have never gone that far away from the caverns, but they suspect it has something to do with the type of ground there."

"That makes sense, if that ground is made of glass. But if they can dig through solid rock, glass should be easy."

"Maybe they cut themselves. No, they would just heal. Maybe they are allergic or something."

Mich shrugged. "Maybe so." It was no use dwelling on that; the worms could surely hold their own, whether or not they could burrow.

10

DEMON

They once more headed south, toward the Shattered-Glass Glade, to find the Welties, with five new friends in tow. They had lost track of the river during the diversion in the worm tunnels, but surely would intersect it in due course.

It wasn't long before they came across a band of marauding crimson-skinned demons. Each one was more hideous than the next. They had stout little horns growing out of their foreheads, the cloven hooves of goats, the tails of serpents, and the bodies of men.

"Well, well, well, look what we have here, folks," said a particularly gruesome one in the front. "It seems as if we've run afoul of a faux basilisk, a couple of walking buckets of glue, a whore and her pimp, and even some escargot! Boys, we shall have some fun tonight!" The demon stepped forward, salivating.

Mich was worried. He had encountered a demon once before and knew how dangerous they could be. They were always looking for women and trouble. They were able to dismember themselves at will and could change instantly to any form they wished, regardless of size. They could be injured if caught unaware, but demons were seldom caught unaware. They could take over a person's mind if that person did not guard himself against it. On top of that, they had a bad attitude—as this demon's greeting had just reminded him.

A warrior worm slid forward and wrapped his tongue around

the demon's neck. The demon reached up, removed his head from his body and let the tongue pass through. So much for the weapon that had given him and Nola so much trouble before! It was no use trying that tactic again.

The demon put his head back on and laughed as he made a grab for Nola. Nola screamed loudly and tried to run, but the demon caught her foot, causing her to fall flat on her face. He yanked her to her feet, leering grotesquely.

Mich felt awkward and useless, again, because there was nothing much he could do. The demons were callous creatures and could hardly care less whether she was a Creator. Perhaps they already knew who she was, so hoped to make an example of her. They might even know that their action would result in the destruction of Kafka, themselves along with it, and still not care.

He drew his sword and kept his mind aware for an intruding demon. It would be sheer folly to blindly attack the demon holding her; maybe that was what they wanted.

It hurt him terribly to see how Kafka was treating Nola. Deep down, he hoped she would be staying in Kafka after this was done. He knew that the hope was a foolish one. She would surely leave as soon as she could. He wished she could have seen his world a few weeks ago, before the arrival of the Fren. He just knew she would have loved it.

He saw that the demon had control of her mind. He had to do *something*. He had to help her, somehow. But any automatic reaction was bound to be wrong. He needed to be cunning, so as to negate the insidious powers of the demons. He combed his brain for an idea, and managed to grasp a faint ploy that just might work. "Spirit," he murmured, keeping his voice low so that the demons would not overhear. "You surely have the power. Read my mind." Then he felt the presence of the unisus's mind in his, fathoming his intent.

The demon pulled Nola to him, savoring her alarm. She was

screaming and trying to break out of his grasp, but the demon was strong. Why wasn't anyone doing anything, she wondered, outrage mixing with her fear. Why was Mich just standing there?

She had her eyes screwed shut so that she could not see the horrible demon's eyes. She could hear the other demons laughing and applauding, goading him on. She felt his tail sliding across her body, touching her legs up under her dress. She wondered again how her friends could let this happen to her.

Then she felt the demon's breath on her neck as his gross lips touched her ear. Her mind whirled with confusion as she felt an electric tingle travel from her neck to her toes.

She decided that Mich must care nothing for her. In fact the whole lot of them were against her. They were all conspiring against her. They wanted this to happen to her. They wanted to kill her.

But this demon, this erotically appealing demon, was trying to help her. He was trying to protect her from the evil ones who called themselves friends. He was holding her tightly to protect her, loving her. His muscular body was pressed close to hers and she could feel him responding to that closeness.

She started to enjoy the demon's caresses. She liked the stroking of that prehensile tail. She searched for his mouth with hers. Her lips traveled across the masculine jaw.

Just as she reached his open mouth, she heard a screaming voice. "Depart demon! Leave this one to those who love her!"

What did that mean? The demon was the one who loved her, wasn't he? She continued the kiss, although she now felt nauseous for some reason and her ears rang.

The kiss sent shivers up her spine and made her feel ticklishly sinful. As the demon lay her on the ground, her head pounded as if she was experiencing the worst headache she'd ever had. She felt the demon's sensuous, black claw on her breast.

Then she heard the voice again:

"I said—*depart!*"

The voice carried such force that Nola's headache turned into a migraine and it pounded at her skull like a jackhammer.

She sat up and held her head. Then she held on to her stomach; she could feel it wrenching, and she vomited from the pain. She realized that she had actually wanted the demon and the thought sent her stomach roiling. She vomited again. How could she have wanted to have sex with something like that?

When the pounding of her head abated, she opened her eyes. She had, somehow, managed not to puke on herself, but she had spattered the demon somewhat. He was lying on the ground holding his head and drooling. He was in pain too, although he looked much worse than she felt. She could feel the demon leaving her mind. The farther away it got, the better she felt, and the worse the demon looked. The other demons were gone.

Something weird occurred to her. That voice, the one that had banished the demon—had sounded just like her own. In fact, she had said those words. But how was that possible?

She looked around for Mich. As she spied him, he came charging toward her with his sword extended. Nola closed her eyes and screamed, fearing Mich had become jealous of her liaison with the demon and was going to kill her.

Mich leaped over her and landed before the demon. With one swipe, he lopped off the demon's head and cut that into two halves. After he was sure the demon was dead he wiped off his sword in the grass and turned to Nola.

She looked up at him, her blue eyes bright with tears. He was sorry that he could not protect her from that experience, but it was the only way to get at the demon. He just wished he knew why the demon had attacked her. There were surely some nymphs around;

the demon could have his pick of those beautiful, stupid creatures.

He was caught by surprise as she jumped up and threw her arms around him. He dropped his sword and held her close.

"It was so horrible!" she cried into his shoulder.

"The demon took over your mind, but you're okay now. Spirit saved you," he explained. He felt ashamed that the rescue had not been completely his doing.

"Spirit? How?" She looked at her huge friend standing nearby.

Simple. The only way to exorcise a demon is to tell him to leave you alone. You, of course, had no idea so you could not have done it yourself. Only one who can speak directly through your mind can do it. He was a tough one, though. Usually, you have to tell them only once. However, my role in your rescue was purely arbitrary. Give credit where it is due, to the one who saw the strategy I did not, and who slew the demon.

She had spoken the words to repel the demon—because no one else could speak them for her. Spirit had sent the words to her, after learning them from Mich. That might not be the old-fashioned, hero-slays-dragon-saves-damsel type of action, but it had been effective.

Nola looked back at Mich and experienced a déjà vu. He might not have slain a dragon, but he *had* slain a demon for her, just as he had in her dreams.

He was smiling, and that made her feel better. Again, she wanted to kiss him, and again she balked. She owed him so much! She could never have made it through this place without him. He was so brave. But part of her just could not believe that he was who he claimed to be, even now. For the moment she let herself believe, she would be hopelessly trapped, in love. Once she was in love, if she found out she was mistaken, it would be too late. Her heart would break and she would probably kill herself. She had lived too long in the real world.

Since demons were naturally rotten, the worms consumed its flesh with delight, gnashing it with their rows and rows of teeth. Then the party traveled on until nightfall, intersecting the river.

They spent the night next to the River of Thought. The water glowed dimly in the night and it was very beautiful. Mich showed her how the colors changed according to how one looked at the water, and she was entranced. She touched the water with a finger and it swirled around almost like an oil slick, only the slick was not oil and it was not just on the surface. It had the viscosity and texture of ordinary tap water, but there was something else there. It gave her a feeling of happiness, as if she were touching every dream ever dreamed by anyone; as if she had shared them all.

They rested in each other's arms, while the others formed a protective ring around them, and they let their minds drift peacefully through the night. Nola thought again of the kind of diversion that might nicely fill such a period, but still couldn't bring herself to suggest it to Mich. She was just too ambiguous about it, not sure what she really wanted.

In the morning, both Mich and Nola felt a call of nature and found a nearby stand of trees, where they answered it. Nola wondered why this should be so in the dream realm, but concluded that wherever eating occurred, so did other processes. They scouted out some food for themselves and for the worms, as the worms could neither see nor smell well.

Mich looked again at the map. He traced his finger along the dotted line. He noticed that it stopped at the Shattered-Glass Glade, not at the source. The source wasn't even marked on the map. The river ran past the glade, through a section marked "Unknown," then ran off the paper. He hoped that the source was somewhere in the unknown section. But if it wasn't he would just follow the river to its end, wherever it led. He had to save Kafka and find his father.

Nola put her hand on his shoulder. "What's bothering you?" she asked, sitting beside him.

"Oh, nothing," he said, folding the map. "I was just thinking about my father."

"Don't worry, Mich. We'll find him. And if not, so what?"

Mich was taken aback. How could she treat the matter of his father's disappearance so callously?

Nola noted his response and clarified herself. "I mean, you say I am a Creator. I can just re-Create him—as soon as I find out how."

She was right! That was within the power of a Creator. Nola had done more with that statement than she knew. He felt so much better about neglecting the search for his father in favor of saving Kafka. Now, why hadn't he thought of that?

At that moment, the group was startled by a strange noise. It sounded like a child babbling. They looked and saw a small, gaunt creature that resembled a troll running quickly toward them. Its little legs carried it so quickly that it was upon them before they could react.

It brushed by Mich and he felt a sudden, sharp pain in his arm. He looked and saw a deep cut, and his blood was welling out. When he looked up the creature was gone. He could hear the faint babbling, then even that disappeared.

"Oh!" Nola cried as she saw the cut. She ripped the yellow sash from her sleeve and wrapped it tightly around his arm.

Mich was confused. "What was that?" he asked Heat.

I don't know. I have never seen that ilk before. Heat's silver orbs glistened with anger. He did not approve of this at all. His friend had been maliciously cut.

Nola wrapped the bandage tightly. The blood would not stop. It flowed until the sash turned red.

One of the worms crawled up and wrapped its tongue around Mich's arm. He could feel the pain disappear. He took off the blood-soaked sash; where the cut had been was now clean, healthy flesh. The worm had extended its power of rapid healing to him. He was coming to appreciate the worms better.

"Uh, thank you," he said awkwardly. He had never been good

with such expressions of appreciation, as the Sorceress Madrid had noted. He hoped the worm wouldn't want to be kissed.

"That wasch a Fren," it said.

"A Fren!" Nola exclaimed, amazed.

"A Fren?" Mich asked, similarly surprised. "I couldn't tell."

"Yesch. They are getting more common."

Mich realized that it was true; they must be getting more common. Not many people had actually seen them. He had seen a picture once but never a live one; he had never thought he would. It was different in the flesh: fast, ugly and pointlessly vicious. It hadn't even tried to kill him; it had simply hurt him in passing, perhaps because he was in its way. This one had slashed open his arm so quickly that he had barely felt it. What would happen when he met a whole army of them? What about when they knew his identity and meant to kill rather than off-handedly maim? Mich was not at all sanguine about the prospect.

They put the incident behind them as well as they could. Mich, Nola and Snort mounted a worm and traveled underground, where they would be safe, while the two unisi galloped full speed on the surface. They traveled in this manner through the morning and most of the afternoon. Everyone was beginning to show signs of wear. All were tired and worried, including the worms. Nola was learning to understand their expressions. Each worm had its own personality and idiosyncrasies.

They arrived at the Shattered-Glass Glade by evening. The worms surfaced and they dismounted, resting. "This is it?" Mich asked, with a confused expression.

"It's beautiful!" Nola said.

Yes, it is, Heat agreed. *The sunset makes it look like broken glass.*

"But it's nothing like what I expected," Mich complained.

"Let's be glad for that," Nola said, smiling.

In front of them the glade stretched out under the western sunset. It was not made of glass after all, but the ground here was marshy with tiny rivulets of water flowing erratically in all directions. The orange and red light of the sun glistened on the water, making the glade sparkle like shattered glass. The whole scene was quite pretty.

"We cannot dig here," one of the worms said. "Alscho, there are Schenticores. Very dangerousch."

Mich did not want to be rude, but he was having trouble understanding the warrior worm's speech. It had an awful accent, but Mich guessed that it must be difficult to talk with all those teeth and all that tongue.

Luckily, Nola had understood his speech a little better and clarified it. "Centicores? What are they?"

Mich's face lit up. At last, a monster he knew a lot about! "They are composite creatures with the rear part of a scorpion, the wings of a griffin, the body of a horse and the head of a wolf. I saw one once, from a distance. It was fighting a dragon." He smiled. "The dragon lost. They have been here longer than any other creature. They date back to when Kafka was still exploring his boundaries."

"Yesch. They have been around for eons," the worm agreed. "We fear them."

Spirit stamped a foot in the muck. *I'd prefer to avoid them if possible. I can defend myself, but I cannot be sure of defending all of you.*

Mich had always wondered what special way the black unisus had of defending himself. Obviously, it took him time to expend whatever it was, in the same way it took Heat a year to charge his laser. Otherwise, he would have used it to save Nola from the demon, before Mich had found a way.

"What do we do now?" Nola asked.

"Well, the Welties should have sent a scout to greet us. I suppose they are occupied, possibly in trouble. I hope they haven't encountered the Centicores," Mich said, troubled. "We will just have to look for them."

"I don't want to go trekking through this place at night," Nola said, looking around. "Is there someplace safe where we can spend the night?"

"Well, I think it might be best if we stay here. There aren't any fruit trees around, but maybe we can find something else." He gestured to Snort. "Snort, do you think you could hunt us some pink bunnies? There should be plenty around here, with all the grass."

Snort puffed steam indignantly. Of course he could! He moved into the bushes to scare up some game, while the others settled themselves down for a chat.

Nola leaned against Mich, who involuntarily enfolded her in his arms. She was quite comfortable. She just wished she could bathe soon; she hoped Mich wasn't appalled by her messy hair and dirty face.

Mich asked the worms about their heritage. He wondered why he had never seen or heard of them before.

"We are reschently borne of the River God," the worm began. "There were few of usch in the beginning, but we have managed to expand our territory in the pascht twelve yearsch. King Kras wasch the firscht out of the river, and I and my comradesch were schecond. I wasch the king'sch concubine, and we have had many children. Our children were all infertile, except our lascht."

"Twelve years?" Mich asked. "But I thought King Kras was two hundred years old!"

"He isch. He emerged from the river age one hundred eighty-eight."

Then he understood. "Just as I was born at the age of eighteen. And you are female?"

"No."

Mich almost choked when he heard that, but Nola explained that worms were bisexual and there were no specific male or females of its kind.

"Afterward, hisch lascht child, Chitie, wasch called upon to become a prince, scho that the king will have an heir. He feelsch he isch going to be Forgotten schoon."

Nola paused, for Snort had returned with several pink rabbits hanging limply from his jaws. He cooked two of them for Mich and Nola. He gave the others to the worms, who greedily sucked them down, gnashing them into tiny bits with their thousands of sharp teeth.

"But now I know the evil onesch transchformed him into a Fren," the worm continued. "They plan to do thisch with all creaturesch."

"You poor things!" Nola said. Nola had compassion for everyone but herself, even for creatures such as these. "How will you survive?" she asked.

"We won't schurvive without a fertile heir to the throne. King Kras isch no longer fertile; I am the only one left who isch fertile."

"Why can't you take the prince's place?" asked Mich.

"I prefer not to involve myshelf in politicsh. Even if I did, I schtill cannot reproduche without another of my kind who isch fertile. The king isch being Forgotten. I muscht be the prince'sch conshort, but I could never reign asch king."

Nola turned in Mich's arms and put her frail hand on his solid chest. "We have to help them," she pleaded.

He squeezed her reassuringly. "We will. We will help my father too, but Kafka is our first priority."

Nola yawned and put her head in his lap. She hoped he wouldn't think she was bored with his conversation; she was just so very tired. She also hoped he wouldn't take this gesture as a pretext to make a move on her, yet at the same time hoped he would. She liked his naivete, and indeed that had been part of his job description, but here in person she was also frustrated by it.

For no good reason, she began to feel a little homesick. She thought of her soft bed and her cat, Kudo. She missed her friend,

Lori, and her mother too. Then she thought of John. She would never be going to find him. Let him think she was dead. She would have to return and take Kudo away from there. But where would she go? She decided she'd rather live in one of those shelters than live another day in that place. But however much she missed her cat and her friend, she had to remember that if she went home now, her dreams would be no more and life would no longer be worth living. Whatever happened, she would stay in this weird world until it was safe.

Mich felt Nola cuddle into him and he reached down to stroke her hair. It was tangled with twigs and leaves, but it remained soft. Her slender body kept him warm. She was constantly amazing him. One moment being soft and delicate, and the next moment seeming tough as nails. She just did what had to be done. Even though she never spoke of Earth, he knew she wished she were home, despite the destruction shown by its magic mirror she called the TV. If he had any choice in the matter, he would get her back safely.

He also wished he knew why she always seemed sad. Even when she smiled, she never smiled with her heart. He struggled with the urge to ask her again. The urge won out. "Nola?"

"Yes?"

"Did something happen to you on Earth to cause you so much pain?"

Nola felt like saying, "What pain? I'm not in pain, I'm just fine," but that would be a lie. If Mich was truly the one whom she would love, then why start out with exclusion and lies? She shifted uncomfortably in Mich's lap. "On Earth, I live with a boyfriend—"

"A boyfriend? I see . . ."

"No, you don't," she said nervously. "I've been living with him. I really cared about him, maybe I still do, a little, and well, he abused me a lot."

"What do you mean, abused you?"

Nola shifted her body again. "You know, he hit me and raped me and all that."

Mich sat deadly still and silent. He was appalled, but had to say something. "He hit and raked you? Why?"

Raked? She decided to let that pass. "Well, he hit me for many reasons, but mostly because he'd had a bad day. He'd, you know, because I would never want to. I never wanted to because I was always sick inside. I mean, I'd have to go to the doctor because he was so rough on me, and the doctor would say no intercourse for three weeks. Well, he couldn't handle that, so I was always sick. Before I came here, he tried to kill me. All I ever did was try to make him happy. Perhaps that was my failing."

Mich was disgusted and angered by the mere thought of anyone treating Nola that way. He didn't understand. Intercourse?

"I should say so! Why did you stay with him for so long? You should have left the first time he struck you. Certainly you should not have remained to talk with him."

"Talk?"

"Didn't you say you had social intercourse?"

This was almost funny! "I don't know. It's kind of hard to explain. The first time it happened, I was in love. He cried and begged my forgiveness and told me it'd never happen again and how he would die if I left him. I loved him, so I stayed. When it happened again, I gave him another chance, hoping he'd change. Well into the relationship, I guess I figured my love would somehow be the magic he needed to change." Nola started crying into Mich's knees. "I was so stupid. I hate him!"

He began to get the idea that intercourse was *not* a harmless act. He now understood her pain, and why she had been so reluctant to tell him. Mich caressed her and wiped away her tears before they could fall. He had no idea what to say. All he knew was that if he ever met the demon, he would not think twice about slicing him through the heart.

He thought about what would happen when the time came for her departure. He would rather die than be without her. With that thought, he suffered a realization: he loved her. He supposed he always had. But he knew he was a fool. She would never love him. He would be surprised if she ever trusted another man again after the pain she had suffered at the hands of her boyfriend. And, of course, she was the Creator.

The next day, Nola felt somehow relieved to have told someone about her life. Mich, however, seemed sad. Nola's fear had come to pass. Her sadness had been transferred to Mich. She gave him a hug, and at least he smiled.

They found some marsh cane, which Snort kindly steamed for them. It was delicious. Nola preferred this type of food over pink bunnies and piglets. They did their morning business behind the reeds, then mounted up. They rode astride the unisi, while the worms slithered easily through the slippery mud. Her respect for the worms was increasing as she associated with them.

A few minutes into the glade, they dismounted and Mich led the party on foot. The unisi were having difficulty walking because of the marshy ground, and preferred not to be weighted down further. They would have flown, but their party now included slow-moving, landbound creatures, and it wouldn't be right to leave them to handle the glade alone.

The going was slow and tedious. There were occasional pockets of deep mud, and they had to be careful not to step in one of those. There was no telling how deep they were, or what might lurk at the bottom.

An hour into their journey, they were forced to stop. The mud pockets became frequent and close together, while the areas that they used to walk on became deeper. Spirit and Heat were knee-deep in brown muck. If they went farther, they would not be able to pull themselves out.

Mich realized why the worms could not travel here. Rock could crumble away, but mud could not; it would simply flow back into the tunnel and drown them.

"Any suggestions?" Mich asked of the group.

There is only one alternative, Heat replied, lifting a sinking hoof. The mud was a stark contrast against his white hide. *I can see the river from here. Perhaps if we walk toward it, the ground will be sufficiently hard.*

Nola couldn't understand that logic, but who was she to argue with a unisus? They were the smartest creatures in Kafka, she thought.

The group changed course and headed toward the river. As soon as they did so, Nola could feel the earth beneath the mud begin to slope upward. Heat had been correct.

"How did you know the ground would be hard here?" she asked Heat.

Simple logic, really. The bank must be dense near the river in order to keep the water from sinking into the ground.

"Oh." Nola felt momentarily dumb.

Once at the river, they stopped to rest and think. They discussed it and decided that they could not go that deep into the glade again. If they couldn't walk out there, then the Welties couldn't either. But where were they, in that case?

As they tried to come up with an answer, a guardian mermaid swam up to the bank of the river. She propped herself out of the water on her elbows and her bare breasts floated at the surface.

"Excuse me, Your Majesty," she said. She seemed very nervous and was looking this way and that, as if paranoid. "Are you looking for the Weltie forces?"

"Yes, we are! Have you seen them?"

"I have a message from Greyden. She gave it to me just before she disappeared." The mermaid handed Mich a tiny vial, then swam quickly away.

He opened it. Inside it was a note. He pulled it out and read:

Your Highness, Prince Michael:
My husband has disappeared. All my friends are gone, I am the
last. By the time you read this, I too will be Forgotten. There is
not much time left. There has been much destruction during your
absence. Save Kafka! You must hurry!
Greyden

They have been forgotten. This is worse yet! What is happening to Kafka? Spirit's green eyes showed white around the edges. He was afraid.

Nola, feeling his fear, stroked his muscular neck in assurance. But she too quailed. "Oh, my God! This is awful! We have to do something!"

Mich was stricken. They could never defeat the Fren alone and there was nothing he could do about the Forgetting of his friends. It was up to their Creators.

I believe, Spirit thought, *that this quest should be directed by you, Nola.*

Nola decided that Esprit was right. She was the one who was supposed to save Kafka, but what could she do? The answer was obvious. She needed to assert herself and motivate the group with a pep talk. That might not be enough, but the cause would certainly be lost if they lost heart.

She stiffened and clenched her fists. "As long as I am alive, I will not let you down. We have lost the Weltie army, but we still have each other. I say we fight the Fren ourselves—and fight we will!"

Mich was always awed at how she stood up under severe pressure, but seemed meek when lesser threats occurred. He wished he had the same backbone. Then, somewhere, deep inside his soul, he found he did. "I'm ready," he said. "We'll do it."

Just then, the group was startled by a raucous cry. They turned to see two Centicores galloping toward them at full speed, throwing muck and water behind them, stingers recoiled for the strike.

The first Centicore swept up two of the warrior worms and cast them into the deep mud, where they struggled uselessly. The three remaining worms were snagged on the beast's stingers and tossed in after their brothers. Then, the Centicores turned their attention to the next weakest-looking prey: Nola.

Nola's dander was up and she, stupidly, stood her ground. The wolf head snarled and lunged for her. She punched it on its tender snoot, and her fist got smeared with Centicore snot.

It yiped, as it was startled by this attack, but it soon lunged at her again, this time with its stinger. The tip glistened with a drop of deadly poison.

Nola felt the wind knocked out of her as an arm swept her backward, out of the way. It was Mich. She felt herself falling and tried to brace herself against him, but he was unbalanced as well and they both splashed, helplessly, into the river. Then everything went dark.

11

TINA

Nola woke to the smell of bacon. She sat up and rubbed the sleep from the canthi of her eyes. She was in her bed at home in her old clothes. The sheets were warm and wrapped around her. Her body was clean and her hair was in order.

"It was a dream," she mumbled. "I can't believe that it was all a dream." She felt rather sad knowing this. She got out of bed and walked into the kitchen.

"Oh, you're awake!" said a feminine voice.

Nola looked. In her kitchen, cooking bacon, was her friend, Lori.

"Oh, Lori, you wouldn't believe the dream I had!"

"Really. Tell me about it later, Nol. Where is John? Did he try to kill you again? Anyway, there's someone who's been waiting for you to wake up." Lori gestured to the couch.

Nola walked into the living room. There, on the couch, in living color, sat Mich.

Nola felt herself fainting, but Lori caught her and sat her down.

"It wasn't a dream! It was all true!" Nola exclaimed. Lori looked strangely at her. "You think I'm crazy, don't you?"

"It's okay, Nola! He explained things to me." Lori laughed. "I didn't believe him at first, until I remembered all those pictures you used to draw and when I saw that cross around your neck and the way you two were dressed . . ."

Nola felt her neck. The cross was there; she had forgotten about it.

"But how did we get here?" she asked, her head still reeling. "We were in the hotel at the beach."

"There must have been some kind of side effect when we both fell into the river together," Mich said. "So we arrived not where we left this world, but where your home is. Where your heart is. Your heart must have guided us. Your friend says she found us here when she came to check on your cat." He made a wry smile. "And your cat reminds me of my basilisk. Isn't that odd?"

"Not really," she said. She took a better look at him. He was also clean and was dressed in street clothes. He looked rather handsome. Oh, how she wished she could let herself believe that he was really the one she was searching for! But—

Her thoughts swung suddenly to Kafka. "But we can't stay here!" she cried. "Kafka needs me!"

"At least eat something first, dummy," Lori said.

"I can't. You don't understand, we have to go back!"

"We can't," said Mich, shaking his head.

"Why not?! We did it before!"

"My father and I were the owners of the last two bed spells in Kafka. They can be used only once, and he has the other one. I've used mine."

"You never told me about that!"

"I never thought I'd have to," he said sadly. "I shouldn't have pulled you into the river, but I couldn't think of any other way to save you from the Centicores. I want to return as much as you do; we just can't." He hated to tell her that. She loved Kafka, despite being born of the Earth.

"We have to! Mich, dammit, you can't stay here, you'll die!" Nola rose from the couch and dashed for the door. "There must be a way!"

Lori intercepted her. "Where do you think you're going, Nol?"

"To the beach!" she said, pushing her friend out of the way.

Nola ran down the hall to the elevator with Mich close behind her. Lori caught up to her and stopped her again.

"At least let me drive you, then!"

Nola agreed. She didn't have any money left for bus fare anyway. So, Mich, Nola and Lori piled into her car and sped toward the beach.

Mich, of course, was totally fascinated with this strange box on wheels, but dared not bother Nola with his questions. He could tell that she was thinking, hard, about something. He wondered what she had in mind. Whatever it was, it was bound to fail. He hated to think negatively where Nola was concerned, but there was no escape. There was no way they could expect to depart Earth without a bed spell.

Lori sped down the highway and into the city. Within two hours, they were just inside the city limits and nearing the coast. Mich still had no idea what her plan was, but he was prepared to help her, even though he knew it wouldn't work.

He watched the things that whizzed by outside. Deep inside the city, he had seen huge glass squares that rose up into the sky, and concrete paths that many people walked on. There were lots of wheeled boxes, like this one. He hoped that he would be able to learn about it all. Surely he'd have to, assuming he didn't fade out in this realm after a week.

Now the buildings were only half as tall, about ten stories. There were a few more trees and the sky was a deeper blue; otherwise, it was the same. The air smelled as stale and the graffiti was just as rude. Though he couldn't imagine growing up in such a strange place, it was easy to see why one might want to dream of other things.

Nola had doubts about her plan. She didn't expect it to work, but she just couldn't sit idly by and let her dreams be destroyed. As far as she knew, Esprit was left to the mercies of the Centicores. She shuddered to think of that. She simply had no choice, she had to go back! She didn't know what she'd do if Mich died here. He would die in her dreams as well, and she'd lose her only possibility for true love.

Just maybe, if she got to the beach, there might be a way. Mich had come up from under the sea the first time, so maybe there was some way into Kafka from there.

Just when the car reached the bad part of town, a squad car seemed to appear from nowhere. The blue and red lights started to flash, the siren wailed and the officers gave chase. There was no doubt they were guilty of speeding.

Lori started to pull over, but Nola grabbed the wheel. "We don't have time, Lori! Drive like you've never driven before or I swear I'll never speak to you again!"

Lori, cowed by her usually docile friend's behavior, stepped on the gas, pressing the pedal to the floor. Luckily, Lori's car was an old souped-up Camero that her father had restored for her, and could outdistance almost any car.

Mich, who was holding on to the front seat and leaning forward, was now thrown back into his own seat. "What's going on?" he asked. "What's that noise?"

"That's a police siren, and it means trouble," Lori said.

"You said a mouthful!" Nola agreed. "See if you can lose him between those buildings up there; he's far enough behind now."

"Oh, demons?" Mich asked. "Trolls?"

"Close enough," Nola agreed.

Lori slammed on the brakes and cut the wheel. Mich was thrown forward again, then thrown to the side. Nola also lost her grip on the dash and slid right as the vehicle squealed around to the left, into an alley. Lori took the next left, before the police car could see where they were going. She had doubled back and they were now headed away from the coast.

"This is no good!" Nola cried. "Go in there!" She pointed to a smaller alley to the right.

They got themselves headed in the right direction again. Mich informed them that the police car was no longer pursuing them. "We outdistanced the demons amidst Fren Cliffs." Naturally he interpreted the close, high buildings in terms of land features he understood.

That was a relief! "It's a good thing you haven't put your new license plates on yet!" Nola said.

Lori drove them out of the city, onto a highway, and drove for another hour. Then she exited and drove through a residential area.

"Let us out—here," Nola said. "The beach isn't far. It will be safer if we walk the rest of the way."

Lori stared at her friend. "What? You don't like my driving?"

"No, no. It's not that. I mean we—as in Mich and I—should walk. You had better get home. But I'm sure that cop will remember your car. You better get home and park it in the garage and cover it. Make sure you're not followed."

"But—"

Mich cut her off. "Nola is right, Lori. We should go on alone, regardless. There is a lot of dangerous stuff going on where we're headed and I wouldn't want to involve you. It is bad enough already, right here. Demons are well worth avoiding, if you can."

"Amen," Nola agreed with a subdued smile.

Lori grudgingly let them go their way. She wasn't sure she would ever see Nola or her new friend again, but the knowledge Mich had shared with her braced her attitude on life. A whole other world where dragons and fairies lived! Maybe she would believe in her own dreams more from now on.

Nola and Mich waved good-bye and watched Lori drive off. Lori was a good friend, the only friend she had here. She was a bitch most of the time and tended to sleep with every guy she met, but she did care about people, and when Nola needed her, she was always right there.

They walked through the housing area, following street signs. Soon they reached the seedier part of the boardwalk, with all of the local bars and drug-infested alleyways.

Nola looked around to get her bearings. They were in a dank, smelly alley. The kind that was usually occupied by winos and junkies. Places like this always depressed her. She knew that some of these people had once been successful in life, but had fallen through society's cracks through no fault of their own.

She started walking, deep in thought. Mich was holding her hand, but she was barely conscious of it. There was something nagging her with increasing strength, almost drawing her along in this direction, though she had never been in this section before.

"*Ooww!*" someone yelled. "Hey, why don't you watch whatchur doin'!"

It was a young woman, about twenty-five years old. She was sitting between a box and a garbage can. Startled, Nola paused to look more carefully.

Her clothes were classic hooker style. Her blond hair was in disarray, and she smelled of alcohol. She held an empty liquor bottle in one hand and a pistol in the other. Nola had stepped on the hand with the bottle in it.

"I'm sorry," Nola said. "I wasn't paying attention."

"Yer damn rightcha weren't! You should be more careful round people who've got one a these!" She held up the gun, then let it fall to the street with a clacking sound.

Mich noticed that her top was ripped, showing some interesting flesh, and she was bleeding from a gash in her shoulder. "What happened to you?" he asked. "Trolls?"

"None of yer g'damn business!" she snapped. "You g'damn

sonofabitch! Why don't you just git outta here an leave me the hell alone? I'm off now, come back later!" She threw the empty bottle on the ground at their feet and it shattered into a thousand pieces. She started crying, and covered her face with a hand.

Nola instantly took pity, as Mich knew she would. "You're bleeding! Why don't you let us help you?" Nola bent down to help the girl up.

The girl slapped at Nola's hands. "Why can't you all just leave me alone! Whaddaya care, anyhow?"

"Look," Nola said reasonably, "I'm not going to tell you that I know what you're feeling, because I can't possibly know, but I do care. I want to help you, and I'm going to. You can't kill yourself." Nola felt an uncomfortable pang of familiarity. She had felt this bad herself at times.

She lifted the girl off the ground by her armpits, being careful not to touch her wound. The girl fought with her and slapped her in the face, but Nola did not release her. This wasn't exactly a demon or a Fren, after all.

"Whaddayou care? Go 'way, just go 'way, damn you!"

But Nola wouldn't let her go. She wasn't sure herself why she was doing this. There was just something that made it seem important, quite apart from the girl's evident need of help. So she persisted. Eventually the girl collapsed in Nola's arms and cried.

"It's okay," Nola said. "I promise, I'll help you." She knew better than to ask a prostitute where her parents were or where she lived. "Do you have a friend you can call?"

"No," the girl sniffed, "I ain't got nobody."

Nola looked helplessly at Mich.

"I think there's some healing spice in the Forest of Imagination," he said. He hated to get Nola's hopes up like that. There was no chance of them reaching Kafka again.

"Okay," Nola said. "You're coming with us. We'll help you." She paused. "By the way, what's your name?"

"It's Tina, not that you care, and what the hell is healing spice? Some kinda new stuff?"

Nola ignored her. "Well, Tina, how would you like to get away from planet Earth for a while?"

The girl struggled free from Nola's embrace. "Are you kidding? What the hell ya think I wuz tryin' to do when you stepped on my hand?" She knelt to pick up the gun and put it in her purse.

That wasn't what Nola meant, but she wasn't about to clarify it. "All right, then, that's what we'll do."

The girl resumed crying as they walked down the alley toward the city limits. The beach wasn't far now. Tina preferred to stumble along without help. Her purse flip-flopped at her hip as she walked.

In due course, they reached the beach. Spirit wasn't in sight, but if he had come here again, he could be walking along the far end of it. Maybe all they had to do was wait for him to come to this end. Maybe. There were a few people on it, so Nola sat Tina down on a bench to talk to her. "Will you tell me what happened to you now?" she asked patiently.

"Well, if you *must* know, I was doin' a trick for a regular. He was a disgustin' one an' I heard he'd been with Frita. That chick has some kinda VD, an' I told 'm I wanted cash in advance. He beat me up and did me real good. I told 'm I'd sic Johnboy on his ass—that's my man—an' he said he wuz gonna kill me." She paused and tried to straighten her torn dress. "But I ain't no dumb ho. I carry an enforcer."

She removed the pistol from her purse and showed it to Mich. Mich held it up to see it better. He put his eye to the little hole in its end, but couldn't see anything inside. He twiddled the little device on one side of it.

"Hey, man! You crazy? Gimme that!" Tina snatched the gun and stuffed it back in her purse. "You tryin' to git me caged?"

Mich couldn't quite understand her strange phrases, but kept his mouth shut.

"As I was sayin'," Tina continued, "he said he wuz gonna kill me, so I pulled out my enforcer and gave him what he deserved."

"You killed him?" Nola asked, horrified.

"No way! I may've had the street drilled into me, but I ain't God! It ain't my right to take life. No, I just gave him a plug in the leg, an' when he was on the floor, I took my pay."

Nola was glad to have the story straight, but she wasn't so sure she liked it.

Mich was fascinated by it. There was never anything like this going on in Kafka. He was glad there wasn't.

After the beach cleared out a little, Nola led them down to it. The section of beach that she reserved for her pondering was devoid of people for miles and the sun was dropping low in the sky.

"What now?" Tina asked.

"I wish I knew," Nola said, disappointed that apparently Spirit had not made it here this time. "Any ideas, Mich?"

"Nope. Maybe we should go in the water?" He knew, with regret, that this was all pointless.

"I ain't goin' for no swim!" Tina said defiantly. "If we're gonna do it, let's do it now!" She pulled out the gun and aimed it at her temple.

Before Nola or Mich could speak, they felt a strange sensation. Nola remembered the only other time she had felt this way. She had been put asleep for an appendectomy.

In moments, all three of them were asleep.

12

REILITY

Mich, Nola and Tina lay on the ground. Nola was glad there weren't mosquitoes, biting flies or other obnoxious insects here. Maybe there were, but there were spells to protect people from such attacks.

Spells? Did that mean—?

As they woke, their first sight was that of a pair of huge black fetlocks blowing in the breeze.

They struggled to their feet, rubbing their eyes. They were back in Kafka, standing before Spirit. They were beside the river at the exact spot they had fallen in.

Spirit's huge, black head towered over them. He lowered it to look Nola over. Heat was nowhere around, but Snort attended to Mich, worrying over him as if Mich were his cub.

Tina stared, disbelieving, into Spirit's sparkling green orbs. She saw her own image reflected back.

"AAAAAAHHHHH!" she screamed, stumbling backward. "What the hell is that thing?!" She pointed the gun at him.

Nola immediately slapped the gun from Tina's grasp.

"I wouldn't," she said.

"W-what the—" Tina stammered.

Nola drew her aside. "Look, I asked you if you wanted to leave Earth and you said yes, so that's what we did."

"But I thought—"

"You thought I meant permanently? No." Nola stepped back and dramatically raised her arms. "Welcome to Kafka."

"Kafka?" Tina looked again at Spirit. She rubbed her brown eyes, still not able to believe what she saw. "Where the hell are we?" she demanded.

"I'll explain later." Nola turned to Spirit. "What happened, Esprit? How did we get here?"

I brought you, he thought happily. *I'm glad to see you are healthy. I missed you.* He nuzzled her face, and she gently caressed and kissed his nose.

At that moment, Mich wished he were a unisus. He wanted more details. He knew he'd finally learn what special magic Spirit had. "But how did you get us here?" he asked.

Heat galloped up carrying some tiny red berries in his mouth. *I believe I can answer that, if I may.*

Be my guest, Spirit thought.

But first, let the girl eat these.

Mich took the berries out of Heat's mouth and persuaded Tina to eat them. The girl seemed somewhat dazed, and put them in her mouth without really paying attention. Her eyes were trying to take in the whole scene at once, and evidently not succeeding.

"Look at your shoulder," Nola told her.

Tina was astonished as she watched the wound on her shoulder heal before her eyes. "Look at that! The pain's gone too!" Then, catching sight of her reflection, she scooped up some water to wash her dirty face and arms, and brought out a comb to do something about her hair.

Now, Heat began, *if I might answer your question—*

But Tina interrupted, still working on her appearance. "How can them horses say stuff but don't move their lips?"

Heat stared at her. *My dear, we are not horses!* He was obviously insulted. *We are called unisi. My name is Heat and this is Esprit; that's*

Spirit, to you. He indicated the black unisus with his bright silver horn. *We two are the lessors of a once complete rainbow and we speak with telepathy. That is, through thought; and I do not appreciate being referred to as a mere horse!* He snorted indignantly.

"Scuuuuze me!" Tina said, daunted but resistant.

Now, he continued, *I was about to say that it was Spirit's power that brought you back. Unlike me, it takes him precisely five years to charge his spells.*

Nola was intrigued anew at her friend and looked at him in awe.

"You say 'spells'?" Mich asked.

Yes. His power is far more versatile than mine. He can perform any given spell, once every five years. He was just a few hours shy of being fully charged when you fell into the river.

"That explains why he didn't try to save us before; he was charging a bed spell! I always thought you had to be in bed, but I guess it doesn't matter where you sleep, or even if you are sleepy. The spell put us to sleep. But how did he know that we'd fall into the river? I mean, if he had been charging a bed spell for five years, how did he know we'd need a bed spell? Or was it just a coincidence?"

Spirit explained, *I didn't know you would fall. When I release the spell, it coalesces into whatever spell I require. As Heat indicated, it is very versatile.*

"That it is," Mich said thoughtfully. "How did you get rid of the Centicores?" Mich knew that they hadn't defeated them, because there were no bodies.

Nola tweaked his arm. "Silly!" she said, laughing. Mich remembered his friend's wings and the answer was obvious. The unisi must have outmaneuvered them in the air.

"I guess we should go before the Centicores return. What will we tell King Kras? His warriors are gone."

"Now, wait just one minute!" Tina interjected, bracing against Snort. "Did you say King Kras?"

"Yes," Nola said, hoping foolishly for something she wasn't able to pin down at the moment. She had been somehow drawn to Tina; was there a reason?

Snort, annoyed at being used for support, puffed steam into Tina's face, and she immediately stood on her own, trying not to sway. The booze was wearing off, slowly.

"Well, well. Ain't this nice? You know, I ain't never told this to nobody, but I used to have a dream about a gigantic worm that lived underground, cuzuva story my grandpapa used to tell me when I wuz a girl. You know, that worm's name was Kras. He was named after a city in the Soviet Union where Grandpa's mom wuz born."

It was true! There *had* been a reason! Tina had dreamed of a giant worm named Kras? There could be only one explanation. Nola realized that she had been drawn to Tina because the girl was another Creator.

Nola laughed out loud. Not that what Tina said was funny, but at the coincidence of meeting another Creator and taking her back to Kafka. The chances were slim. Maybe Nola's luck was turning good, for once.

Heat realized what he had done. He had snapped at a Creator. Heat cuffed the ground with his silver shoes. He was embarrassed, but still too proud to apologize. Instead, he offered her a ride behind Mich. She accepted, saying that she loved horses. Heat wasn't insulted, being loved like that.

Mich remembered their important business. "We must return to the Fren Cliffs and fight them ourselves. Are you ready?"

But what of their mission to locate the source of the River of Thought and destroy the dreamstone dam? Nola thought they should attend to that first. But she didn't voice her thought. For one thing, if they didn't do something about the Fren soon, they would never reach the source.

Spirit trotted north, back the way they had come. Mich followed with Tina clinging tightly to his waist. Snort flew ahead to watch for danger.

Nola was just a little green. Tina, despite her status, was very pretty, with her long blond hair and more than adequate bosom. She had been a mess when they arrived in Kafka, but her clean-up job had been effective. Now Nola worried how she herself looked. As if she didn't have more important things to be concerned about.

Tina was frightened by just about everything they saw. When they stopped for a snack, she was even frightened by the spotted oranges, but she enjoyed them. Nola told her to be careful not to eat any mushrooms, but Tina reminded her that the mushrooms were her own idea. Tina found Nola's story of eating the worm eggs hilarious.

When night drew close, they were near the worm tunnel where they had been abducted. They discussed it and decided they should inform King Kras of his warriors' fate.

They soon discovered that King Kras's kingdom was in ruin and the king himself was deathly ill. His pedestal lay in a crumbled, tarnished heap.

"I feared that when I hadn't had word of them. Do not worry, they are not dead," he mumbled.

"What's up with you, Kras? What happened to your kingdom and your pretty silver throne?" Tina asked.

"I was preparing to send you a message when I learned that you were here, my dear Christine. When I called forth the royal cavanymph to carry the message, I was attacked by the Fren. There were many here. I fear they have made off with my son. His enclosure had been ripped open. None of my loyal subjects remain. I fear they are all dead or run off." He coughed up some green goo, and turned an ugly shade of brown.

"Don't worry!" Tina cried. "I will help Nola fight the Fren and I'll bring back your people. Just don't die!" She embraced the slimy worm.

King Kras jerked back and blinked his red eyes. *"No!"* he coughed. His voice, despite its cracking, was still authoritative. "I must insist. You cannot fight the Fren alone. You must enlist the dragons. They reside in the unknown region of Kafka."

"But the dragons won't help us," Mich interjected.

"They will if you have the right credential. Here, carry this to them. You must continue south." He looped his tongue up to remove his crown. Inside the silver bowl was a medal. It was made of iron and was in the shape of a crescent moon. Resting inside the curving moon was a six-pointed star.

Nola heard Spirit whinny for the first time. His voice was sweetly terrifying. *The Kahh!*

"Yes. Take it to the dragons. They will not refuse you. No one will." He tongued it to Mich. He coughed feebly and rolled his eyes, which had now turned black. Tina hugged him again, gently, and his skin tone looked better where she touched it. She was, indeed, his Creator.

Mich turned the star over, looking closely. "But what is it?"

Kras grimaced with pain. "Leave me. There is danger here. Go—now!" he gasped.

"But I can heal you!" Tina protested. "It will take some time, but I know I can do it. You're my creature."

"Yes. That is why I will not let you take the risk. You are immeasurably more valuable than I am. You must go."

"Do it," Mich recommended. "We must protect our Creators at all costs, and we of Kafka appreciate the dangers better."

"But you can't really want me to go," Tina protested to the great worm.

"Yes. I want you to go. Instantly!" Kras sagged, seeming to deflate, and his color deteriorated even more.

Tina's expression changed. "Well, if that's the way you feel." She let go and stepped away, hurt.

The group left Kras behind. Tina seemed not to care anymore. "I never liked him anyway," she commented sourly.

Nola believed that most Creators would be strange people, but this girl gave new meaning to the word. Nola did not question her. She thought it better to give Tina time to adjust to being in Kafka. Then something shifted in her mind, and she realized that she had been looking at it the wrong way. Tina simply couldn't handle rejection, even for good cause, so she pretended she didn't care. Even to herself.

Once outside, they foraged for food. Mich was too nervous to eat so he sat and waited. He hoped that he could find his father. It was likely that the Fren had killed him, but he put it out of his mind. What kind of hero was he? Kafka was falling and he could only watch. He hoped that whatever special power Nola and Tina had would manifest itself soon.

The group gathered around the tunnel entrance in the dark. The night was unusually quiet. Nola lay huddled against Spirit's flank and Tina sat beside her. Snort rested his serpentine head on Mich's lap while Heat grazed.

Mich took the medallion from his pocket and handed it to Nola so she could give it a close inspection. The edges were sharp, like a knife.

"Esprit, you called this a Kahh," Nola said. "What is it?"

It was a gift to the dragon Kafka, from the Great Wizard. You know him as God.

"From God?" Nola wasn't sure she understood that, but decided to let it pass. "What is it for?" she asked, still confused about how it would get dragons to help.

Reading Spirit's thoughts, she knew that dragons were the worst monsters in Kafka. They were numerous and often attacked in swarms. A few were so large that one could easily kill a Centicore with one chomp.

It is the hope symbol. It is the sun rising over the moon, representing light overcoming darkness. In legend, it is used whenever Kafka is threatened, to unite its denizens for the common good. Whoever you show it to will offer his help unconditionally. But only to the one who holds it. It is the one law by which humans and dragons alike must abide.

Heat lifted his head. *That is true. However, should it be shown to one who is truly evil, such as the Fren, the symbol will be forever destroyed and all hope with it. Ones like the Fren have no hope and will destroy all they can find. There is a saying. "When the Kahh is lifted high, your enemy will be your friend, all good creatures will be your brothers and hope will satisfy." As long as a creature has hope then it must obey this law.*

Mich hadn't heard that part, but it made sense now. That, perhaps, might be the reason none of them had ever heard of the worm king. If he was meant to protect the Kahh, it would be wise to remain secluded. He hated to think what would happen if Reility ever got his hands on it. He stuffed it back into his pocket.

Nola had an idea. "Could we use it on the Centicores instead?"

Come to think of it, we could, Heat thought. *The Centicores are a rare species, but we could use them too. The dragons are better at fighting large numbers than are the Centicores, but we could accumulate quite a fighting force with those.*

Yes, Spirit agreed. *It's too bad that we cannot use the Welties. They would have turned the tide in our favor.* He glanced at Nola. *Perhaps Nola will find the strength to remember them back into existence.*

Nola suddenly felt the burden of saving Kafka weigh heavily on her. Why didn't she know what to do? There had to be someone who could help her.

The group rested, somewhat uneasily. Mich wished the night was colder so that Nola would seek shelter in his arms. He really did love her. He would much rather have a cushiony, warm girl like her in his lap than a scaly basilisk. If all was lost and Kafka fell, he swore to himself that, somehow, he would get her home safely, though she would take his very soul with her.

Tina, who was not used to this, tossed and turned until Nola finally explained things to her. They talked together for some time. In the morning, Tina seemed more at ease, and the booze had worn the rest of the way off. "You know somethin'?" she remarked musingly. "I'm all the way sober now, and not only no hangover, I don't even want to get crocked again."

"I think those healing berries healed more than your shoulder," Nola said.

Tina squatted behind a tree to answer nature's call. She had consumed a lot of alcohol, but now it had cleared. When she was done, she found a luberry bush and sat there, eating and thinking.

She wished she hadn't gotten involved in all this. It was barely believable, but she had pinched herself several times. She was not dreaming. Not in any ordinary sense. She wished she were.

Kafka was certainly better than the street. She just wished that her grandfather were alive to see it all. He had a wonderful imagination. After his death, she had no one. It hadn't been long before the money ran out and she was evicted from her home. She found work on the street. She hated it, but it paid her bills and kept food in her stomach, so why should she complain? It was certainly better than being homeless, like her friend Martha.

Martha had turned old and weak from sickness. The last time Tina saw her, she was sick but too weak to vomit. Tina blamed society for that and swore she'd never let it happen to her. But she had been well on the way there when this happened.

Now she wondered: had it really been coincidence? She had felt a tug at odd moments. Could it have been when Nola passed within her range, or dreamed of Kafka? Had she been tuning in on another Creator? And Nola had felt the tug too. Otherwise she would never have befriended a drunken prostitute.

Tina hoped that her new friends never found out that she was ashamed of herself. That was no way to be around people. Once people found that out, they used her, then left her to the dogs like leftover table scraps. She couldn't figure out why Nola had been so nice to her, even with the tug of Creation. She decided it was pity. Tina wasn't too proud to accept pity now and then, but she knew that pity didn't last forever.

"Hey, you okay?" Nola asked, stepping through a bramble bush to reach Tina.

"Yeah, yeah, I'm fine. Why don't you go back to your friends now?"

"Let's not start this again. We had such a good talk last night. Why don't *you* go back to *your* friends?"

"I ain't got no friends, girlie."

"I don't have any friends," Nola corrected her, annoyed more by her attitude than her vernacular.

"Whatever. I don't have and never did have 'friends.' All I got is Johnboy. He protects me and he ain't never asked me for too mucha my change, so I give him some merchandise free a charge."

Nola, despite herself, was disgusted. Tina was really a pretty girl. It was too bad that she had wasted herself that way. Yet at the same time she realized that others might say the same about Nola's own abusive relationship with John. How much difference was there between Tina's Johnboy and Nola's John? So maybe she couldn't afford to be judgmental.

Tina sighed as if she were being forced to do something difficult and got up to join the others.

"Well," Mich said, "I'm glad you're all right. It's not safe to go off by yourself around here, especially with the Fren population on the rise."

Tina turned away. "Yeah, right," she mumbled.

Mich was unsure how to react. He did care about her. Without

Tina, he wasn't sure that King Kras would have parted with the Kahh, and they might have been doomed. He decided it was best just to ignore her bad attitude and get on with the journey. "Let's go. It will be another half day before we reach the Unknown section of Kafka and there is no telling what we'll find there. We'd better get there before it gets dark. It's time to locate the source of the river."

Nola didn't understand. "I thought we were going to find the dragons." Though she did feel that it was best to get to the source rapidly, if they could stay clear of the Fren long enough to do it.

"Oh, I almost forgot," he said. "I thought it would save time if I gave the Kahh to Snort. He will inform the dragons, then they will meet us at the edge of the Unknown tonight."

Heat stamped a foot. *You gave the Kahh to Snort?! Did you realize that when those dragons get here, they will devour us!*

"Not if I have the Kahh," Mich explained. "Snort will fly back early and bring me the Kahh."

I hope Snort doesn't run afoul of a Fren or a Demon.

Mich hadn't thought of that. He could see the worried look on Nola's face. He still wasn't quite used to this leadership business, and didn't want to make too many bad mistakes. But he really didn't think this was a mistake. "No, he will stay in the air. As long as he is airborne, he will be fine."

Heat persisted. *What if he runs into a transformed demon?*

Heat had a point there. Damn that equine sense! "Let's just hope the demons learned their lesson last time. The demons are mean and cruel, but they are cowards."

Nola wasn't sure about that. And what had happened to their agreement that she would lead the mission? She knew she ought to assert herself, but somehow she didn't—and was disgusted with herself. Mich was a nice guy, but his well-intended actions were almost suicidally risky.

She smiled, privately. *She* was supposed to be the suicidal one! But maybe she would get up her gumption, or whatever, before Mich blundered too badly.

So they had to be satisfied with Mich's decision. Tina mounted Heat behind Mich and the group traveled due south, into the unknown. Nola noticed how the young woman's breasts and thighs pressed against Mich's backside as she rode, holding on close. Neither of the two gave any evidence of noticing the contact, and Nola was disgusted at herself for being bothered by it, but she was. She wished they could find a separate steed for Tina. She would have traded places with the girl, but knew that Spirit would never allow it.

Mich was sorry that he had not explored his father's kingdom before. He had simply lain around the castle most of the time, letting his friends wait on him. They really were friends, he decided. He had long thought of them only as servants, but he came to know each of them by name. His favorite was Misty, the palace ghost. He wished she weren't so shy. He would love to hear some news from the castle, but Misty would never show herself to all these people. Besides, she and Snort had some sort of rivalry. Mich had never quite understood about that and he didn't want to be nosy, so had never asked for details. What could a ghost and a basilisk have to be competitive about?

Nola sat confidently on Spirit's back. They conversed wordlessly. "How can everyone expect me to save Kafka? I can't even save a dollar!"

I would not worry, Nola. I know that you will find the power within yourself soon. But, you will not find it until you let go of your reality. I can see in your mind that you still have doubt. This is not good. The Fren feed on doubt.

"What do you mean, the power within myself? I have no special power."

Spirit shook his mane and snorted. *I never thought I would use this word, but that is spurious! You are a Creator!*

"So, what does that have to do with anything? If I have some kind of power that only a Creator has—"

Not a Creator. You. You are different from the others. I can feel you pulsing with it.

Nola was getting frustrated. She calmed herself, then phrased her thoughts better. "What is this power that you are speaking of?"

Spirit tossed his head, laughing with equine mirth. *Why, imagination, of course! I thought you knew that.*

Nola thought about it. She did have an imagination. Even her parents and her high school teachers thought so, but they also thought she used it for the wrong things. She used it to daydream a lot. It brought her nothing but trouble.

"But what did you mean about letting go of my reality?"

You have been born and raised on Earth. Everything you do, everything you say and how you act are all dictated by an Earthly reality. You know no other way than the ways of Earth.

Nola was confused. "So?"

You must learn that the rules that apply on Earth do not apply elsewhere. You must believe in Kafka and you must disbelieve the Fren and their dams. You are the only Creator with an imagination strong enough to disbelieve things from existence.

"Oh," she said, brightening. "I have a really good imagination. That should be easy!"

That, my dear friend, remains to be seen. Then he added, *I hope you are correct.*

Nola wondered what would become of Esprit and Mich if she didn't pull through for them. As long as she believed in them, they would always be there, wouldn't they? And what would happen to her other creations, such as the nymphs and the sea horses?

Spirit had read her thought. *I'm afraid we will all be gone. If Kafka is destroyed, all its creatures will be destroyed with it.*

Nola was appalled. "But I can't let that happen! I love you!"

Spirit's thoughts were tinted red as if he were blushing. *And I you, my friend. Michael would be lost without you as well. He loves you too, you know.*

Nola was taken aback. "He does? But how could he? I barely know him!"

Untrue. You know him well, you just cannot accept him for what he is. As I have said, you have been trained to an Earthly reality.

Nola could not refute that. That was, indeed, how she felt. But what could she do? She was what she was, an Earthling.

I hate to interrupt, Heat broke in, *but it seems we are coming upon the Unknown.*

Nola craned her neck to see. Up ahead was the river and, as far as the eye could see, nothing but golden grasslands. There were no trees, no bushes, no flowers and no signs of life, not even a gust of wind.

Something was strange, though. The river had dwindled to a mere stream. It must have been getting less and less deep the farther they traveled down it. Nola had been too busy with her thoughts to pay much attention. What could account for this?

They traveled farther down the river until the landscape looked the same from all sides. The grass grew tall and, except for the river, the land was featureless in all directions.

They continued on until Mich halted them. "This is no good. We're going nowhere. I'm going to look at the map again."

They dismounted and studied the map together. There was nothing to tell them which way to proceed. They had gone off the map's edge. Disgusted, Nola walked away.

"What now?" Tina asked.

"I don't know," Mich admitted.

"Did you notice the river?"

Mich turned and stared. "The dam must be finished! It must be drying up! I knew this would happen! We've got to find that dam! There must be some clue on what to do next in this map."

They stood for a while, stymied. If only the map extended farther!

Mich practically tore the map as a scream came, and Tina jumped. "What was that?" she asked, alarmed.

"It was Nola!" he said, throwing down the map. "It came from over there."

He looked in the direction Nola had walked. She had been standing on the bank of the river, but now she was gone. He hoped she hadn't fallen in. The water was low, but the muck beneath could be deep. She couldn't have been that careless!

As he stared at the empty spot where her voice had come from, he heard her scream again. He rushed over. Just as he reached the sound, he was blinded by a sharp and stinging flash of light, and Nola stood before him.

He went to embrace her. "Stop!" she cautioned. "You're going to push me back through!"

Mich drew back, confused. "Are you okay?"

"Yes, I'm fine! I was just startled. I think I found something."

"What? What is it?"

Nola took Mich's hand and walked him to the spot where she had disappeared.

"Feel this," she said, guiding his hand. He felt a wall beneath his fingers. It was smooth, like glass, yet there was nothing there. His hand was pressed against air.

"How can there be a wall here? I don't see anything."

Nola moved his hand across the invisible wall's surface and it disappeared with a spark of light. "It's okay!" she said, seeing his concerned look. "Your hand is just on the other side."

"The other side of what?" he asked as his own hand disappeared. The wall apparently had a hole in it.

"The other side of Kafka, I think."

"What are you talking about?"

Nola decided she would have to show him. She led him through the invisible doorway.

Suddenly, they found themselves in a vortex of air that sucked at their bodies like a vacuum. Kafka's landscape was rushing around them in a great circle as if they were in the eye of a tornado. The wind pulled at their hair and clothing and threatened to separate them. Nola wasn't as afraid of it as she had been. It was actually kind of fun, like a ride at an amusement park. Mich, on the other hand, had a terrified expression on his face.

There was a loud cracking noise like the sound of lightning striking a power line, and in a few seconds they stood before the Mangor Mountain range, both slightly dizzy. "Do you know where we are?" Nola asked.

"Yeah, that looks like Mangor, where Madrid lives," he said, pointing south. "And look, here is the river." Then he did a double take. "But how can Mangor be south? It's always been the most northern point in Kafka. No one has ever been beyond because of the monsters that live there. How have we gotten north of them?"

They turned north, away from the mountains, and saw the unknown. The River of Thought stretched as far as they could see and the landscape looked the same as the one they had just left.

Nola found the wall behind them and they stepped back through the doorway. They returned, near to the spot where they had exited.

Spirit, Heat and Tina were standing nearby. All were amazed by what they saw. Snort had returned, and was staring similarly. "Just exploring," Nola said brightly. "We're all right."

Snort, relieved, got back to business. He gave the Kahh back to Mich, who put it in the pocket of his sweatpants. Snort reported that he could not find the dragons. When he searched the mountains, he only found Fren.

"What happened to us just then?" Nola asked before Mich could ask about the Fren.

"I'm not positive, but I think we entered some kind of warp. We just stepped beyond the northernmost region of Kafka!"

I understand that portholes like this exist, Heat thought. *When you went there, did you find the source?*

Mich became worried. He should have seen the source, but had not. "We were at Mangor. I saw the river, but it never ended."

"What the hell d'ya mean, it never ended?" Tina demanded. "All rivers end!"

"I'm sure they do. But I saw no end." Mich contemplated what he had seen. If this was a porthole, why did it bring them to Mangor? Why not some other part of Kafka, or why not another world, for that matter, as was the nature of portholes? Unless it was some kind of magic loop.

"Heat, do you think it could be a magical loop?" he asked.

I suppose it is possible. If you went through it here, which is as far south as the map shows, and then came up just north of Mangor . . . He trailed off and walked over to the invisible wall. *Let me conduct an experiment on this wall. Perhaps I can find out more about it. Would you mind assisting me, Tina?*

Mich was shocked that Heat would ask for her help instead of his. She was a Creator, but Heat was his best friend. He felt a little jealous for the relationship that had begun to form between the two during their trip down.

"Sure, why not," she said wryly.

Snort. The little dragon perked up. *See if you can locate some life form, such as a pink bunny or a rat, but do not harm it.*

Snort bounded through the grass in his usual way, trying to scare out some critters, but nothing appeared. The plain was barren of game. Snort finally came back carrying a purple cricket. He was disgusted that he couldn't come up with anything better.

It's kind of small, but it will have to do. Give it to Tina.

Snort did as directed. He was glad to have the bug out of his mouth. It had taken great restraint for him not to chomp it and swallow it. He was starving!

Now, place the cricket on the wall.

Tina gently put the cricket on the vertical face of the wall. The cricket slipped down, but scrambled back up and slipped again. It managed to stay on the wall with difficulty. It hung there, in the air.

Now, Tina, cut the cricket in half. Make sure that it doesn't fall off the wall.

"Ewww!"

"Just do it!" Mich snapped. He was immediately ashamed for that outburst. He was somewhat miffed at her for an obscure reason that made no sense to him. He was also anxious to see what Heat was getting at.

Watch carefully, Heat told them.

Tina fished in her purse and produced a tiny pocket knife, just the right size for slicing up crickets. She gingerly held the cricket to the wall and pressed the knife across its midsection, separating it into two halves.

The others looked at the halved cricket as its lower half slid disgustingly down through the air, leaving a string of guts on the wall. "So, what about it?" Tina asked.

Just keep watching the two halves. The cricket is not yet dead.

Everyone was extremely interested now. They all stared at the cricket, which still twitched an antenna. As it twitched for the last time, something strange happened.

"Look!" Mich said. "It has multiplied, like the worms. There are four of them now!"

Not so, Heat thought. *Look closer.*

They did.

It is not four crickets, but two halved crickets.

The group exchanged bewildered glances. "What good are two halved crickets?" Nola finally asked.

Then Mich caught on. "Oh! I get it now." He doubled over, as if someone had punched him, and he stomped his foot. "Why didn't I realize that before! Damn! Misty uses one of these when she gets ready to go spooking!"

Nola saw that he was going through his cute little dramatics, but the curiosity was getting to her. *"What?"* she demanded.

"Don't you get it? It's a death mirror!"

The others were blank. He decided he had better explain before the girls became furious. "It's a mirror, really. It reflects only dead things."

"But it reflects everything," Nola said. "It reflects the grass and the river so that it looks as if it goes on forever."

"But the grass is brown. It's all dead here, and the river is not a living thing," he said.

"That's true."

Mich turned to Heat. "Can we fly over it?"

I'm afraid the lack of even the slightest breeze would make flight impossible. We need wind to help lift our bulk.

"Can we go around it?"

Let Spirit and me check.

Heat leapt over the drying river and galloped a short distance away, while Spirit galloped to the other end. They stood for a moment, checking the dam, then ran on again. They repeated this until they were over the horizon and out of sight. In a few minutes they came galloping into sight and rejoined the group.

The dam seems to extend infinitely. Perhaps it makes a circuit around the whole of Kafka. The Fren have surely been planning this for a long time.

"Do you think the source might be behind this mirror?"

Indeed, it seems quite possible. However—

"Then all we have to do is smash it!" Mich found a large rock and heaved it at the mirror.

Uh, I wouldn't advise— Heat warned, but it was too late. The prince was still too impetuous for anyone's good.

The rock flew toward the mirror, struck it, and began to fly right back to him. He ducked, just as the rock flew over his head and landed with a splash in the river, causing its colors to mix.

Mich looked at Heat. He felt like a fool. Why did he always act first and listen later? He should be more patient.

I apologize, Heat thought. *I should have warned you about that. It seems that this death mirror has been constructed of dreamstone, the type which cannot be destroyed by any Kafkian.*

Mich was stricken. What would he do if the source were behind it? He couldn't destroy it. No Kafkian could, and neither Nola nor Tina were ready.

Just then he felt a wonderful notion creep up inside his head. It grew and grew and grew, until it burst out of his mouth as joyous laughter. He laughed so hard that he was forced to sit down.

He was jolted out of his enraptured state by two silver hooves being stamped down beside him. He looked up. Heat was glaring at him, his ears flat. Mich could see his distorted image in his friend's silver eyes.

I fail to behold the drollery of this predicament. Heat was gritting his teeth, trying not to be angry with his friend.

Mich tried his best to keep from smiling, but could not. He knew that Heat rarely lost his temper, but when he did, his words became almost too large to comprehend. "We found it."

Spirit stepped closer as he saw Mich about to laugh again. *Found what?* he asked blithely.

Mich looked at Tina, then at Nola, who was now smiling also. "We found the source!"

Nola's smile turned to a look of astonishment and confusion. "We found the what?"

"The source! You still don't get it? This death mirror wasn't put here to reflect the dead; there is nothing here for it to reflect but bugs, grass and sky."

"Would you just get to the point? I'm going nuts!" Nola said. His bright green eyes were wide with excitement.

"This is the dam," he said, almost crying for joy. "This mirror was built to trick people! *This is the dam!*"

Nola realized, finally, that he was right. The mirror did extend across the river. She bowled him over in her rush to hug him. She lay atop him and kissed him.

Mich enjoyed her happy kiss and held her close. Her body was soft and warm and cushioned in all the right places, so this position was hardly uncomfortable.

The kiss was excruciatingly sweet and long. He felt a hot flash travel up from his toes. When it finally reached his heart, she pulled away. "I'm sorry," she whispered to him. Then she spoke louder to the others. "This means Kafka is safe!"

"Far from it!" a nasty voice howled.

Nola looked up and found herself gazing into the mirror. In its reflection was a small, scraggly-looking creature. It looked like an ugly little dog with a man's head. It stood on its hind legs and in his paw was a scourge. Across its forehead was a diadem of thorns. Behind him were several more creatures, each with a dangerous-looking razor that was shaped like a jag of lightning. Their black eyes glinted ominously.

She disengaged from Mich and stood up. "What——?"

"I have come to kill the ones who may aspire to halt my takeover, and it seems I have found you."

Reility! Spirit whinnied. He reared up, his hooves stroking the air, his teeth bared.

Reility whipped Spirit's flank with the scourge. The assault was so swift and accurate that Nola didn't see it until Spirit's black hide was turned red with his own blood. She winced as she felt his pain.

Reility's face showed no emotion, neither malice nor pity. Something in his face seemed horrifyingly familiar.

"Next?" he said, smiling an artificial smile.

Nola slowly backed up against Mich, who in turn backed against the dam. One of the Fren was instantly between Mich and the wall, holding his jag at Mich's back.

"You realize that you cannot escape death," Reility informed them. "It comes, ready or not."

This was awful. It had come down to this at last. Nola had thought it would. The Fren would destroy her and her friends, just as they had the rest of Kafka. The Fren would conquer and this wonderful place would be a world of pain, despair and hopelessness— and the blame would be laid at her feet. It was just like her to screw it all up. Why couldn't she discover her power?

Nola felt Spirit's voice speak to her, privately, carefully. *Nola, you must jump into the river. You must go home. Take Mich and Tina with you.*

Nola started to cry. *I can't leave you here!* she thought back. *I can't come back until you recharge! That's five years; please don't make me go!*

Please, Nola. By my troth, I swear you will return soon. As for me, if you truly love me, my friend, you will do as I ask and do not worry; just go.

Nola could feel the sadness in his heart, but she knew that if she did not take his advice, he would be even more unhappy and they might never see each other again. It seemed that five years wasn't so long to wait after all. She would have to leave, though her heart was breaking.

Tina was surprised when Nola took her hand. Did she, after all, care what happened to her? Maybe. She would have to remember to thank her one of these days for it, if they got out of this alive.

"Well, Lady Nola, who will be first to taste death?" Reility asked. "Perhaps your horse?" He whipped Spirit again across his tender nose.

Nola was angered beyond control. "You cannot kill him! He's a dream!"

"No, but he can feel pain and feel what it's like to wish he were dead. And I can do worse to him than inflict pain. Perhaps you'd like to see?"

"I will destroy you!" she yelled. "I know where the source is. Did you think you could trick us with this mirror?"

"You fool! Your stupidity is astounding; the river *has* no source. It is never ending and never beginning. The only source is your own tiny brains! And as you can see, they are not enough. My people grow stronger every day, and you are helping us!"

"Helping you? Never! I am here to wipe you out!"

"Don't think that I don't know about you and your misguided friends. You have not yet fathomed the secret, and don't think I will give you the chance to do so. Take her!" he yelled to his minions.

"Bite me!" she cried back.

As the first Fren reached her, she threw herself into the river. She felt a razor graze her side as she plunged, headlong, into the tepid water. Tina's hand was wrenched from her own when she fell in, but Tina had already lost her balance. Mich was caught by surprise and was pulled in with Tina.

They found themselves in the sea, struggling to reach the surface.

They were deeper than they had been before, and Tina blacked out immediately. This time, both Mich and Nola were wide awake and swimming mightily to the surface, trying to drag Tina.

Nola's head came above water and she filled her lungs with clean air. Her heart rate suddenly increased and she too blacked out.

13

JOHNBOY

When Nola came to, she was lying on a beach towel on the shore. Mich was kneeling beside her, speaking softly.

"Nola, are you okay?" he asked, stroking her forehead.

"Yes," she answered, smiling weakly. The razor wound had been bandaged up. She could see that it had bled a lot. The bandage was soaked. Too bad she couldn't have remained in Kafka long enough to have it magically healed. But of course that was the point: to get out of there in a hurry.

Nola thought she had better be cheerful for the sake of the others, considering what had happened, but inside she was sad and angry. Somewhere in the back of her mind, her suicidal voice cried out for the escape of death. She did her best to ignore it. Reility had taken her away from her heart friend, possibly forever. She felt as if a vital piece of her soul had been torn out. But no matter how long she was here, she had to have faith in Spirit's promise that she would be able to return to Kafka one day. What, then, would become of Mich? Was she going to lose him forever?

She tried to hold back the torrent of tears, but one slipped loose. She quickly wiped it away.

"Are you sure you are all right? You look flushed."

"It's okay. I'm just a little upset, that's all. Where is Tina?" she asked, changing the subject.

"She's okay. She's here."

Nola sat up and looked. Tina was standing behind her.

"How you feelin' girlie? Lemme change that bandage for ya." Tina ripped another long strip from the bottom of her skirt. She removed the old bandage, and when Nola saw the cut she felt squeamish. Tina quickly applied the new bandage, tying it tightly.

"That was some trip! I ain't felt nuthin' like that since—well, since before I wuz in rehab." For the first time, Tina was embarrassed. It meant that she cared what Mich and Nola thought of her, and it was a step in the right direction.

"Hey, man, I'm starvin'. Whacha say 'bout hitting the deli downtown for a sub or something?"

Nola wasn't very hungry. She was worried about Mich. However, for the sake of herself and her friends, she faked optimism. "Sounds great! It'll be a nice change from luberries." She noted Mich's expression and quickly added, "Though luberries would be great on some ice cream."

"Better yet, you gotta let me cook you guys a dinner."

Nola looked at Mich and he looked at her.

"Hey, come on, I'll fix us some spaghetti—homemade, my grandpa's recipe," Tina said enticingly.

Nola laughed at how hard she was trying to convince them. "Oh, okay!" she said. "Where do you live?"

"Where else d'ya think a ho like me would live? Park Avenue or sumthin'?" She laughed. "I live on North Fourteenth Street. Come on, we can take the subway train. It oughtta be fun for you." She smiled, looking at Mich.

He wondered what a subway train was. It was apparent that he was going to find out.

The trio walked through the suburbs for some time, then into the city and hailed a cab. Fortunately Tina had change for it. The cab carried them to the closest subway station.

It took the girls time to coax Mich onto the escalator. He was afraid that if he fell, the teeth at the bottom would eat him. Once they were on the train, Mich was full of questions about how the train ran, which led them into a discussion about the magic of electricity. Mich commented that it reminded him of riding the worms in their caverns.

When they arrived at Tina's apartment, the day had waned. She took them first to the roof of the twelve-story building and showed them the view. The night was warm and breezy and the skyline was alive with manmade stars. It was hard to tell where the city ended and the sky began. Nola explained to Mich that each light belonged to someone's home or workplace and he was astounded that so many people could live so close together. He had never seen a high-rise section during the days they had spent near the beach, so perhaps had thought that multistory buildings were rare. Here they grew like weeds.

Inside her huge apartment, Tina cooked the spaghetti. She stewed her sauce for an hour while they discussed recent events and future plans. The room filled with the delicious smells of food. She served them warm brandy tea and cheese and crackers.

Nola noticed how much nicer Tina's apartment was than the one she had shared with John. It had two bedrooms, a kitchen with a separate breakfast nook, a small dining room and a large living room. She had matching furniture and a wall unit with bookshelves, a big-screen television and a nice stereo. Nola couldn't understand how someone who had all of this could be unhappy. Sure, the way she got it wasn't too great, but even Nola would be proud to have a place like this, no matter what she did.

Tina understood her thought. "Sure, here's where I'm halfway happy. It's the street I don't like—but that's where I gotta be, every night, if I don't want to lose this."

Just as Nola had to be with John, if she didn't want to be on the street herself. It did make dismal sense.

"So, what goes on from here?" Tina asked Mich.

"I wish I knew," he replied. "I guess the only thing we can do is wait. I hope we can find a way back before it's too late."

"What'll happen if ya don't get back in time?"

Mich shook off that unpleasant thought. "I suppose there will be no more Kafka."

"And no more dreams for Earth," Nola said.

Tina shrugged. "Who needs 'em anyhow? I sure as hell don't. I do just fine without 'em."

Mich shook his head. "No, you don't."

Tina leaned forward, feigning interest. "Whadaya mean, I don't? I got all this stuff, don't I?"

"Let me answer your question by asking you a question: What were you like as a child?"

Tina looked shocked by the question, but settled herself to ponder. "I suppose I wuz a pretty good kid," she said. "I mean, I got good grades and I had a lotta friends." She sipped the warm tea. "I didn't actually rebel until my dad died and my mom remarried. I wuz a bitch cuz I blamed her for my dad dying. He died in a car crash, ya know," she said, sipping her tea again. "He wuz wasted and my mom let'm drive to the store to git more beer. He passed out at the wheel and drove off a bridge. He died instantly." She looked down into her cup. "Then it was just me 'n' Grandpa. He brought me up from a teenager. I wuz happy then. I went on through high school getting straight *A*'s. I was never not on the honor roll." Tina sniffed. She wiped her eyes with a napkin. "My grandpa was always proud of me. He'd brag to all his geezer friends 'bout me. Then, at my graduation, he was huggin' me and screamin' so loud, so that everyone could hear'm. He was so happy. But I guess the excitement was too much for him. He had an attack and died in my arms."

"Oh, Tina, that's so awful!"

"I ain't finished yet, girlie!" Tina snapped. "Well, I couldn't handle it so I turned my back on everythin' I'd learned and took up drinkin' and drugs. I done everything from pot to ice. That last shit almost killed me. My grandpa left me well off, so I was able to buy lots of it, and I did. But the cash started runnin' out an' I needed more ice, so I tried to git me a job. I couldn't even git my damn foot in the door. So I sold the only thing I had left, my body, and I made money. Lots of cash. Then one day, I had been doin' so much ice that I passed out in the street and lay there for three days. I wuz awake, but I couldn't move an' I didn't even realize how long I wuz there until I saw the paper. It only felt like a few minutes. I was skin and bones while I was on that stuff cuz I wuz never hungry. Eventually, I guess somebody didn't like my body stinkin' up the place, so the cops came an' put me in rehab. You know, they had to tie me to a damn bed so that I wouldn't get out to get more ice. I think it was illegal and it was a nightmare on that bed. I was on it for a whole week, going through the most painful and emotional withdrawals I'd ever gone through. The time I spent in that place comin' down was one of the worst times of my life, but it was worse being puppet to them crystals. I was glad for it later. Then I wuz straight for a while, till I hooked up with that fat bastard that raped me after being with a VD chick. Then— you know the rest."

Tina looked at them for comments. Both had concerned looks on their faces, but neither spoke. "It's okay. I'm done now," she said.

"Are you?" Nola asked.

Tina nodded. "Uh, yeah. I dreamed. I didn't tell nobody, because nobody would've believed it. But you know about that, seein' as where we've just been. And sometimes I felt this weird tug, like somewhere I had to be, but I couldn't find it, and anyway, I wuz busy. I guess you know that too, cuz I didn't find you, you found me."

"Yes," Nola agreed. "I didn't even know I was looking for another Dreamer."

"Oh, well," Mich said. "That's quite a story. Do you understand, now, why you need dreams?"

"No."

Nola smiled, knowing that Tina was having another fit of perversity. She had quickly bloomed in Kafka, souring only for a while when it seemed that her Creation rejected her.

"When you were a child, you had dreams and wishes, but people destroyed them and dragged you down. They destroyed your dreams and—no offense, they turned you into someone who doesn't care about herself or others."

Nola broke in before Tina could come up with a snide comment. "You know, I had just as much reason as you to have my dreams crushed. My father disowned me and my mother could have cared less what I did. I was pregnant at sixteen and was forced to make a tough and heartbreaking decision to abort the pregnancy. One of my last boyfriends, who I loved very much, beat me up constantly until he strangled me and left me for dead. But I tried to handle it differently from you. The more people brought me down, the harder I tried. I relied so much upon my belief that somewhere, out there, was Mich. If it wasn't for that belief, and the thought of someday meeting him, I would be dead by my own hand."

Mich was touched. He hadn't realized how much she believed and relied on him. Why, then, couldn't she trust him? Had Earth had that much of an effect on her? From what he knew of this world, it would probably affect him the same way. He felt out of place because he was the only one in the room who had an easy upbringing. The easiest possible! He hoped that they wouldn't be prejudiced against him for it.

"That's pretty sad too," Tina said. "I suppose I can understand whatcher sayin' now. You mean, if Kafka is gone, then everyone will be like me?"

"That's the gist," Mich said as he stuffed a cheese-laden cracker in his mouth. "But it's not too late for you. King Kras is still alive. Maybe."

"Ha! Holy crap!" Tina laughed. "I didn't know it was that bad! We gotta get back there! We don't need a whole planet full of people like me!"

Tina was laughing, but, somehow, she didn't feel like laughing. It wasn't funny. No matter how bad it treated her, Earth was her home and the only place she ever wanted to be. If people had no hope and no dreams, the whole world would be covered with the blood of people slitting their wrists and everyone would get whacked out on drugs and start killing each other for another hit. She decided she'd have to give serious thought to fighting back and regaining her hope. Maybe with the help of these two quirky friends, she could do it. Whatever happened, it would take her a long time to heal enough to be in fighting condition.

Tina looked up and sniffed the air. "Oh, fudge! My sauce is burning!" she said as she dashed into the kitchen.

When she was gone, Nola held Mich's hand.

"Mich," she said, "I know she's a Creator, but maybe she should stay here. I mean, if she has any dreams left, there aren't that many. Maybe Reility would just destroy any she has left."

"I know what you mean, Nola, but she could be a big help if she finds out how to use her ability to Create, as will you. She's just too valuable. Besides, I don't think she'd let us leave without her."

"Soup's on!" Tina said, smiling. Those smiles were rare, but when they happened, they could light up the room.

She served the dinner steaming hot, with garlic bread and sodas. The smell made Nola's mouth water. She didn't realize just how much she missed the food here. Mich had never seen food like this before, but the smell got to him too. They were all hungry.

Suddenly, there was a knock on the door. Tina sighed and got up to answer it.

It was a man wearing dark glasses, a wide-brimmed hat and a black trench coat. Nola thought he looked like something out of a Humphrey Bogart picture, only fatter.

"Johnboy!" Tina cried happily. The two embraced. "Whacha doin' here?"

Nola felt a cold shiver. This was Tina's pimp? He reminded her deviously of Kras, the worm king, perhaps by no coincidence. Who could say where a Creator got her inspiration?

"I came to check on my girl. Where you been?"

Tina held the door open so that he could come inside. "I been on vacation."

Johnboy laughed at the joke. He scanned the room and noticed Mich and Nola.

"Who are these two?" His tone took on a seriousness that made them nervous.

"Oh. Them two? They're okay. That's Nola and that's Mich."

Nola pushed forth a slight smile. Mich reached for Johnboy's hand. The large man came forward and pumped it a few times, then let go. He continued to study them for a moment, then looked back at Tina.

"So it seems I'm just in time for dinner!" He lifted the lid that covered the sauce. "You made this? Smells good. You always were a good cook."

He took a seat next to Mich and served himself some spaghetti. He watched Nola out of the corner of his eye with an intensity that made her want to excuse herself and run into the bathroom. She was afraid he might be thinking of her as a potential employee.

Tina must have been thinking the same thing. Tina checked her watch as if she had just noticed what time it was. "Would you look at that! It's already ten-thirty." She looked at Nola as if she was disappointed. "It's time for us to go. Maybe I can get us a ticket to your friend's house, uh, Lori," she finished. Nola had mentioned her friend, Lori, so that was where that name came from. Tina must figure that they needed all the concealment they could get.

Tina looked expectantly at Nola, praying that she had caught on and would not give her away. She didn't. "Oh, that's right! I almost forgot. We'd better get going, Mich."

Mich looked up from his plate. "Huh? I thought—" Nola nudged his arm. "Oh, yeah! Lori! We are already late; we better get to the bus house, uh, station," he said quickly and started for the door.

Johnboy rose and slid his dark glasses down his nose so that he could see Mich's eyes clearly. His own eyes were bloodshot. "There's no reason to take the bus." He smiled, showing uneven teeth. "I got a perfectly good Cadillac downstairs. I'll drive you."

His tone deepened with his last words. It was obvious that he suspected something. It was also obvious that if they refused, they might never get back to Kafka.

Nola didn't see any reason why they should not go with him. He seemed nice enough, on the surface. Her years of life had instilled in her the principle never to trust a stranger, but she had never been betrayed by one. It was always those who knew one best who hurt one most. However, she was afraid of him and it was that fear that decided her. Better to play along than to risk giving herself away and ending up on the streets like Tina.

Tina noted her hesitation and said, "It's okay, Nola." She hugged the man. "He's as sweet as a teddy bear. He won't hurt ya if you don't want him to."

Johnboy laughed and Tina was smiling. Nola knew that Tina's smiles were genuine. It seemed as if she had no choice. Still the doubt nagged at her. There was something phony about this situation, and

Tina had given her warning in her fashion. She looked to Mich, who just shrugged. This was her world, not his.

"Okay," she said a bit uneasily.

Johnboy took a step toward the door. As soon as his fingers touched the knob, there was a loud crash and the door flung open, throwing Johnboy back onto the glass coffee table, shattering it.

Tina screamed, but the scream went unheard. Both Nola and Mich were staring, disbelieving, frozen with fear.

Johnboy looked around, dazed. "What the hell?" he said as he tried to sit up.

"Click" went the hammer on the revolver that was now held between Johnboy's eyes. "You move, boy, and you die."

Three men had broken in the door and were standing in the foyer. One man held the gun at Johnboy's forehead while the other two stood by and watched.

Johnboy cringed and cowered beneath the weight of what, he felt sure, was death's hand. All his pride, fearlessness and strength could not help him now. *They* had found him. In seconds, his tall, portly body was reduced to a shriveling mass of sweat and tears. He was afraid that this would be the end of him. He hoped Tina would escape. The only thing he could do was buy some time.

Johnboy tried to inch away from the barrel of the gun, but it only pressed harder, cutting his flesh. "Look, man, I don't know what you want," Johnboy said, quailing.

"You know exactly why we're here, boy."

The two men grabbed Johnboy's arms and lifted him up. "We're here to collect."

Tina gasped. She could see from behind that Johnboy's arms and back had several cuts from the glass of the table and were bleeding. She knew why the men were here. Johnboy had some kind of partnership going with these men. They imported several types of drugs.

Johnboy distributed them to dealers. But he made the biggest mistake a distributor could ever make: to get hooked on the drugs he sold. Now Johnboy owed money. A lot of money. He was her friend and she had tried hard to help him come up with the cash, but he just popped, snorted, shot, drank or smoked it up, along with the rest of his money.

Nola's mind was spinning. She had never gotten hooked on drugs, but she had seen enough to have a fair notion of Johnboy's situation. He had been looking for more girls to pimp for, because he had heavy debts to pay off. Nola might have found it very difficult to get out of that Cadillac without having something addictive forced into her, and Mich might have left it dead. But that was no longer the real threat. All of her conscious thoughts were blinded by fear. Her eyes were fixed past Johnboy's bloody back, fixed beyond the gun, fixed beyond the men, fixed beyond the open door. She was praying that someone, anyone, would walk by and offer some kind of help. She kept trying to scream, but her throat was blocked by her heart.

Mich stared in disbelief at Johnboy and the men. He was well aware that a life was about to be taken right here in front of him. He too kept glancing at the door, though not for help, but escape. If only he were offered a chance, just one second of distraction. The doorway was so close.

"You choose. Pay up or say your prayers," the man said calmly.

There was a look of sheer terror in Johnboy's eyes. He did not have one cent to give, but he did not want to die. Not like this. There was too much left for him to do. He wanted to die a clean man, not a broken one. He scraped the deep recesses of his brain for an answer, any answer. Anything to get that gun barrel away from his head. Deep within, he found a way out, but it was an evil way. It was a way that would save his life but, later, would take it from him in another way.

"I don't have the money."

"Then you die." The man cocked the hammer.

"Wait! You guys got me wrong! I can pay!"

The armed man turned and looked at his comrades, then back at the beaten dog that was Johnboy. He was smiling wryly. "Whatchoo got, then?"

"Your boss, Charlie, he likes girls, don't he?" he stammered.

The man laughed. "Yeah, so?"

"So I got girls for him! Nice girls, beautiful girls!"

"You mean her?" the man asked, gesturing with the gun at Tina. "She don't look like much to me."

Tina was horrified. "Johnboy, how could you?" she pleaded.

Nola saw a tear run down her face for the first time. It was quickly wiped away and her stricken face was replaced by one of terrible anger, bordering on madness. Nola could see Tina as she fought herself to keep from doing something foolish. She wanted to give Johnboy the beating of his life, because it seemed that the man had sold them out to the trolls of Earth. Maybe even the Fren of Earth.

It was odd how Tina had deceived herself about what her pimp would do when hard pressed. It had been clear to Nola in an instant that this was what it was all about. But probably her friend, Lori, could say the same about Nola's own relationship with John. It was hard to see clearly when encumbered by one's own emotions.

"You know, this one here ain't such a bad deal," the man said, looking Nola up and down. "Maybe he'd take her as payment." He paused and seemed thoughtful for a second. "But there's no accountin' for taste. We'll take both of them."

"Johnboy!" Tina screamed again.

In that instant, while the man was distracted by Tina's scream, Johnboy knocked the gun from the man's hand and lunged for him.

Mich saw his chance. He made a mad dash for the door. He whizzed right by the startled men and down the stairwell. Nola screamed after him and tried to follow but one of the men caught her and held her fast. She could do nothing but submit to the brute. The other man went after Mich.

Meanwhile, Johnboy had scored on the gunman's stomach with his head. He lifted his head and drew back his fist. The gunman recovered at the last moment and stuck out his free hand. The hand grasped Johnboy's throat like an iron vise and it held him fast. Johnboy struggled and grappled with the hand; he couldn't breathe.

"Let's tie up the bitches," the man said to his friend while smirking at Johnboy. He let Johnboy go. Johnboy collapsed to the floor, coughing and sputtering, grasping his neck.

Tina tried to run, but did not get one step. The man who held Nola pointed a gun at her. The other man retrieved a telephone and removed the cords. He wrapped the cords around Tina's wrists so tightly that her hands turned purple.

"Owww, you bastard!" she said and spit at him.

He grabbed the hair on the back of her head and pulled it back. When her mouth opened to yell, he stuffed in a handkerchief.

He turned to Nola and bound her as well. "Maybe we should give this one a strip search!" he said, smiling.

He put his hand on her neck and ran it down to her blouse. Nola would rather have been fondled by a worm's tongue, slime and all. But that wasn't an option. She brought up her knee, but, sadly, not fast enough. He caught it, and fondled her thigh.

"Oooh, she's a dangerous one, fellas! Look out for her!" he said mockingly and jerked her roughly out the door. The other man bound Johnboy as well and dragged him at gunpoint through the door while pushing Tina.

A station wagon waited on the street outside. Nola was still kicking and trying to slow the man down. She didn't like the way he was holding her. It was as if he had her in a love embrace. He held her much too close to his own body, still trying to sneak in some good feels. She braced her feet against the car door. That caused him to release his hug so that he could deal with her feet. She knew why he didn't simply club her halfway senseless, so she couldn't resist: bruised goods didn't make a good impression on the boss. She tried to push against him and make him lose his balance, but he was too strong and he shoved her into the backseat.

Tina put up a fight as well. Her feet were flailing and kicking at the car and at the man who held her. But his friend aided him, and soon both women were in the car, sitting close to each other for what comfort they could get. Johnboy was shoved in behind Tina and the door was slammed shut.

The two men sat in the front and waited. Soon, the big one became impatient and honked the horn. The third man appeared. His clothes were torn and he suffered a busted lip and swollen cheek. He walked to the car and got in.

"Well, where is he?" asked the driver, irritated.

"I'm sorry, boss, but he got away from me. He got my gun too."

Nola could hear the driver sigh deeply. He reached over and struck the man several times with a rolled-up magazine. "You stupid jerk!"

"It's okay, it's okay!" the man yelled. "I shot him in the gut. He was bleedin' pretty bad; he won't live too long."

Tina's gaze locked on Nola's and showed genuine concern. Nola's own eyes clouded over and filled with brine. She felt a stab in her chest, and she cried.

The car moved off down the street, away from town.

Johnboy reached up with his teeth and removed the handkerchief from Tina's mouth. He looked at her apologetically. There was hate in her soft brown eyes. He knew to speak an apology to her would only make her angrier, but he wished he hadn't done what he had. He wished he knew something to say that would make it all right, but he knew there was not. Tina looked as if she wanted to kill him. How could he apologize for what he had done to her and her friend? Now his life was being destroyed; he had lost his only friend. He felt the tears coming and had to turn away.

Nola, Tina and Johnboy sat silently as the car sped down the street. It bore them on through the city. An hour later they were in the suburbs and, an hour after that, in the country.

Nola could think only of Mich. She hoped that he would be okay. She was just getting to know him. She was even beginning to feel that this was not a dream. Maybe it was all real and she just couldn't see it. If that was the case, then she must be torturing him by withholding her love. But as long as one tiny doubt remained, she would not commit her heart to him and his world. She wouldn't walk into the same trap twice. If she did, she would die. With such thoughts of Mich in her mind, she fell asleep and dreamed.

14
DREAM

She dreamed of Kafka. The land was black and charred. It was being overrun by the Fren. They were killing people and burning the land, laughing all the while. They taunted and teased her for not knowing the secret to destroy them.

The survivors of the raids yelled at her and shook their angry fists and screamed, "Why are you letting this happen to us? Why are you just standing there, letting them destroy our land? It's all your fault!"

Nola ran away. She ran past the villagers, past the stench of death to the river. The river's splendid colors were gone, replaced by a murky black water that smelled of rotting sulfur. She ran on until she found a patch of green grass on a hilltop, far away from the commotion. The last small piece of life left in the ruined land.

In a moment, she saw Spirit emerge from the thick, dark smoke that was the sky, winging his way down to her hilltop. He landed beside her and looked down disapprovingly.

Why do you sit here, when you are needed down there? he asked.

Nola burst into tears. "I can't do anything about it!" she sobbed. "I don't know the secret!"

Do you realize that if you do not learn the secret, Earth will die too? The secret lies within you.

"Earth too?" she asked, appalled.

Earth without dreams.

Now she understood, in the intuitive way of dreams. "Yes! I know. All human life on Earth will be managed by people with no dreams. We will lose hope and love and we will kill each other and ourselves—become extinct."

Nola stood up and hugged Spirit's muscular neck. His hide smelled like smoke. She suddenly felt so ashamed that she wished she were dead. She cried and Spirit's neck became moist and salty.

I feel your sorrow. It is painful, he said, blinking tears from his green eyes.

Nola realized it was true. They shared their souls and shared their emotions as well. He felt her pain, and she could feel his stubbornness. She released him and composed herself.

You know the secret, you need only apply it. Look, he said, gesturing with a toss of his head.

She looked down and out onto the blackened field below the hill. The Fren had surrounded a group of fairies. Nola winced, as she expected them to be killed, but the Fren just stood there. The fairies collapsed into a heap.

Nola tried to turn away, but she felt Spirit's mind watching intently. She was compelled to watch also.

Slowly, she saw the fairies change color, turning light brown, then dark brown, then black. Their bodies changed also. In a matter of moments, they were completely different creatures. The fairies got up and joined the Fren, for that was what they had become.

Nola looked up at Spirit with sudden realization.

"The Fren, they didn't kill them. They didn't even touch them! The good dreams, they became bad, became Fren. The Creators of fairies, their dreams were crushed. Esprit, people like me are destroying Kafka by giving up hope!"

Suddenly, the whole hilltop was lifted and tilted, causing Nola to be thrown to the side. She woke.

15

CHARLIE

The car had just pulled sharply into a driveway. Beside her, Tina and Johnboy also woke. The car stopped and the three of them were dragged up the steps of an enormous farmhouse. Once inside, they were released. Two men shut and blocked the door.

The interior of the house was extravagant, to say the least. Everything looked expensive. There were wool rugs covering the floors. To the side was a living room filled with expensive toys, such as a sunken bar, a huge stereo system and some kind of TV whose images were projected onto the wall, but with no projector in sight.

"Come upstairs, Johnboy," a man's voice said.

They followed the voice up a winding staircase, down a hall and into a den. Once inside, a huge man sat them in chairs in front of a desk. Behind the desk was a grotesque figure of a middle-aged man. His black hair was streaked with gray and he held a tiny pipe between his teeth that looked as if it was made of ivory. Kneeling on the floor beside him was a beautiful, frail woman wearing nothing but her own hair and a G-string. She was stroking his leg.

The man puffed his pipe and leaned forward. "So, Johnboy, to what do I owe the pleasure of your company?"

The muscular bodyguard spoke up. "He don't have the money, Charlie."

"Doesn't have, you idiot!"

"Sorry. He doesn't have the money, boss."

Charlie sent two rings of gray smoke through the bowl of his pipe. "Can't pay, eh?"

He stood up and walked over to Johnboy, who was being held down in a chair. The woman crawled behind him, her full breasts dangling. It was obvious that this man was rich in both money and power, and poor in human decency.

He put his hand on Johnboy's shoulder. "You know, John, we've been working together for a long time. I trusted you so much that I gave you one of my best jobs, a home and a new car. We were friends, you and I, and we had some good times. You remember that time when you got arrested on a robbery charge and I helped you out? Remember? They were going to kill you in that place. But I looked out for you and you were free. Then we picked up those hookers and got drunk, you remember, right?" He laughed gruffly. "We had a good time, didn't we? You remember?"

Johnboy was so nervous that he was ready to wet his pants, but he managed to squeeze out a fake laugh, then added, "Yeah, I remember. You—you really helped me out, Charlie."

Suddenly, Charlie grabbed both his shoulders and wrenched the fat Johnboy from his chair. "And this is how you thank me?" he yelled.

Johnboy just hung there, not responding. This wasn't defiance, but inability. The question was rhetorical, anyway.

Charlie seemed to rein in his temper and went back behind the desk, with the woman still clinging to his legs, her hair shifting now and then to expose her buxom flesh. Nola could hardly imagine a more pathetic creature—unless it was herself. He made a quick gesture and three men came forward, releasing them from their bonds.

Charlie's face was red and he was trying not to snarl, but he didn't do a good job. "I treated you like my son and you took my drugs, smoked them up yourself instead of selling them like a good boy. You promised to pay me, and now, now you come to me telling me you can't. Now I have to punish my son."

"B-but Charlie, I b-brought you these girls!" Johnboy stammered.

Tina burst into tears beside him. "Johnboy, how could you? I hate you!"

Charlie walked out from behind the desk again. He looked down at the lovely woman who was clinging to his leg, massaging his inner thigh. She looked up at him and smiled sweetly.

"It seems to me you've overlooked the fact that I *have* girls. What would I want with a couple of your sluts?"

Again, Johnboy couldn't answer. It was obvious that Charlie was playing cat and mouse with him, and would do whatever he chose to do the moment he got tired of posturing.

Charlie looked at the woman and stroked her hair. "I'm tired of you now. Wait in your room."

"But, Charlie, I want to serve you, you are so distressed, let me help . . ." she pleaded.

"I said get out of here, bitch!" he said, kicking her cruelly. But the woman knew better than to cry. She absorbed the blow and left, wrapping her hair tightly around her. If she had any sense of pride, it had obviously been beaten out of her long since. And this, Nola knew, was what she herself would become if she didn't find a way to escape.

Charlie motioned to his bodyguard, who pointed a revolver at Johnboy's temple. Tina sat on the opposite side of him, with Nola next to her. Both girls were too frightened to say a word.

Nola was afraid that if she pleaded in Johnboy's favor that it just might get him shot sooner and herself as well. But Tina, despite what he had done to her, still cared for him. "Leave him alone! I'll get you the money!"

"Shut up, you walking social disease! This is between me and my son."

Charlie stepped forward and leaned close to Johnboy. "As my daddy always said to me, 'This'll hurt me more than it'll hurt you.' " Charlie leaned closer and kissed him on his forehead.

"No!" Tina cried.

Nola had a really ugly feeling about this. "Tina, I think we'd better keep quiet," she said urgently.

"No!" Tina repeated, staring at her wild-eyed. "He's going to—"

Nola rose and turned away, trying to draw Tina along with her. Tina hung back.

The gun sounded, deafeningly loud. Nola whirled, shocked.

Johnboy's head had been pushed to the side as the bullet ripped through his skull. Blood and small pieces of flesh and hair spattered Tina's face and blouse. Johnboy's tear-streaked face was twisted into a look of horror, going slack as his head dropped down.

Tina's scream echoed forever in Nola's mind as everything slowed down. Both girls were in a state of shock and terror. They were easily led downstairs. Though she was numb, Nola's mind still functioned, and she knew Charlie had done the murder in their presence for a reason: to impress upon them the likely penalty for defiance. So that they could be more expeditiously reduced to the nude girl's state, without bruises.

Nola's eyesight was double as she tried to fight off her heart palpitations. She was in what seemed to be the basement of the farmhouse. It was dark and musty, except for moonlight streaming in from a small window high on the brick wall. She held on to Tina's hand after the men left, locking the door behind them. They both sat in silence for a long moment.

"Are you okay?" Nola asked, still staring into space.

"Where are we?" Tina asked as the shock wore off.

"I—I think we're in the basement or something," she replied, looking around.

Then Tina's awareness rushed back in with a vengeance. "John-boy!" she cried, putting her face in her hands.

Then she looked up and seemed to stare at a vision of him in her mind. "All the better for ya, you dumb bastard! How could you? How could ya do this to me?" It was much the same reaction she had had when leaving Kras the worm king.

Nola wasn't sure what to do. Should she console Tina or should she shake a fist and curse as Tina had? She decided that neither would help. She had to try to keep her friend's mind occupied. It was obvious that Tina was teetering dangerously back and forth between grief and rage. Neither emotion was likely to be much help right now.

"We have to find a way out of here," Nola said calmly. She looked around. There was the door, but when she tried it, of course it was locked. The floor was concrete and the room was empty, except the window.

"There ain't no way outta here," Tina sobbed bitterly. "I been here before and believe me, there ain't no way."

Nola got an idea. "Were you alone when you were here?"

"Yeah. So?"

"Well, I think we might be able to reach that window up there," she said, pointing.

"You know, I think it's wortha shot." She looked at Nola, then back at the window. "But how we gonna do it? I ain't that strong, ya know."

"I think I can boost you up. Here, stand on my hands."

Nola locked her fingers together. Tina stepped onto them and Nola lifted her up. She was somewhat shorter than Nola herself, and therefore lighter despite her fuller figure.

"The window is barred on the outside, but the inside is unlocked," Tina said as she opened it.

At that moment the door was opened and a man came in with a

shoe box. "Aha!" he exclaimed. "I see the boss was right. He thought you might try that."

Nola sighed. She let Tina down.

"What's he gonna do with us?" Tina demanded.

"He don't want you two to die yet. He's got some internationals coming in and he needs you two to do a job," he said with a wry smile. "He told me to show you this."

He opened the box and withdrew a yellow butterfly, wings pinched between two fingers. He let go, and the butterfly immediately flew toward the light of the window. It struck a bar and tiny sparks flew from it as the life was zapped out of it. The butterfly fell to the floor.

"Isn't the symbolism deep? The boss just loves doing that!" Then the smile on his face vanished and he nodded. "There's no way out, unless you do the job." He turned and walked out. They could hear the clicking of the lock.

Nola sat on the floor, all hope gone. "He's going to kill us, isn't he?" she asked, picking up the dead butterfly.

"Soon as we finish the job, unless he figures we're worth the effort."

"What did he mean by that?" Nola was pretty sure she knew, but hoped to be refuted.

"He'll take us to meet some foreigners and make us turn tricks for them."

"Turn tricks!" Nola exclaimed, anguished by the confirmation. This was no slow brainwashing effort, but a fast action. Like a mugging—or a rape. "I'm no—"

"Better learn. Charlie can really make you hurt, if he wants to. At least you get taken care of, as long as you perform well."

Nola sat for a time staring at the butterfly in her lap. She thought of Mich and of Kafka, and of what Esprit had told her in her dream. As she stared at the lifeless little body she realized that, like the butterfly, she'd end up dead very soon unless she was careful. If she ever got free of this prison she knew she could find a way to save Kafka. It was up to her. What a burden it was to save a world, and more so to save two worlds. If she ever got out of here alive, maybe . . .

A tear fell onto the bright wing. She wiped it off, removing some of the brilliant pattern. She felt a hand on her shoulder. "It's okay, Nola," Tina said, sitting down beside her. "You got a prince who loves you. It's like a fairy tale. It ain't right for a fairy tale to have a sad ending. It just ain't right."

Nola could only nod her head. This wasn't the way a fairy tale was supposed to begin either. She hoped Mich was okay, but somehow, she didn't believe he was. How could he survive being shot in the gut, in a foreign world? The people they were dealing with played for keeps. This was no longer the adventure she had thought it would be. This was the ugly reality of the world. She couldn't even imagine what kind of chaos would come if people lost their dreams. And what of poor Tina? Nola really couldn't blame her for losing her hopes and dreams. She was beginning to lose her own.

Tina was no better off. She put her head in Nola's lap and silently wept. At first she had been sad for the loss of her friend and the cruel way that he had been killed, but then she realized that her love for him was false. He had brought her nothing but misery all her life.

Sure, he was good to her, not taking too much of the money she earned, but whenever he owed someone money, he used her to pay. Well, this time he had been the one to pay. She was glad for having made new friends. But now she was sad for getting them into this mess. Nola and Mich could, indeed, have a fairy tale relationship if it weren't for her. Why did they care so much about her? She was nothing but a worthless slut.

"I'm sorry," she murmured. Unable to say anything else, she closed her eyes and slept.

Nola understood. She knew that Tina must be ravaged by guilt, but what could she say? It's okay? It wasn't okay. So she just stroked her hair.

Dawn was coming, and soon Charlie would come for them.

Tina stirred in Nola's lap. Nola was glad that she was able to sleep. She wished she herself could get the same rest, but her heart and mind would not let her.

Tina sat up as she was wakened by the sound of a motor and of a loud zapping. The two girls jumped up. The sound came from the window above. They watched as the metal bars were pulled away from the wall. Large sparks shot out in every direction and the bars fell away. A rope ladder was lowered through the window and then a smiling face appeared.

"Mich!" Nola cried. "You're alive!"

Tina was aghast. "You're alive!" she echoed.

"Yes! Now come on, before the dogs come again!"

Tina climbed the ladder to the window. The window was small, but she was able to fit now that part of the wall had been torn away with the bars. Mich helped her out, then he helped Nola.

Mich was overcome by her touch on his arm. He had been so worried that something was going to happen to her and he'd never get to touch her again. When she was through the hole, he pulled her into his embrace. He held her close and kissed her.

"I was so worried about you," Nola said, dazed by the kiss. "I thought you were dead. What about the shot?"

"Never!" he said and kissed her again.

A female voice shouted to them. "Come on, will you? Here come the dogs!"

That was Lori's voice! Nola turned and saw the car with a rope attached to the bumper. Attached to the other end of the rope were the electrified window bars. Tina was already in the front seat and

Lori was behind the wheel. Nola saw four boxers running toward them, snarling and barking loudly.

Nola and Mich dashed for the car. The dogs arrived just as they slammed the door shut. Mich's window was open and a dog stuck in its head and snapped at him with its white fangs as he rolled up the window. The dog couldn't get its head away quite fast enough and the rising window caught the creature's tender nose and upper lip. It howled with pain and jerked away.

Lori slammed her foot on the gas and the tires skidded for a moment on the grass; then the car sped across the lawn. Nola and Tina sagged in their seats, overwhelmed by relief. Thank God for good friends, Nola thought weakly.

"But how did you ever find Lori?" she asked Mich. "You don't know your way around this world, and she's in another city."

"Ah," he said, pleased with himself. "I used the magic she explained to me when we talked before. The magic box number."

"Magic number?" Nola asked blankly.

"The phone," Lori explained, laughing. "I told him how to use the phone, and how to call collect, in case of emergency. I didn't realize he would remember my number."

"I would remember anything to save Nola," Mich said.

"But how did you know where to find us?" Nola demanded.

"I felt your presence," he said. "You are my Creator."

Just as Nola and Tina had felt each other's presence, when coming together. It must have been stronger for Mich.

"Well, you took long enough!" Tina said. At that, they all laughed.

Lori drove them back into the city to her apartment. Once there, she made them some food and they sat talking.

"So, that guy killed Johnboy?" Lori asked as if this were routine, but her face was grim.

"Yes, and he would have killed us also if it weren't for you two," Nola said, stuffing her face with chili. This was mostly to conceal her own reaction to the killing, but it had another cause: she hadn't realized how hungry she was. It was good to eat again.

"After making us turn tricks for his clients," Tina added.

"Tricks?" Mich asked. "You perform tricks? I would like to see some of them."

Tina opened her mouth to explain, but Nola cut in first. "Never mind!" She also felt much better knowing Mich was safe, his innocence almost intact. "Mich, I thought that guy had killed you."

"Killed me? Ha!" he said, assuming a macho pose. "He didn't know who he was messing with! I gave him a few punches and he ran away as fast as a pink bunny."

Nola saw that his shirt was bloodstained in the midsection. "How did you get the bullet out?"

Lori interrupted with the explanation. "I've been working part-time at the hospital. I took it out for him with a razor and a pair of needle-nosed pliers. Fortunately it was superficial. I expected him to scream his head off. He didn't even say ouch."

Tina turned somber. "I'm sorry I got you all into this mess. You should have just left me."

"Don't be silly," Mich said. "You're too pretty to—" He caught Nola's look, and changed tack. "We need your help. You're a Creator too. You can't lose faith, no matter what happens."

"If you do, you'll make more trouble and we'll all be dead," Nola said.

Tina, Mich and Lori turned to look at her.

Nola saw that she should elaborate. "Mich, do you remember what the worm king said about the Fren?"

"Yes. They are the product of a shattered dream." He suddenly realized the enormity of what she had said to Tina.

"Yes, they are. I realized something. The Fren are borne by a shattered dream; that means that they don't actually kill certain creatures. It is the faltering Creators who make the Fren strong, and unless we do something about it, their numbers will increase."

"Maybe we can do something here," said Tina.

"I thought about that too, but the more I thought about it, the less sense it made. We can't just walk up to people on the street and say, 'Hey, are you a Creator?' Even if we can tell by the tug of their minds, the chances of getting close enough are remote. The world is just too big. We were lucky that the two of us found each other, even considering the affinity we felt. Maybe we could train ourselves to tune in from afar, as Mich did on me, but that would still take so long that the battle would be lost before it started. The best thing to do is to work through their minds in Kafka—through the cumulative dreams of mankind. That way we can reach all Creators without having to search for the individuals. Even if we could find every Creator on Earth, we could not convince them to have faith and not let people smash their dreams into Fren."

"What are you saying?" Tina asked, clearly interested.

"I'm saying that we have to attack the Fren directly."

"Isn't that what we have been trying to do?"

"Yes. The only problem is, how can I destroy them? To destroy them you have to disbelieve them. I can't disbelieve someone else's dream. That's up to the other Creator. How can we contact the other Creators, once we're in Kafka, and tell them how to destroy Fren if we don't know ourselves?" No one could answer that question. "Well, it's a problem we'll have to deal with in due course."

"Why don't you all get some sleep?" Lori said. "I'll pull out the couch for Tina and myself, and you and Mich can take my bed."

"Thank you for your help," Mich said as he led Nola to the bedroom. Lori winked. She evidently liked him, and in other circumstances might have done something about it, as she had with some of Nola's prior boyfriends.

Mich showered while Nola changed. He found the shower another novel experience. He just turned a knob and not only did the water pour out, but he could pick how warm he wanted it. His hair was tangled and dirty, but a little squeeze of this liquid soap fixed that. Like the wheeled, speedy vehicles, this was novel magic.

When he was done, it was Nola's turn. She was glad to have a shower. The water seemed almost to wash away her cares. Almost. When she was done, she blow-dried her hair.

She stepped into the closet and found an oversized night shirt with Mickey Mouse on the front, and donned it. When she stepped out, Mich was waiting for her under the blankets. He smiled when he saw her. She wondered what he could see in her. She was about to destroy his world, literally. She wasn't sure if she'd ever discover a way to cure Kafka of its shattered dreams.

She climbed into bed and sat up next to him. He put his arms around her and put his head on her shoulder. She could feel a hank of his black hair fall against her skin. It felt like cool silk. She couldn't resist running her hand through it. He closed his eyes and seemed to drift off. There was no way she was going to let him go. He was, after all, the man of her dreams. Too bad he hadn't yet gotten up the nerve to take proper advantage of opportunity. Maybe she should nudge him a bit under the covers and see what happened.

She lay for a moment in silence and tried to fathom the secret of destroying the Fren. In her dream, Spirit had said that she had to disbelieve them. How could she do that? Should she just walk up to them, one by one, and say, "I don't believe in you," and they would disappear? That was too easy. It couldn't be that simple.

She pictured Kafka in her head, in all its splendor. She pictured the River of Thought and all its changing colors. She pictured the Shattered-Glass Glade and the Centicores. Not wild and terrorizing, but going about their business in the glade, grazing and sprinting about with their babies. She thought of the castle, and being there with Mich and her friends.

She looked down at the shining cross around her neck. The moonlight that poured through the window bathed the star sapphire in its center. The stone seemed to almost catch the light and play with it; then it released the light in a dazzling display of bright, laser-like beams. She was surprised as one shone in her face. This seemed familiar. When had she experienced something similar?

Suddenly, there was a loud *Crack!* and a ball of swirling lightning bolts appeared in front of her, then disappeared.

Mich was started awake. He stared. In a moment, there was a louder *Crack!* and a hole appeared, hanging just over the bed. There was an actual gap in the air. Wind started coming from it, and it brushed their faces with scent.

Nola remembered what it was that was so familiar.

Tina rushed in, holding her billowy robe shut with one hand, clutching her purse with the other. She stopped short, behind the swirling hole. "What's that?"

"It's a bed spell," Nola said, smiling. "I've seen one before."

Mich jumped out of bed, his hair blowing into his face, and noted the splays of light that emanated from Nola's cross.

"Where did you get a bed spell?" he demanded.

"I don't know. I didn't know it was a bed spell. It's different."

"Yes, it is. The light, it's moonlight, not magic light. How'd you do that?"

Nola looked bewildered. "I don't know, but let's go through it before something abolishes it!"

Both Tina and Mich hastily agreed to that. One by one, they jumped into the black hole and were immediately whipped by a magic wind that dropped them gently into . . .

16

VOLANT

Suddenly they were standing on a landscape, Nola in her Mickey Mouse nightshirt, Tina in her billowy robe, and Mich in white undershorts. They would have been embarrassed, but there were more pressing sights to see.

"Where are we?" Tina asked, looking at the blackened ground. "It looks like Kafka, but everything is burned!"

And so it was. Kafka had been decimated. Nola felt as if she was going to collapse; the scene was just as it had been in her dream.

"What happened to——?" Mich asked of no one in particular. He was too abashed by the sight of his ruined home to finish his statement.

It has been too long.

The three of them turned around to see Spirit, accompanied by Heat. They scuffed the ash-covered ground with their hooves.

"Is it too late?" Nola asked sadly.

It is never too late, Spirit thought, but he seemed doubtful.

"What happened?" Mich asked.

Heat stepped forward and nudged Mich lovingly. *The Fren have destroyed most of Kafka. They have been multiplying in your absence and it seems there are half as many Kafkians and twice as many Fren. The Fren are running rampant and destroying things.*

"I was afraid something like this would happen," Nola said.

Spirit focused a green eye on her. Its horizontal pupil contracted and expanded. *Congratulations on your fathoming of the secret. Now our world may be saved.*

"But I don't know it!"

Of course you do! What do you think converted that celestial dreamstone into a bed spell?

She looked down at the cross that dangled on her chest. "Celestial dreamstone? It's just a star sapphire."

No. It is one of the rarest types of dreamstone in Kafka. I have yet to see another like it.

"How did you know about the stone and the bed spell? That happened on Earth."

I watched it in your mind. My mind can touch yours anywhere hope exists.

"Oh," she said, remembering that they shared minds. "But I don't know what I did." Nola could feel that Spirit was disappointed. "I'm sorry, I just have no clue," she said.

Replay the scene in your mind. Perhaps we will be able to find out what you did.

Nola closed her eyes and remembered as Spirit watched, tuning in on her thoughts.

She saw herself getting into bed with Mich and she remembered the feel of his hair, and her wish that the innocent lunk would do something. She held the cross in her hand and closed her eyes, missing Kafka.

What are you doing there? he interrupted.

Nola was startled. She had forgotten that Spirit was in her mind. "I'm looking at my cross," she said.

No, your eyes are closed.

"I was just thinking of Kafka, and wishing—" She broke off as she caught on.

You were here, he finished for her. *You see, you have found the power within yourself.*

"I understand!" she cried and jumped up and grabbed Spirit's neck. "Thank you, Esprit! Thank you! Now I think I can do it!"

I may be wrong, but the cross you wear seems to be a catalyst that amplifies your thoughts. I had not known its nature before, but I assumed there was a magic about it because it appeared before me one day, at my feet.

"So you think the cross had something to do with it?" She paused in thought. "That seems feasible. This cross means a lot to me. But why did you get it? Why not me?"

Your world is too corrupted for magic ever to work there. There is no room for magic in a world of science.

Mich hugged her. "I knew you'd figure it out," he said. "But you said the Fren don't kill people, so that means they can be saved. What about the Welties? I figured they were—Forgotten." He hesitated on the word, dreading the thought of it.

Nola thought about that. The Fren were crushed dreams, but it did not mean that they were Forgotten dreams. "The only reason I can think of for that is that they were also transformed into Fren. Maybe if the Fren remain in that state for too long, they get Forgotten. It could also be that when a Kafkian creature is destroyed, or crushed, it happens in degrees. For example, if you are a child with an imaginary friend and your parents tell you it is not real, that is a light crush, but if you believe wholeheartedly that your dream will be real, only to find it isn't, that could be a big crush. Maybe the big crushes are Forgotten faster."

"So, you think that they were Fren when they disappeared? But why, then, would Greyden send us the note?"

"The note?" she asked blankly.

"The note Greyden, the Weltie woman, sent to the mermaid for us," he reminded her. "Saying that they were all being Forgotten, including her."

That stumped her. "I don't know. Maybe she was the last to be converted."

That sounds plausible, Heat thought. *But if that is the case, then the Fren would eventually disappear entirely, and that would be no better than having Kafka full of Fren. Earth would surely be destroyed.*

The group looked solemn. Mich tried to help. He knew if his friends lost hope, the battle would be lost. He couldn't let that happen now, not when they were so close to a solution.

"Well, now we can get on with Kafka's salvation. Let's find the dragons—if they still exist."

I don't believe that would be possible tonight, Spirit cut in. *The night is growing short and our moon has ceased to glow. Perhaps tomorrow.*

"Now wait a minute," Nola said, looking thoughtful. "From what we've discussed, it seems to me that there may be a way to save the Fren instead of just having the dragons chomp them to bits—"

"*Save* the Fren!" Tina cried, shocked. "Are you out of your Creative skull? What good would that do?"

Nola stifled her ire at being interrupted. Tina tended to be annoying at times, but she was a good person. Nola tried not to smartmouth her, but couldn't cut it off entirely.

"I will be able to tell you as soon as you stop interrupting me!" she said, biting her lip so as not to yell. "Now, if you will let me continue, I was going to say that we can save what the Fren once were and even, possibly, revert them to their original form with a nonphysical method."

"Oh, you mean like reinforce them and make them 'uncrushed,' so to speak. Like, with your mind, right?"

"Yes!" Nola agreed. She was relieved that someone finally had it straight.

"Oh, that's easy, then!"

Nola shook her head. "We'll see."

"Say, I'm hungry. Snort!" Mich called, looking around. The little basilisk came slithering into view from the nearby brush. "Let's go see if we can get some food while the girls set up camp. In the morning, we'll go in search of the Fren and put Nola's theory to the test."

"Wait!" Tina said. "Why not test it now? Maybe you should give it a try. Nola, you turned that stone into a bed spell; why not see if you can think up some Chinese take-out for us?"

"I can give it a try," Nola said. She wasn't very hopeful, but she was anxious to test her newfound power. She had learned the hard way not to take too much on faith, and not to count unhatched chickens. The sooner she tested herself, the sooner she would know, one way or the other.

She stood amid her friends and closed her eyes. She took her cross in hand and tried to think of Chinese food. She thought of a white paper carton with a red dragon printed on it and the little metal handle on top. She imagined herself opening it and a cloud of steam coming from it along with the smell of pork fried rice.

She was jolted from her concentration by Snort's surprised honk. She opened her eyes and saw a huge Chinese take-out box sitting on Snort's tail. She walked over to it and found it open and steaming hot. It was filled to capacity with pork fried rice. There was enough for all of them.

"Let me try!" Tina said. Tina closed her eyes. In a moment, three cans of soda appeared next to the food. "Wowee!" Tina said when she opened her eyes.

Nola was filled with excitement. Could this be the answer they had been searching for? She wanted to test it again. "We need some place to sleep tonight too!"

This time she thought of a fine, large house with huge windows and many rooms. When she opened her eyes, she was disappointed.

Next to the river was a much smaller house than she was thinking of. It wasn't even a house, really, it was more like a shack with a thatched roof. It had no windows and only two rooms. It looked as if it had been through a hurricane.

Spirit approached it and looked at it with distaste. *Apparently there are limits,* he said. *You must practice. Your power will grow.*

"I hope so," Mich said, inspecting the inside. "This has no magic shower."

Nola laughed. It certainly hadn't taken him long to get used to the comforts of Earth culture! "Put in a magic-number call to Lori," she suggested. "Maybe she can send you a shower."

He shook his head. "No. There's no magic box either."

"I hate being inadequate," Nola said, cheered. "When my power grows, I'll be sure to install a phone system."

"For now I will settle for some clothing," he said.

"Oh. Of course." She conjured him a halfway-decent princely outfit. As an afterthought she conjured herself some clothing to substitute for her nightshirt, including a comfortable halter. Tina made herself a shirt and slacks. After some tinkering, they were all reasonably garbed, and far more comfortable.

The group dived into the carton of rice, stuffing the food in their mouths by the fistful. Snort really seemed to like the new treat. He almost fell into the carton, at one point, in order to reach the fast-disappearing rice. Nola practiced, conjuring up some luberry bushes for the two unisi to graze upon. She knew the bushes wouldn't last through the next day, with no water or soil to sustain them. Everything was delicious and welcome in their growling stomachs.

"At least we don't have to worry about finding food in this burned-out place," Mich commented when they were finished. "Let's go in."

They settled in for the night. Nola and Tina took one room of the shack while Mich took the other. Snort rested in the doorway as "watchdog" and the two unisi rested in a copse of burned trees.

Mich lay there for a while in his room, staring at the ceiling. He felt rejected. Why had Nola chosen to bed with Tina instead of him? He was a man of honor and respect. She knew that he wouldn't try to touch her, or even kiss her. Did she still distrust him so much that she could not even be alone in the same room with him? Maybe he should face the fact that she might never trust him. He had believed that since she had Created him, her dream man, that she would fall instantly in love when they met. He loved her, of that much he was certain. Maybe she would forget about him when this was all over. As much as he hated to think of it, the possibility remained. Anyway, what was the purpose of being a dream when she did not love him the way he loved her? Maybe it would be better to be Forgotten. For the first time, he cried.

In the other room, Nola sat quietly against the wall. Tina, beside her, was resting peacefully, her eyes shut. Nola felt uneasy. She was happy about finding the answer that for so long had eluded her, but she wasn't sure what she would do once Kafka had been restored, if she could restore it.

She stood up and crept to the door. Snort was ever alert and stared at her with bright, yellow eyes. She reached down and gave him a loving pat. "Stay here and look after them. I'll be back." Snort snorted affirmation. She stepped over him gingerly and went out under the night sky. She wandered silently around the shack, looking at the stars blinking behind a mist of clouds.

Night was her favorite time. The air was clear and cool and the silence was comforting. Mich kept entering her mind and she kept refusing to think about him. She did not know why. She let the clear breeze brush her face.

She was startled by a nudge from behind. It was Spirit.

What troubles you?

Nola laid her hand on Spirit's flank. "It's stupid," she mumbled.

I see. You are troubled about Prince Michael.

"Yes." She sighed. There was no pretending with Spirit around. She could feel the tears starting.

There is no need for sadness, my friend, he said.

He raised his head and put his nose to the wind, his velvety nostrils flaring. His mane floated gently in the night breeze. His forelock was swept about his ridged horn as it caught the starlight and sparkled. Nola found it difficult to distinguish him from the night. His hide was so black that only its starlit sheen could be seen, outlining him, and his green eyes glowed like a cat's. His wings were slightly more visible, neatly folded and protruding well beyond his tail.

Nola caught her breath at his beauty. She turned her eyes to the stars once again. "He is all I could want and more," she said, stroking Spirit's neck. "Why am I so afraid of him?"

Maybe it is not him you are afraid of. Maybe it is reality.

"What do you mean?" But on some level, she already knew.

I can feel your heart, Nola. I see there that if you accept him, you will be giving up all you've ever known to be the truth, and you are confused. He breathed heavily the sweet breeze. *There are many truths in this place and time. You needn't be tied to just one.*

Nola wiped a damp eye with her dirty hand and sniffed. "Yes, but I accept you; why can't I accept him?"

I have always been with you and you knew that one day you would meet me, even if it be in death, but you were untrusting about him. The men you've been with let you down. They abused you physically and mentally. I've often felt your pain when one would strike you. I hated them for that. Now, I hate your reality even more. Reality made you not trust men, but you must realize that yours is not the only reality. And not the only truth.

"I suppose that's right," she said, sitting down and putting her arm around his foreleg, "but I'm still having trouble. I want to trust him. He deserves that. But I also want to—to get physical with him, even though I'm afraid that after that he'll turn possessive and violent and ruin everything. And he keeps ignoring me that way. So I just don't know."

You have spent twenty years in one reality. I know it is hard for you to trust a new one in only a few weeks. It will take time. Spirit folded his forelegs, being careful about her arm, and lay down beside her. His size still awed her.

"I'm so glad that you understand," she sobbed. She reached up to hug the massive neck and kissed him on the cheek as he lowered his head. "I love you so. Will you always be here for me?" she asked, even knowing the answer was yes.

Forever, he thought to her.

"Yes!"

Then she turned back to the house. She toyed with the notion of going into Mich's room instead of Tina's. But he was probably already "asleep," and might resent being disturbed. She owed it to him to leave him alone, at least to that extent. So, with mixed, possibly scrambled feelings, she went to the proper room.

In the morning, Nola summoned some bacon and hotcakes and they all ate their fill. Mich accidentally let a burp slip and blushed from embarrassment. Nola giggled. She was glad he liked the food she produced.

He reached into his pocket and pulled out the crescent-shaped object that was the Kahh. "What should I do with this?" he asked.

I believe it should be stored for safe keeping until this war is over, Heat thought.

"But where? No place is safe from the Fren."

"Oh, yes, it is!" Nola said, taking the Kahh. She stuffed it down her halter top between her breasts. This time, Mich was the one to laugh.

Heat's equine lips twitched and he looked as if he was trying not to grin. *That may not be sufficient. We must find a place that will be unknown, yet well guarded.*

"Where can we find a place like that?" Nola asked.

Perhaps Castle Edward would suffice, Heat thought helpfully. *The Kahh would be well hidden in the catacombs.*

Mich was uncertain. "But who would guard it? The castle is probably deserted."

Snort slithered up and jetted a small flame. He aimed his snout at a bush and jetted a larger flame that engulfed it and left it a pile of ash. It was obvious that Snort wanted to guard it.

"Do you really think you can do it?" Mich asked. "What if the Fren come?"

Heat broke in. *All he has to do is snap up the Kahh and lose them in the catacombs.*

"That is true," Mich agreed. "No one has ever been able to find his way out of the catacombs, unless he was a resident of the castle. That's because it requires the use of secret doors."

"Good," Nola said. "Now that that's settled, I'm still not sure that we can do this. I can summon food and shelter by using my imagination, but transforming evil back into good is another story."

Tina had a thought. "Mich, Heat, Esprit, do you know of anyone who might be able to help us out?"

Mich shook his head. "Madrid might have been able to help us, but she's gone. What about you, pal?" he asked Heat.

There may be one. However—

"Who?" they asked together.

Spirit caught on. *The Volant, the goddess of the sky. But her price for information is steep. You do not want her help.*

"Who is the Volant? And how could she demand payment? This is a worldwide emergency!"

Figuratively, she is our mother. She is the one who released us from rainbow service when she discovered that our colors were not true. She governs the sky, the air, the sun and the moons, Spirit thought. *She is the goddess in charge of the other minor Volants and she governs the skies of many worlds. She has always demanded a price.*

"What kind of price would she ask? I can give her anything she wants," Nola said as she conjured a credit card. But she winced internally as she thought of the charges she had piled up on Earth; the trolls there would be after her for sure, when the time for settlement came. At least they wouldn't be as bad as the thug Charlie. She hoped she wasn't incurring some similar magical debt in Kafka.

There is a story that long ago, a wyvern captured a child. The child's mother went to the Volant to ask how she might save her child from being eaten. The Volant told her to drive the wyvern from its nest with a smoke fern. When the woman had saved her child the Volant demanded payment, but the woman had nothing to give. The Volant took her child.

"Ouch," Tina mumbled. "That's a steep price, all right."

"That's okay, maybe she will deal with me," Nola said.

We must test your ability first; you are strong, but if you fail, Tina will do no better. Then we will have to seek the Volant.

Tina stifled her ire at that comment, but knew it was true. "Well, then, let's get goin' and find the Fren before we lose what's left of Kafka."

They turned to go, and found themselves face-to-face with a group of expressionless Fren. The group contained about five creatures; each one looked uglier than the next.

"Well," Tina said with a sour face. "That didn't take much time."

Spirit's quick mind spoke silently to Nola. It was time for the test. She nodded her head. She closed her eyes and tried to think of something that the Fren could not escape. She thrust her hands forward as if throwing something.

Her friends watched as a metal mesh net appeared just above the Fren, and settled over them, clamping down with barbed spikes into the blackened ground. The Fren spit and hissed at one another as they were drawn close to the ground. They tried to saw through the net with their metallic lightning jags, but Nola had imagined a magic net that could not be cut with anything, no matter how sharp.

She had worried that it wouldn't work, thinking that she had to do something special to create something magical. Instead, she simply believed in what she was doing. She had faith in herself and her abilities. She was happy it worked.

"Now what?" she asked.

Go on with the experiment, he thought.

Nola remained nervous about this. The Fren frightened her. What if she just made them angrier than they were? As it was, they were so angry that they were eliminating on one another and chewing viciously at the net, and each other, while uttering strange sounds.

"Oh, crap! I'll do it first!" Tina said. She closed her eyes.

"Wait!" Mich said. "What if you change one back and the others attack and kill it?"

"That's right!" Tina said. "We'll have to let one out."

"I've got an idea," Nola said. A single Fren was released. She closed her eyes and made another throwing motion, and it was netted. "Now try."

Tina concentrated on it. She tried to imagine what kind of creature it must be. She concentrated harder and she began to see an outline. It was some kind of dragon, but she could not make out the details. She opened one eye. The Fren stood there, unchanged.

"Looks like I goofed. I thought it might've been a dragon or something."

Nola gathered her strength. "Let me try."

She looked hard at the Fren, then shut her eyes. The image of a large reptile was firm in her mind. "It looks like a dragon, but I don't think it is. It's too fat."

She tuned in and intensified what she could see. The fuzziness went away and she saw the rear of a huge dragon. She imagined it turning to face her. She was shocked. It had three golden horns on its head and small dark eyes. For a moment, she locked mind's eyes with—a triceratops, with red spots.

The image wavered. There was a flash behind her lids and it was gone. "Damn! I lost it!" she said as she opened her eyes.

There, before her, stood the dinosaur, horribly cramped. It was covered by the net. The Fren had been transformed!

Nola waved her hand and the net was gone. The dinosaur trotted over to her and nodded its armored head in a gesture of thanks. Nola nodded back and it galloped away into the burned wilderness.

"You did it!" Tina said. "But why couldn't I?"

Nola was getting a notion. "Try it again."

She brought a second Fren forward and netted it. Tina closed her eyes. This time she saw an image right away, but could still not make it out.

"It's a bird," she said, squinting her eyes. "It looks familiar."

She concentrated harder. She saw a color, red. The color of the bird grew brighter and brighter, until it was almost blinding. "I've got it! It's a phoenix," she said and opened her eyes.

It was indeed a phoenix. The net was gone; the bird had fried it to ashes with its magic fire. The phoenix squawked, spread its flaming wings and leaped into the air.

Tina and Nola hugged each other with girlish excitement. This was a good start, but there was much, much more to do.

Nola pulled back, smiling. "We'd better finish these off," she said.

Tina tried again with a third Fren. This time, she couldn't make it out. Nola tried. She put forth a great effort but came up blank.

Try the other two, Heat suggested.

The last two were equally difficult. The images remained blurry and they were unable to tell even what species the creatures were.

"Try to make 'em disappear," Tina suggested helpfully. "I tried and I can't do it."

Nola tried, to no avail.

I fear that you may not be able to do that. To disappear, they must be forgotten, and only their human Dreamers can do that, Spirit thought.

"Say, that's right. Maybe only their Creators can change them back."

The more she thought of it, the more sense it made. In fact, she remembered dreaming as a child of a dinosaur just like the one she had changed back. She had long since suppressed it because her mother said she was foolish.

"Tina, did you recognize that bird?" she asked.

"You know, it's funny, it looked really familiar, but I can't remember where I saw it."

"Well, what do we do now?" Nola asked the group.

"I don't think we have a choice," Mich said. "How do we call the Volant?" he asked, turning to Spirit.

You must recite an incantation, Esprit thought. *I shall put it in your mind. Speak it to the sky.*

"Why me?" Mich asked, surprised. So far, he had been kept pretty much out of things. He hoped he could do something valiant to impress Nola.

You are the king of Kafka now. She will be more apt to listen to the one who can legally represent this world. She would simply be annoyed if one of us were to call her.

Mich had almost forgotten about his royal blood. It was true. With his father gone, it was his responsibility to be king now. The realization was almost overwhelming, when he thought about it, yet he knew he must do all he could to save Kafka. Even if he died trying.

"I'm ready," he said, straightening his shirt. He felt for his sword. He forgot that he had left it and his clothes on Earth. Their return had been so abrupt that he just hadn't thought to gather his things. He didn't want to ask Nola to make him a new sword, so he would get along without it for now. It hadn't served him terrifically well anyway.

Suddenly, his mind was filled with words. He looked to the sky and repeated the spell. "Lady of the sky, Lady of the air, hear me now, listen to my prayer. You are needed here, on the ground. Only in you can help be found."

He dropped his head. "Kind of corny, isn't it?" he asked of no one in particular.

Almost instantly, there was a slight stirring in the air that grew stronger and stronger. Ashes from the burned-out ground were swirling into dust devils. The wind swept their hair and caused their eyes to tear as it picked up horrendous speed.

It soon turned from a gale into a hurricane. The two unisi kept their wings tightly clamped to their bodies, lest the wind catch their wings and hurl them, uncontrollably, into the air.

"Look at that!" Nola cried over the roaring wind.

The others looked and saw a shape in the distance. It was a white tornado. It was as high as the highest peak of the Mangors and as fast as the wind around them. It wiggled in the air like a serpent on a string.

Nola looked harder and was surprised to see that the tornado had no cloud feeding it. The sky above it was clear and blue. The tornado itself was very pale, almost like snow or steam. In a moment it was upon them.

Just when they thought they would all be blown away, the tornado exploded. They found themselves lost in a thick fog that settled around them, blocking all vision.

"Where are you?" Mich called.

"I'm over here!" Nola called back. She held out her hands so that she wouldn't bang into anything.

"Where?" he cried as he felt through the fog.

The fog started to open up and he saw her and his friends. The fog continued to open until there was a hole in the middle where the group stood. The fog completely surrounded them, even above. It was like being in a giant igloo. The light from the sun filtered faintly in so that there was barely enough illumination to see.

"Who calls me?" inquired a sultry voice.

Mich nerved himself and responded, "King Michael Edward!"

"You mean the prince who dwells in the Forest of Imagination? The human prince? Are you now a king?"

"Yes. Until I find out what happened to my father."

"What do you want of me?"

"Kafka is in peril. The king is unable to act, so I must speak for him. As king, I must save Kafka at any cost."

"Then, for you, I will show myself."

The fog above them swirled around somewhat as a pair of dainty feet showed. The woman moved slowly down through the fog, revealing herself from the base up, as if descending through an invisible hole in a cloud. Her legs were slender, long and firm, yet very dark skinned. As she descended, Mich noticed something strange. She had a pair of huge silvery wings.

The Volant was a winged woman with dark brown skin, flowing black hair and brown eyes. She was wearing a tight white gown that flared widely at the knees, so that when a breeze whipped it up, it exposed her shapely calves. She was slender, stately and beautiful. Nola was just a little jealous. Well, maybe a lot jealous.

On her left shoulder was a huge hummingbird. It seemed to be three feet long from beak to tail tip. Mich wondered what flower that bird would pollinate.

On her right shoulder were two tiny hummingbirds. They seemed to be of all colors, but mostly red and green, and their feathers sparkled like morning dew.

As her feet touched gently on the black ash, she folded her wings behind her back and looked at the group. She noted Snort and reached out a lovely brown hand to pat his hot head. Then her expression shifted from wan smile to scowl as she saw the two unisi. "How dare you give that incantation to a human! I thought I expelled you two."

Spirit and Heat both bent a foreleg and arched their necks in a half-bow.

We know that we are not welcome in your presence, Mistress Volant, Spirit thought. *But we have done nothing to harm you or the sky. We are sorry that we could not be a part of your rainbow, but we cannot help the colors we were born with. You of all people should be sympathetic. Please, do not let our presence here affect my friend's situation. We have great need of your assistance.*

"You are a noble animal to speak to me thusly," she said, impressed. "I have never harbored resentment toward you. It is my job to design the rainbow with colors chosen by God, and your colors were not selected. I know how you must feel. There are some who say a Volant should not be so—well tanned," she concluded, casting a glance at her arm. "I will listen to your friends."

Thank you.

She turned to face Mich. "You called me. Now, what is it you wish?"

"I wish information," he said a little nervously.

"I am the goddess of the sky, not a muse of information!"

"Yes," he said, clearing his dry throat. "I was told you would give help, for those willing to pay."

She approached him and looked him in the eye with an icy stare. It was all Mich could do to keep from backing away and making a break for it. Her face was chiseled and serious. Then she seemed to become thoughtful. Finally, she retreated again.

"Yes, this is true," she said, her gown sweeping out as she turned to face them. "I sometimes take payment, if the cause is worthy. Is your cause worthy?" The Volant gave him such a hard look that Mich almost choked. He looked away and tried to cough.

Nola stepped up and took his hand. "This will work," she whispered reassuringly.

He started to explain about the Fren.

The Volant held up a hand to silence him. "I know of this. I don't care."

How could she say she didn't care? The life of his friends as well as his own were at stake here, not to mention planet Earth. How could she be so callous? "But if you don't help us, you'll die too!"

The Volant laughed sweetly. "Young man, this is not so! I am not of Kafka. I am of the skies of the universe, a goddess! What is one world lost? That's just less work for me to do."

Nola couldn't stand it anymore. "Look, if you don't help us, I'll— " But she couldn't kill the woman, because goddesses were eternal. "I'll capture you!" she said, thinking of throwing a net. She felt silly after saying it.

The Volant seemed unconcerned. "And who are you?"

"I am Nola Rollins of Earth."

"Ah, a Creator. I'm afraid that capturing me would not be possible, but you could complicate things for me and possibly delay me. I am on a to-the-second schedule, you know. Let me consider."

The woman walked through the fog wall. No one tried to follow.

There was no telling what would happen if they did. They might lose each other in the fog. So they waited, and waited and waited.

Half an hour later, she returned. "I have decided to help. What have you to pay me with?"

Mich spread his hands. "I have nothing but the crown."

"What would I want with kingship?" She nodded to the two small hummingbirds perched on her shoulder. The birds immediately flew toward the group.

One landed on Tina's purse and removed the pistol. Tina was amazed that the bird could lift the gun, which was twice its size. It carried the gun to the woman and hovered before her, turning this way and that, showing her the gun. The woman shook her head, her thick hair tumbling slowly. The tiny bird took the gun back to Tina's purse, then flew back to its mistress's shoulder.

The other bird flitted among the group looking in pockets and in socks. It flew to Nola and hovered for a moment. Then it made a bee-line for her halter top. It perched on the fabric and stuck its long bill inside.

Mich glanced over and saw the bird on Nola's chest. It looked as if it were sucking nectar from her bosom. Nola had a surprised look on her face and was reaching up to shoo it away. Her hair was tangled and wild and her blue eyes were wide with amazement. The bird pulled free before her hand reached it, and it flew back to the woman with the Kahh in its bill.

Nola reached after it but missed. What would happen now? She knew the woman would surely take the Kahh as payment! But what good would it do to pay her when she would just use the Kahh to destroy Kafka anyway?

"Excuse me, Volant, but we cannot pay with that," Mich said.

The woman looked up from the Kahh in her hand. For a fleeting moment, the woman had an expression of mischief on her face, but it was replaced with a sweet smile.

"My name is Ventus, Prince; call me Ventus." She gestured to him. "Come, sit. I think we can deal. You too," she said, pointing to the others.

Nola sat down next to the woman. Ventus Volant; that was a nice name. "You have a pretty name, Ventus. That's Latin for 'wind,' isn't it?"

"You compliment me." She blushed, which was hard to do, considering her dark skin. "Thank you. Yes, it is."

"And Volant, that has something to do with flight."

"You're a smart girl. Perhaps my information will, after all, be useful to you. I will tell you all you need to know."

"But the Kahh—" Mich began.

Snort jetted flame into the air. Guarding the Kahh was his job!

Peace, friend, Heat thought. *She will not use the Kahh on an evil creature. We have no fear from that, and she will keep it safe. We will have two problems solved.*

"Let's see, how do I begin," Ventus said. "Have you discovered the way to convert the Fren into the creatures they once were?"

"I think so," Nola said. "Tina is a Creator too, and we tested ourselves. We started with five Fren and were able to turn two of them back, but not the other three. Why?"

"You see, you cannot fight the Fren alone. You must have the help of the other Creators. There are a few more on your planet, perhaps ten or so. You must help them come. They may know what is happening, but they cannot stop it. They are all like you, Tina and Nola: they've lost faith. Their dreams have been destroyed but most of them have not yet Forgotten their dreams, and there is still hope."

"But how do I get them here?" she asked.

"You can bring them, my dear; you are the gifted one. You are the one who can imagine magic, the only Creator who can do anything with magic Creations, and with that talisman you wear."

Nola fingered the cross around her neck. "You mean, all other

Creators can Create new dreams and re-Create old ones, but I'm the only one who can Create magic dreams, like spells and stuff?"

"Yes, and magic is needed to destroy the dam. You can Create magic dreams that work on other worlds as well. You can bring the Dreamers here."

"You mean with a bed spell?"

"Yes, or something like that. You can give them all one, and those who wish to come, will."

"But what do I do once they get here?"

"You must simply join hands and cast your minds across Kafka. Once the damn is destroyed, the Fren cannot reproduce. Every Fren must be contained until the dam is destroyed; otherwise, they will kill you. You, being human, can be killed. Only you have the ability to destroy that dam. All will be restored if you make haste."

"How do I find the others? There are billions of people on Earth."

"With magic. Use your imagination."

"You say there are only a few Creators left on Earth. Why is that?"

"You silly girl," the Volant laughed, "do you not know the nature of the very world in which you were born? Nearly all on Earth are simply passive dreamers. They see the things and creatures of Kafka, yet do not take them for more than a mere dream. They do not believe. So you see, only the ones who truly believe are keeping this world alive. If much more time passes, there will be only you two to keep this world from dying, making you an easy target for the Fren. They will never let you leave now. They will be watching."

Nola felt her heart go cold. "Thank you, Ventus," she said tightly. "One more thing, though. Is King Edward still alive?"

"He has not been Forgotten, yet. Now, you must act quickly, but you must prepare. Go to the castle and arm yourselves. You will not be able to capture all of them in nets. The ones that slip through will try to destroy you. When all the Fren are captured, you will face Reility. Beware of him; he is strong." The Volant smiled, somewhat distantly. "Good-bye, mortals, and I wish you luck."

Mich felt a great relief to know that his father was still alive. He also realized that Nola must care greatly for him. He would not have thought to ask the Volant about his father. He cast a glance and a smile at Nola, who returned it in a deeper fashion.

As they sat there, the woman opened her wings and lifted into the sky, carrying the fog behind her. The sun shone down once again, although it was now lower in the sky.

17

LOVE

Spirit and Heat stepped forward to nuzzle Nola. Tina gave her a hug, Snort rubbed his body on her legs like a cat and Mich kissed her uncertainly. They were all, it seemed, proud of her. She just hoped that their faith was well placed, knowing that it was not over yet. They wanted her to know that they would stand by her, no matter what came to pass.

"What is the best route to the castle?" she asked.

"The safest way to get there would be for you to conjure us there. Why don't you try it?" Mich asked, smiling.

"Hmmm." She considered, realizing that the notion had merit. "Now, there's an idea."

She thought about conjuring. If she could Create a magic spell, would it matter how she went about it? "Maybe we should mount up and join hands," she suggested.

They tried it. Snort sat in Mich's lap. The two unisi had to squeeze together because their barrels were so large that Mich and Nola had to lean over to reach each other.

Nola asked Mich to describe the castle to her so that she could picture it in her mind. She knew what the castle looked like, of course, having Created it, but she found it easier to picture when he spoke to her. Once she had it fixed, she began to concentrate. She pictured the dreamstone castle with its tall battlements, ramparts and parapets with high flying pennants, its tall outer wall an imposing barrier to its enemies, in its own section of the Forest of Imagination. This part of the forest seemed untouched. The trees rose majestically, opening their arms to the sun.

When she opened her eyes, they were there. Castle Edward stood before them as huge as ever. Every brick gleamed as if it had just been polished yesterday.

The drawbridge was down. Mich called out, but of course no one responded.

"It looks empty," Tina said. "Let's go in."

Mich took a step onto the drawbridge—and fell through it, into the moat. He coughed and gasped with surprise as he scrambled onto the bank and stood there dripping.

"What the hell happened?" Tina asked as she felt the drawbridge with a hand. "There ain't nuthin' there! It's fake!"

Mich looked at it. The drawbridge was opaque and he could even see the splinters of wood that had flaked off from use. It looked perfectly real, until he reached down and his hand passed through. "She's right. It's illusion."

"But how can it be?" Nola asked, stunned. "I conjured us to the real castle, not a pretend one. This is another kind of magic."

Mich thought for a moment. "You must be Forgetting it."

"I haven't forgotten it!" Nola said indignantly. "Why would I try to conjure us to a place I didn't remember?"

"Forgetting isn't a matter of awareness," Mich explained. "It's a magical state. On some level you are losing your power over the castle. Maybe because of the distraction of this adventure."

"We'd better get inside, then, before it disappears," Tina said.

"It's too late. Look," Nola said, pointing to a high parapet. The parapet had disappeared and adjacent ones were blinking out as if they had never existed. Then the keep went, and the outer wall.

"But that's dreamstone! That's your castle," Mich said, reconsidering. "You created that, Nola; how can that happen?"

Nola looked stricken. Her face twisted as if she were about to throw a fit. "I'm sorry," she said. "I can't explain it. I don't know what to do."

"Better figure it out pretty quick," Tina advised her grimly. "This looks to be getting worse."

"An ongoing process," Mich agreed.

Nola had had her doubts through this whole adventure and suddenly they were coming back to haunt her. The only reality she had ever known was her little apartment, John and her cat back home. She wasn't sure if she remembered how she got here. She wasn't even sure if she was dreaming. She had thought she wasn't, but now she was uncertain. Oh, why did she have to break down now?

She started sobbing. "It's me," she said. "I want to believe . . . " She trailed off, too upset to continue. She sat down and put her face in her hands.

Tina bent down and shook her sternly. "Nola, you can't do this! Not now, not when we are so close! Snap out of it!"

Nola just sat and sobbed. She knew it was silly of her to do this, yet she also knew that she was dreaming. No matter what happened here, she knew it wasn't real. Something nagged at her mind and her head started to ache. Nola threw Tina's arm away and stood up.

"Look," she sobbed. "I can't help you! I'm just a suicidal girl from a stinking city. I'm not a Creator, I'm just a silly, self-destructive girl with nothing better to do than live in a dream world. I've gotta get out of here." The reality of the words she spoke cut her deeply.

With that, she took off running. Spirit tried to gallop after her, but disbelieving as she was, she spelled him so that he could not follow.

She ran into the trees and let the forest surround her. There was no sound except for the crunching leaves and her breath as she ran. The farther out she went, the less trapped she felt. After a while, when she felt she was safely away, she sat on a rock for a rest, panting heavily.

"What is wrong with me?" she mumbled. "I shouldn't be acting this way." She took a hank of her hair and pulled on it in frustration. She wiped the tears from her eyes, but then replaced them. She knew this place wasn't real. She should just let it fall from her mind and keep her feet on the ground, just as her parents and teachers always told her. What a fool she was being! She felt as if she was no longer thinking rationally, but she had no control over it.

She covered her face and cried, silently. After a moment, she heard the sound of footsteps coming through the forest. She peered through the trees but couldn't see anything. Though she was confused and tired, she got up and lumbered, once more, into a run.

The footsteps did not fade. Instead they grew louder and closer. Whatever it was, was following her and was intent on catching her. She was just as intent on losing it. She dodged around trees and hopped over low roots. She spied a rocky cliff ahead and went for it, hoping that there would be someplace to hide over the edge.

Her head pounding, she shifted into high gear and ran as fast as she could. Suddenly, her foot snagged on a tree stump and she came crashing down. She tried to stand, but the wind had been knocked out of her. She listened and heard the footsteps coming closer. She felt a hand on her shoulder. It turned her over.

"Are you okay? Why are you acting this way?" Mich asked, with tears on his face. "Kafka needs you. I need you. I don't want you to Forget me. I love you."

At that second, Nola felt a sharp pinch on her head. She closed her eyes and bashed it with her hand. She looked at her hand and saw a flea. In her mind's eye, she glimpsed a red, barbed tail. Then she knew the flea was a demon. It had hidden in her hair to get close enough to take her mind.

She sat up, her eyes wide. "Get out!" she screamed.

The tiny red flea sprang from her hand. It grew larger and larger and assumed the form of a demon, clasping his head as if suffering from a migraine headache.

Nola herself was unsteady only a moment. She slapped her hand to her head, uttered a strained "Ouch!" and turned on the demon.

Mich watched as Nola's eyes lit up like flames. She looked so angry that he was afraid she might shoot fire out of her mouth. She ripped her cross from her neck and held it in her hand. "Sword!" she said, forcing her concentration.

The cross formed the hilt of a lightweight broadsword. She immediately beheaded the squirming demon and butchered his face. She slashed it over and over again. "Die! Die!" she screamed.

Mich finally pulled her away. She dropped the sword and fell into his embrace.

"I'm glad you're on my side!" he laughed.

"I'm sorry," she sobbed. "I should have known better; I'm so sorry." He squeezed her tightly and she looked up at him. "Did you mean what you said? I know you told me before, but did you mean it? Do you love me?"

He laughed, somewhat bitterly. "Of course I love you! How could I not? You're the most beautiful person I've ever known."

"Then why did you never try to touch me, when you had all those chances?" she demanded before she thought.

"You're my Creator! I wouldn't presume—if you had been an ordinary woman—oh, the times I've wished you were! But I have to treat you with utmost respect, so you won't be annoyed. I wouldn't even dare suggest—" He broke off, flushing.

Nola was overwhelmed. This time she did not balk. "Annoy me," she murmured. Then she gave him the sweetest kiss she could manage, holding him all the while. She touched his face, which was rough with stubble, but it was the most handsome face she'd ever seen and she never wanted to touch anyone else's.

Mich shivered in her arms. Their kiss held such force that his head was spinning. He had wished so long for a kiss like this, and until now thought he'd never know what it was like. He had been with girls before, but he had never loved them. It was different, he discovered, to kiss the one he loved. The emotion that was lacking before, he found with Nola, and it was fantastic.

After a short eternity, they broke. "I—I love you too," she whispered. "My God! I never thought I'd say that again to anyone."

Mich's heart leapt. They held each other awhile longer, unable to speak. Then Nola recovered her cross, which had reverted to its natural state. They made their way quickly back to the castle, which was now a huge clearing in the forest.

Mich stared at the empty spot with his jaw dropped open. "We're too late."

"Oh, no, we aren't," Nola said. This time, she felt daring and did not bother to close her eyes.

"Castle!" she yelled, holding the cross out, clenched in her fist.

The castle started to reappear, beginning with the outer wall, then the battlement. Bricks began popping into place. Nola could glimpse furnishings appearing, then disappearing as the new walls covered the rooms. The castle was soon complete, ending with a waving red and gold pennant.

Nola took a deep breath. "I did it! Last time I tried to make a house, I could only make a shack. I guess I just needed the strength of faith. I have that now," she said, looking into Mich's sea-green eyes. "Maybe having an existing pattern, that of the former castle, helped too. Certainly I don't really know how to build a castle, I mean with the foundations and support structures and all. Maybe re-Creation is easier than Creation. Anyway, it worked."

Tina came over to her and patted her shoulder. "That's great, girlie, but what happened to ya? You have a breakdown or somethin'?"

"It was another demon," Mich informed her. Mich had been surprised by that; he had assumed that they had all been turned into Fren.

"I have a confession to make," Tina said soberly. "The demons—they're mine."

All eyes turned to her. "What?" Nola and Mich asked together.

Both Heat and Spirit crowded in to make certain they were hearing right, and Snort snorted at her. Could this be possible?

"The demons are mine. I invented them. They come around whenever I'm scared. They always hurt me and make me do things I would never do. But I noticed that they don't bother me here cuz I think they are scared of me, but I'm more scared of them. Maybe they know I care about you all and they hurt you to get at me."

"If that is true, can't you just get rid of them? I mean, Forget them or something?" Mich asked.

"Uh-uh, I don't think that'd be a good idea. The demons are supposed to prey on people who got warped minds. Everybody dreams and sometimes someone creates an ax murderer. Their weak minds are easy to control."

"But won't that just make them more evil?"

"The demons make a creature the opposite of what they are. Like, if you have faith," she glanced at Nola, "then you have no faith when the demon takes over. So if a demon controls the mind of a murderer, then that person will probably value life above all else."

"I hate to admit it, but I guess we really do need the demons," Mich said, looking as if he'd just tasted dragon dung.

The group went into the castle.

Nola and Tina were in awe. Neither had ever been in a castle before. There was the warm smell of burned wood and dust. Their footsteps echoed as they walked beneath the arched ceilings. Huge tapestries hung on the walls. One was a picture of a maiden sitting on the ground. In her lap was a unisus that had been speared. All around her were dogs and hunters on horseback. Nola was impressed and Tina dawdled, trying to look at everything. Snort skidded on the polished floors, his long claws making clicking noises as they struck.

"This had to be re-Creation," Nola murmured. "I didn't actually know about any of this. Maybe the whole castle was there, just too thin to be seen, and I just restored substance to the outline. Like pouring cement into a mold."

Mich didn't give them enough time to take it all in. He led them through a door. Behind the door was a dark staircase that descended into a room filled with all sorts of weapons, from cat-o'-nine-tails to catapults. There was armor for horses and men; shields and garments of mail.

"There's so much here!" Tina said as she donned a mail hood.

Mich suggested that they all spend the night in the castle, and in the morning, they would choose their armor.

"That sounds okay to me! I want that whip over there, and—"

"No weapons," he interrupted. "It wouldn't have any effect on them."

"It sure would affect 'em if I whip them in the crotch!"

Mich shook his head. "It won't affect them. They heal instantly. Weapons would just encumber us."

"Oh, yeah. Well, where's my room? I'm beat."

"Go upstairs; you can pick any room you want. After all, there's no one here to complain."

The friends dispersed and went upstairs to their selected rooms. Snort found his old basket in the foyer and curled up. Mich and Nola went to Mich's old room. It was huge and ornate.

"You lived here in this created castle all your life?" she asked, running her hand down a gold-framed mirror.

"Yes. Nice, isn't it?"

"It's a little extravagant, don't you think? I mean, isn't it boring here?" Nola had created a room she had thought worthy of a prince, but now realized how worthless it could be without love.

"I never thought of this place as boring, but I guess compared to my time with you, I've been barely living. I used to think all this stuff and all of the attention from maids and such was the best life I could have. But, when that demon got you, I was afraid you'd Forget me and it really woke me up. You are more important to me than any of these things." Mich held her close. "It's as if I had this emptiness inside that I never knew was there, until you came; then it wasn't empty anymore."

Nola felt so much love in his tender arms that she knew she'd never want to leave him. Their love was a sweet one that neither time nor distance could tarnish. But she suspected she would have to leave him. When all this was over, if she still lived, she would have to return home, and he could not accompany her. That hurt her beyond words.

Nola looked at him and tried to say what her heart was feeling, but she couldn't find the words. There was nothing she could think to say that could describe her feelings of joy and sadness.

Mich gently held her face and brushed her lips with his own. They kissed more deeply and fell on the bed together. They spent the entire evening holding each other closely. They both knew that if they stuck together, things would work out fine.

The two of them rested quietly most of the night. Though they were not fully asleep, their senses were numbed somewhat, due to the lack of motion and good circulation. They were tired. And the matter of sex had no importance; that wasn't what had drawn them to each other. So Nola's main fear had disappeared the moment her love was realized.

Yet despite this, it wasn't perfect. Normally a long night of rest did Nola a world of good. But for some reason, tonight was different. She lay still with her eyes closed, trying to think of all the things that could happen to mess up her efforts. With the realization of her power had come also the realization of her responsibility, and that was an awesome burden to adjust to.

Just before dawn, the next morning, Nola felt a sharp little prick on the side of her throat. Her hand shot up and smacked it, thinking that it was probably a bug.

She brought her hand before her eyes. As the bleariness cleared, she saw red blood on her fingers. As her sight cleared further, she saw what stood at the foot of the bed. It was Reility.

He stood there staring, black eyes glinting evilly. In one hand was a razor jag, and the other grasped a strap of leather that had been cut. Her cross dangled and turned at its end. Its pallid dreamstone sparkled as it caught the early morning light.

Nola's voice was caught in her throat. She couldn't move or even breathe as she stared back at him. She wished Mich would wake up, but he rested silently beside her, not stirring. There was probably a spell keeping him unaware.

She watched the evil creature as he moved to her side of the bed. He leaned his hideous face next to hers until his gross lips were moving against her ear. He spoke in such a low whisper that she could barely hear his words.

"Fool! Did you really think you'd win? This world will die. Your world will die. Your friends will die. You will die."

Not saying another word, he turned and disappeared. The Fren traveled so quickly that they were simply a blur, then nothing.

She sat in the growing light, unable to grasp the severity of the situation. Soon, her lungs could take no more and her breath pushed past her lips in a rush.

At that moment, Spirit's demanding whinny sounded shrill in her ears as it floated through the open window from below. Spirit had felt her sudden anguish as if it were his own.

Mich bolted upright, looking wildly around. He saw Nola's throat and the scratch that still oozed blood. Then he saw her face and eyes. What he read there sent chills up his spine. "Nola?" He touched her shoulder.

She turned and looked at him, tears filling her eyes. "I—I—I lost it. Oh, my God, I *lost it!*" she cried, throwing her arms around him.

"What's going on?" Tina asked, stepping through the door. "I heard those damn horses screaming like they'd gone crazy!"

Mich glanced at her through Nola's hair. "Something happened to Nola. Something awful."

Nola's mind whirled as she tried to explain, through her sobs, what had occurred. She had tried so hard, and now they were all going to die. It was all her fault. She should have known better than to display her cross to everyone. It should have been as well guarded as the Kahh.

"So he took your cross, huh?" Tina asked. "That bites! Whad're we gonna do now?" She threw her hands in the air and sat on the edge of the bed.

"I'm sorry, guys, but I figured we'd be safe here," Nola sniffed.

Tina patted her arm. "It's okay, girlie. This is as new to you as it is to me. We just dunno what to expect."

Mich nodded his agreement. He released Nola and dried her tears. "You know, we are not going to be safe anywhere we go. Reility obviously knows what our plans are and he will do anything he can to stop us. I feel lucky that he didn't try to kill you."

"Why should he?" Nola asked. "He has my cross. I'm no threat to him now."

"That's not true!" Tina said. "We are a smart group and if we organize ourselves right, I'm sure we can take it back. My grandpa always said, 'Never say never!' and he wuz right!"

"Take it back? Are you crazy? What if he kills us? All hope will be lost."

"Tina's right," Mich said, sitting a bit straighter. "There's got to be a way, somehow. This world is based on faith. If we lose ours . . ."

"I get the point." Nola stood and looked out the window. The sun was almost visible over the treeline. From up here, she could see a great deal of the land around the castle. Most of the forest remained, yet the mountains seemed smaller and blacker. Their once snow-covered peaks loomed blunt and dark.

"I suppose we don't really have a choice, then, do we?" she asked, turning back to face Mich and Tina.

18

CAPTURE

That morning the group circled the grounds in search of forage. Both Nola and Tina were too stressed to conjure any proper food. They spent much time in the armory, while Nola perfected the armor as well as she could. Without the cross to make the armor magically strong, they would be taking chances.

Nola clothed herself in mail armor of steel scales down to her feet. Tina preferred to wear mail over a leather vest and leather trousers. She also wore a solid-steel gorget. Nola thought she looked like a wild warrior woman, with her blond hair all tangled. Mich clad himself in leathers, a mail gorget and a pair of thick leather gauntlets. He preferred the freedom of movement.

Nola could agree with that. The armor was extremely heavy. She knew that she wouldn't be able to run very well in steel pants. She disbelieved her armored trousers. Tina liked hers, so was welcome to them. Nola was sure Tina could handle the mail trousers, so left it at that.

"Now we need a plan," Mich said, leading the way to the drawing room.

They sat throwing ideas at one another and eating luberries. None of their ideas seemed viable.

They finally decided the only way was to search out Reility at the Fren Cliffs. Mich knew that they were left unguarded during the day, but that was because the Fren would surely be busy there, converting hapless creatures into their own kind. He decided that their best bet was to try to sneak in at night.

"But why can't we try it during the day?" Nola asked. "Last time we were there, we passed through unmolested."

"I don't think that the Fren knew your nature then. Besides, there were a lot fewer of them. The Fren must now outnumber the Kafkians by a hundred to one. So I think it's better to tackle them when fewer are alert, though that still won't make it easy. I'm sure the cliffs will be guarded at night, while the Fren rest. What I'm not sure of is how we will get past them."

"Can't you transport us directly there?" Tina asked Nola.

"I can't. That requires magic and I can't do that without the cross."

"Oh, yeah." Tina sighed. "I wish there was some other way, but I guess Mich is right. We should take our chances tonight."

So it was decided. The group would start traveling within the hour. With luck, they would be at the cliffs in three days, providing they didn't run afoul of any Fren on the way.

Nola rode Spirit while Tina rode behind Mich. Snort stayed to guard the deserted castle. He was proud to do his part and would surely make a good guard.

The trip was grueling and painful. After six hours of riding at a quick, trotting pace, Nola's buttocks and thighs ached with every bounce. They slowed to a gentle walk in the late afternoon and finally made camp well into the night.

Their first day behind them, Nola realized that they had made surprising progress. They were in sight of the once prosperous Welton Town. Now there was nothing but an empty blackened field.

Nola lay close to Mich, next to the glowing embers of the fire. The night, as always, smelled sweet, despite the ruined land around them.

She let her mind search out Spirit's. He was dozing, head down, ears lolling, on the opposite side of the camp. He opened his eyes.

Yes, friend?

"I just wanted to apologize for all that's happened."

You have no need to be sorry. You are doing well.

"But I'm *not* doing well! I lost my power through sheer stupidity. What good am I now? I know I should have faith, but it's so hard. The main reason Reility didn't even try to harm me is that he knows I'm impotent now without my cross, so he can just let me squirm. I know we are walking into disaster. I don't think we'll even get as far as the Fren Cliffs before we are found and killed."

I, above all others, know what you are feeling, Nola. But, my dear friend, you must press on if we are to have a single chance. Reility is strong, but I feel once we have released his people from his grip and return them to their original states, he will become weaker. He may, in fact, die. When the good outnumber the evil, the evil is driven off. I believe in our endeavor. We will find your cross and you will summon the other Creators to your side, and together we will turn the tide.

"But without real magic—"

Reility is surely overconfident now, so perhaps careless. We are doing what he least anticipates: attacking him in his stronghold. The element of surprise gives us a better chance.

"Thank you, Esprit. I can always count on you for an encouraging word."

"Of course you can. Remember, we all love you and are here to help. We each have our own reasons for helping; however, we all have Kafka in common. Now get some rest; we will be riding long tomorrow. Heat and I hope to carry you to the worm tunnels by tomorrow night.

Nola was grateful for Spirit's ever-present advice. He seemed always to know best. He was a good friend and there was no way she would let him die. In order to save him, she must save herself. Spirit was right; she had to have faith in her own efforts if she was to have any hope of succeeding. She blew a kiss to him and curled up as well as she could in her leather and armor clothing.

The next morning, Nola found some burned bushes and squatted behind them. Mich gathered oranges from the small tree that Nola believed into existence. She knew it would not live long in the ashy soil, but it served its purpose. Tina was busy disbelieving their camp, making sure that even their footprints were gone. She left no trace of their passing, in case they were being followed.

They ate their oranges in haste and left their camp as empty and desolate as they found it.

They traveled through Welton Town. Technically, it could no longer be called a town. There were no ruined buildings to mark its borders, only a pale, dusty road going through the center of the dark, ash-covered ground.

The sun had been joined in the late afternoon by twin moons, one large full and one smaller gibbous. The group was becoming exhausted.

They came to a halt, knee-deep in the muck. They had been traveling close to the badly shrunken River of Thought in order not to lose sight of it. They dismounted to study the landscape.

Nola's ankle turned slightly in the thick mud, causing her to tumble into it with a splat. She rose, covered in disgusting mud. "Yech!" Tina remarked for her. Her ankle was a bit sore, but was okay.

The water had been absorbed by the ash and all around them was mud, as black as coal. The river still flowed, telling them that all hope was not lost, but compared with its former glory, the river was now a mere trickle. If there were any worms left in the tunnels, they had surely drowned.

"How should we go about setting up camp?" Mich asked.

"Maybe I can make a thick stage of wood and sit it atop pontoons. That way, we stay dry and we won't sink."

I smell— came Heat's desperate thought.

Nola glanced at him. His nostrils were flaring wide and his silver orbs rolled back.

Then the attack came. The entire group was surrounded by Fren. At least seventy of the noxious creatures closed in on them, jags flashing in the twin moonlight. A few of them carried heavy cudgels. They formed a ring around the travelers.

"Wait a schecond!" said one of them as he prevented the ring from closing further. He seemed to be in charge of them and he spoke with a strange accent. "Ischn't that one there the one Reility warned usch about?"

Another Fren stepped forward. "No, these are nothing. Look at her, she is as black as we are, and that other, she could never be so simpleminded as to weight herself down with armor!"

Nola was thankful that she had fallen in the muck, which covered her from head to foot, hiding her face.

"You are right. Reility would not be afraid of shuch nothingsch asch thesche."

They began closing in again. "I think that they should be strong enough for a week's worth of work before we recast them."

"Yesch. And look at those fine creaturesch," he said, advancing on Heat and Spirit.

Four more Fren rushed forward with ropes. Heat spread his wings and tried to lift into the air, but he was too slow. Ropes of seemingly infinite length were lashed across his withers and over his wings, pulling them tight to his body.

This overbalanced him and caused him to fall. He had the bad fortune of falling on one of the Fren. When he stood again, the flattened Fren filled out before their eyes, like a cartoon figure recovering from an encounter with a steamroller. He struck Heat's cheek with his club, cursing at him in some strange language.

Nola figured it would be best for all if they surrendered, as the Fren weren't actually trying to kill them. "We'll have a better chance if they think we're of no account. Maybe we can catch them when they're off guard."

The others agreed. Surely they would be taken to the cliffs, which was where they wanted to go anyway.

But it wasn't comfortable. Heat and Spirit were hobbled and haltered with the ropes. The rest of them had their hands tied tightly, and their feet were hobbled as well to keep them from running away. They were forced to move out with the points of jags in their backs. The two unisi were whipped mercilessly with ropes, even though they were cooperating with their captors.

They were pushed, prodded and poked along over the swampy ground. Many of the Fren seemed to quiet down during the journey, as if speaking was against some unwritten law. There were several "Shhh!"s passed between the creatures. All was quiet by evening, when the head Fren shouted for them to halt.

At this point, it was obvious that they were to make camp. The head Fren shouted orders and the others milled about, searching for fodder. When the scant available firewood and food were gathered, the Fren sat around in a circle, with Nola and her friends inside, close to the fire.

The Fren tore apart live animals before them. Their still-screaming bodies were passed from one to another as each took his share. Evidently some sort of magic prevented the animals from dying immediately, despite dismemberment. Trust the Fren to find a way to make eating fun!

At one point, a still-twitching leg was thrown in Nola's direction. She shoved it away with her foot. Another Fren rushed up and snatched the leg. "Don't waste our food on them! They won't live much longer anyway!"

"Perhaps she'd like the head?" another said as a rodent head was thrown into her lap. Nola shrieked and quickly lifted her leg, causing the severed head to fly into the air and land in the fire. But a

Fren quickly fished it out, relishing its toasted quality. Burned fur seemed to be a delicacy to these creatures.

The Fren gave them each a drink of water, but no other food. They teased the group, often throwing things at them, laughing and taunting them endlessly. One of the Fren went so far as to touch Spirit's hide with a flaming stick.

Spirit bucked, and his linked hind feet hit the Fren dead between the eyes with a sickening crack. The thing flew outside the circle and landed in the river.

Every creature went silent and all eyes turned to the river. The river's murky waters began to shine brightly in the moonlight, yet the water was still as if it had simply swallowed him. Then there was a loud gurgle and a bubble floated to the surface. It did not burst. It kept growing.

Inside the bubble was the Fren. Its mouth worked open and closed and his fists clenched. He had such a pained look that Nola was forced to turn her head away.

As the Fren struggled inside the multicolored bubble, something started to happen to him. His body went from opaque to translucent. He was turning into gray smoke that swirled within the bubble. After a moment the bubble burst, spewing smoke into the night sky. It mingled with the smoke from the fire and was gone.

The Fren immediately went back to their business as if nothing had happened. In fact, one of them grabbed the dead Fren's supper and gleefully gorged himself. Nola wondered why they did not lash out at Spirit.

Spirit's mind came to Nola's. *They are creatures of pure evil. They care no more for their own kind than they do for us. They do not attack me because they feel I am too valuable as a work animal to harm.*

"But the river—what happened?"

The Fren are not Kafkians nor are they humans. They cannot lie in the river. The river works only for humans and their dreams. Spirit closed his eyes, and for a moment Nola felt his sadness. *I wish I hadn't lashed out that way.*

"But he hurt you! I'm glad you did. We should push them all in the river!"

You don't understand, he thought, lowering his huge head to look at her. *We need to keep them alive. These evil creatures have a Kafkian seed deep inside them. They are tortured and they need our help. If we destroy them, there is no hope for Kafka's survival. And no hope for your world.*

Nola bit her lip. He was right. Her purpose was not to destroy them, but to restore them. She had to make sure she kept that in mind. It was just that whenever she met these creatures, they radiated evil and malice. Her reflex action was to hurt or kill them. It was as if they evoked evil that was in her. She had to fight that evil, rather than the creatures who were already its victims.

After the episode, all went quiet again and most of the Fren lay down to rest. Several stood guard over their "guests," facing outward, while four stood guard outside the ring of travelers.

Mich moved closer to Nola in order to whisper to her. Tina also moved in to hear. They did not look at one another, in order to avoid suspicion. The Fren who guarded them stood with their backs turned and were far enough away so that they could not hear their whispers.

"I discussed this with Heat. He seems to think that we should just go along with them. They don't have any idea who we are," Mich whispered.

One of the Fren turned his head and looked at them, grinned and turned back. They seemed more concerned with who might approach them than who might escape them. Perhaps they were expecting an attack from the Nola whom they believed was still out there somewhere.

Tina lowered her voice below a whisper. "You know, I just can't believe how we lucked out!" she said. "If they knew it was us, we'd probably be dead. I have an idea." She paused, then said, "I think we should give ourselves new names to call each other, you know, for safety's sake."

"That's a great idea, Tina," Nola whispered. "I'll be Wilma. That is my mother's name."

"That's good," Tina said. "I'll be Joy. That was my friend's name when I was little."

"Okay," Mich said, "I'll take Richard."

With that taken care of, they all sat quietly through the night, unable to rest. None of them had any idea of what lay ahead for them, or how they would get themselves out of this fix.

After an eternity of dead silence, the morning sun's rays descended upon them. The Fren rose and moved on. Nola and the others got moving with alacrity, so as not to attract any hostile attention. This wasn't entirely successful, but did cut down on the abusive behavior.

The Fren took them along the river and it wasn't long before they arrived at the cliffs. The sheer stone rose above them, seemingly deep into the sky. The cliff face was riddled with tunnel entrances.

They stopped at a point near the center of the cliffs. Nola heard a bellow from somewhere far above.

"HOOO!" the voice floated down.

"Incoming!" yelled the guard next to Mich.

They stood a moment, waiting for something to happen. In a moment, they could see a huge wooden crate descending on ropes. As it neared the ground, the three humans were pushed forward toward it.

Spirit and Heat both whinnied loudly as they were hauled away from their friends.

"Esprit!" Nola cried. She hadn't anticipated this. She struggled to follow but was roughly held back by two Fren. "Where are they taking you?" she called.

I don't know, came his thought. *I cannot read the minds of evil creatures, nor would I choose to. Do not worry for me, my friend! It is bad enough I should worry for you.*

Spirit's thoughts came quietly. Nola had to concentrate in order to make them out. Perhaps the evil of this place prevented telepathy. She was losing him.

In one last rush of thought, he managed to say, *Don't forget, my friend, never lose faith! Never!*

And with those words, he disappeared into one of the lower tunnels and his thoughts came no more.

19

TREK

Nola stared after them, the tears coming painfully to her eyes once again. She was shoved into the box with Mich, Tina and four Fren. The door was pushed closed from outside.

She hung her head in the darkness of the crate as it began to rise. She felt an emptiness she'd never felt before. She'd gotten used to Spirit's reassuring thoughts, and she felt as if a large piece of whom she was, was gone. How could she be strong now? She was no longer a whole person. She'd lost her dreamstone cross and her best friend. She felt the walls of the box closing in.

The crate rose in silence. The only noise was that of the Fren's harsh breathing. Nola's ears were popping as the crate jarred against something. The door behind them fell with a loud crack against the tunnel floor.

Beyond the doorway was nothing but dust-filled blackness. The three friends were forced into the tunnel. As they stumbled along, they could still see rays of light that squeezed between the planks of the crate and around its edges.

Nola was afraid as she once again faced forward. Her eyes strained, trying to penetrate the darkness. The walls around her were dark and rough. They seemed to feed hungrily on any light that shone on them. Nola searched desperately for her feet and hands in the dark but could see nothing.

She could feel that the tunnel had begun to wind to the left. She kept her shoulder close to the wall, touching it occasionally with her hands. She tried to keep a mental map of the tunnel. However, when the tunnel became steep, it twisted right, then left again; then it seemed to double back. Nola had lost all sense of direction. It was weird enough to be hauled way up to enter a tunnel that then wound steadily down, without trying to figure why it curved all around instead of going straight to its destination. But maybe the Fren were just naturally crooked creatures.

"Wilma?" came Mich's whisper. He brushed against her back to let her know he was close.

"Yes, I'm here."

"Don't be scared," he reassured her. "I don't know what's going to happen to us, but as long as we are careful to keep up appearances, I think things will work out."

It occurred to her that it shouldn't be hard to keep up appearances, when it was impossible to see or be seen in this black hole. Maybe the Fren could see in the darkness; she could not be sure of that.

"Joy?" Mich asked.

Tina answered with a cough. She was at the front of the procession, while Mich, Nola and a Fren were bringing up the rear.

"Schilenche!" yelled one of the Fren, prodding Mich with his razor jag. "Now we are taking you inferiorsch to schee the chief. He will dechide which schector you are to work in. I would schuggescht that you schpeak when schpoken to. Otherwische, keep your mouthsch shut."

There was something familiar about that particular Fren. But what did it matter? All Fren were enemies, until she had the magic to revert them to their true forms and natures.

As time passed, Nola's feet began to ache. She tried to keep her feet from shifting unnaturally on the stony floor. The tunnel continued its deep descent for some time. Nola was positive that they were no longer in the cliffs, but far below Kafka's surface.

At one point, Nola's ankle turned inward as she stepped on a sloping rock in the dark. Mich managed to keep her from falling by bracing himself between her and the wall. However, the pause in movement caused the Fren to show their impatience. One of them pushed Nola forward and she fell, again twisting her sore ankle beneath her. She knew her ankle was sprained, and the rope that tied her feet together cut painfully into her skin.

She was forced to struggle to her feet and move on. She limped badly and was bound to fall again on the loose stones of the tunnel floor.

She suddenly felt a pair of hands moving over her own. They belonged to Mich. He was walking backward so that he could use his bound hands to untie hers. It was very difficult, as Nola kept stumbling on her injured ankle.

He walked that way for a moment, face-to-face with a Fren. It was a good thing that it was so dark. Mich wasn't sure if he could stare into its face for more than a few seconds without vomiting from the ghastliness.

Finally the rope loosened and slipped off her wrists. Nola felt the blood rushing to feed her starving hands. She rubbed them together to help the circulation. Then she tried to untie Mich's hands but she couldn't even loosen the rope. Her limp was so bad that she had to keep moving her hands away to keep herself from falling.

"It's all right," he whispered. "Just brace yourself on me."

Nola put her arm around his neck and he helped her steady herself. This made walking much easier and more comfortable. She was so grateful that he was there to help her. He seemed to know just what to do. She wished *she* knew.

"Reility will recognize me," Mich whispered.

Nola hadn't thought of that. If they were being taken to Reility, he would surely recognize Mich, and therefore Nola's mud covering would not help her. As it was, her mud was drying out.

"Halt!" a Fren snapped. "Get in there."

They were shoved to the side, where there turned out to be a hole in the wall. They found themselves in a musty chamber barely large enough for the three of them. Was this their destination?

Tina was the last to be shoved in. "They're ahead of schedule, so they're taking a break," she muttered. "I heard them talking. We just have to wait."

"That's great," Nola said. "We can use the time."

"We can?"

"Yes. Ti—I mean, Joy, sit so you're blocking the entrance, so they can't see in."

"Okay," the girl agreed dubiously. There was the sound of her body shifting around. "Done."

Now Nola got busy. First, she created a tiny hooded flashlight, then she created a small spray bottle filled with water. These things appeared in her hand. She sprayed the mud and worked it over the places where it had dried and flaked off. She then disbelieved the bottle. She was learning how to make her talent work effectively for her. She didn't have to perform great feats of magic, just make little efforts of the right kind.

She imagined a pair of scissors and a bottle of hair dye. "Mich, I want to change your appearance pretty drastically, so you won't be recognized. Okay?"

"Very well," he agreed with resignation.

She hated to do it, but she sheared his long black hair so that it came down no farther than the back of his neck. She squirted some of the brown hair dye into her hands and tried to apply it to his face and arms. She worked hurriedly, as there was no telling when the goof-off Fren would decide to resume the hike. That meant an imperfect job of makeup. His skin was a bit splotchy and he'd have a heck of a time getting it off, but at least he looked nothing like himself. She labored to improve the details, but this just wasn't the ideal laboratory for such an operation.

"Douse light!" Tina hissed. Nola disbelieved the items immediately, to avoid discovery. She would have done so anyway, in due course, so that she wouldn't have to carry them.

There was motion at the cave entrance. "Out, captivesch!" the naggingly familiar Fren ordered.

They obediently crawled out. Nola wondered whether she should have focused on untying the other two, but realized that the Fren might check their bonds. In fact, she would have to conjure more rope for her own hands the moment they entered any lighted region. So she did that now, knotting the cord around one wrist and leaving a loop, so that she could quickly slip her other hand in when she had to. The Fren probably wouldn't check it for looseness, because they would figure she'd have freed her hands if she could.

They resumed the trek, wending down. Nola realized that the slant wasn't as bad as she had thought; they were going into the mountain behind the cliff face, rather than down below it. Still, she had the impression of enormous depth.

At long last, it seemed that her eyes were adjusting to the darkness. She began to see dark shapes ahead of them.

Nola felt they were at least two miles beneath the surface (though she knew better) when she noticed the crystals. The walls of the tunnel were lined with tiny glowing crystals that cast a dim bluish light in the dusty air.

She began to hear noises. She could hear banging sounds through the thick walls, as well as far-off voices. The echoes of their footsteps took on a deeper tone. Soon she could see well enough to realize that the tunnel was slowly widening. Ahead of them was a huge cavern.

Inside the cavern, they were told to stand at the end of a short line of creatures. Tina was first, Mich second and Nola was third. She slipped her free hand into the loop of cord, and tried to work it reasonably tight. She hoped they wouldn't notice that her wrists were no longer cruelly constricted.

In front of Tina was a huge brown rat. In front of the rat was a medium-sized Dalmatian with bright orange spots. Next was a small boy with strange ears and shaggy pants. Nola saw, upon closer inspection, that his ears were really stubby horns and his pants were really furry legs ending in cloven hooves. She decided it was a faun. She had read about them in her mythology book.

The first creature in line, a gray mule with a single sharp, slender horn between its eyes, stood before a small desk. Behind the desk sat Reility. There were several guards standing around.

The friends watched as Reility stamped a page in a book, made a note in pencil, then waved to two guards. The guards escorted the mule into one of the many tunnels that circled the cavern.

"Next?" Reility said.

The faun stepped forward.

"State your name and race," the Fren king said in a bored tone.

"Saffron Quandrey, Cava faun, sir."

"Territory?"

"Mangor."

"So, you are a Cava faun? Then you have experience working in caves. You'll be an asset."

The faun bowed his head. In the process, he showed a rather large wound across the back of his neck. No doubt it had been put there by the Fren.

"Sector one," Reility said, stamping his book. "Next?"

The faun was led through a tunnel as the Dalmatian stepped forward. It seemed to have an injured paw. It looked at the ground, and never turned its eyes up.

"State your name and race."

"Bow-wow!" the dog barked.

Reility nodded to one of his guards. The guard stepped forward and lashed the creature's back with a whip. The dog yelped.

Reility stared at the dog as it whimpered. The guard stepped back again.

"I have no patience for your ilk today. So, I ask you once more: state your name and race."

Nola was shocked as the dog began to speak in a male human's throaty voice. "My name is Curbie Martin. I am a Dalmatian." He growled sarcastically, showing his canines.

"Territory?"

"Welton Town."

"Ah. You guarded pigs?"

"No. I guarded the town."

"So, then you are a coward. You were not there when I invaded."

The dog growled, his hackles raised. "Who is the coward? Why do you not dismiss these flunkies and face me, Fren to canine?"

Reility laughed. "Such effrontery will not go unpunished, runty puppy. Sector seven!"

Two guards approached the dog with their jags. The dog looked furious, but relented, and was taken out of the chamber.

Reility was still laughing nastily when the rat was called. It was taken to sector three without incident.

"Next?"

Tina stepped up to the desk. Reility did not look up from his book.

"Name?"

Nola prayed that Tina remembered to use her phony name.

"M-M-My name's Joy Cooper. I'm a h-humanoid," she stammered.

Nola flinched as Reility glanced at her friend. Tina's hair was snarled and her face was dusty from their journey, but she still looked decent. "I assume your territory is Welton Town?" he asked, not looking up.

"Wh-What?"

This time he stared at her directly. "I see from the amount of bruises on your body that you are not a fighter. Perhaps a lover? Maybe a sexual slave?"

This time, Tina flinched. That statement had cut a little close to home. "Yes, that's what I do."

"We have no need of that type of service. However, you seem to have strong limbs. At least strong enough to last a week or so." Reility paused and looked thoughtful. "You look very familiar to me. Have we met previously? Perhaps in the town?"

Tina decided to do the opposite of what was normally done in a case like this. She hoped she was not being stupid. "Yes, I think we did meet. Y-You destroyed my baby daughter," she lied.

Stupid or not, it worked. "Oh, I see." He paused briefly. "I destroyed many children that day. Oh, well." He looked back at his book.

Tina was never happier to see anyone stamp a page in her life. "Sector twelve. Next?"

Nola had been thinking desperately of something to say, when Mich was called forward. She came up with a crazy plan. While Reility and his guards were distracted by Mich, she disbelieved her clothing and armor, but kept the mud wet and in place.

Mich felt very apprehensive as he approached the desk. He kept his eyes turned down. His biggest fear was that the moment he met Reility's gaze, his charade would crumble.

"Name, race and territory?"

Mich kept his voice low. "Richard." He panicked as he tried to think of a last name.

"Last name?" Reility asked.

"No last name," Mich said at last.

"Race and territory?"

"Uh, I am humanoid, and, uh, I'm from the Forest of Imagination."

Reility looked up. "There are no humanoids in the forest except those in the castle. What was your job?" He cocked his head and looked intently, as if trying to see through Mich's blotched skin.

"Groom for the horses."

"Sector eight. Next?"

Nola too kept her eyes down as she approached Reility's desk. She had a good idea of what she would say, but wasn't sure if it would work. When she did glance up, she saw something flash. It was her cross. It dangled around his ugly neck. She was enraged.

"Name?"

"Wilma Roberts of the Shattered-Glass Glade. I am a Terra Nymph."

"A nymph of mud? I've never heard of such a creature." He peered at her, and she could feel the weight of his stare.

"If you please, sir, I don't understand. We have always been there," she said, trying to look dismayed and befuddled.

"Where are you from?"

"The mud, of course."

"No, I mean, where were your ancestors born?"

"The same."

Reility became very frustrated and it began to show in his eyes. Nola hoped she wasn't carrying the stupid bit too far. "Were they not born of the river like all others?"

"What others?"

Reility sighed deeply and leaned forward. "All Kafkians are born of the river. Is this not so for your family?"

"Forgive me, sir, but are you trying to suggest that my ancestors were born in water? That makes no sense to me. I am of terra!"

Reility finally settled back in his chair, a look of complete frustration on his face.

"You must be a nymph! Only a nymph can cause one's mind so much turmoil! Sector seven!" He stamped his book and grinned. "You'll like that sector. I know you nymphs are always concerned with your figures; you should have no problem dieting in that sector."

Nola was escorted through another tunnel. This one was not as brightly lit as the chamber, but she was glad she could see at all.

The Fren kept a jag close at her back. If she lost step, she was poked. With every poke, a new wound was formed beneath her coating of mud. She lost step many times, as she was still limping badly. Her ankle had now swollen and the slightest weight upon it caused her to flinch with pain. However, she did put weight upon it. If she did not, she would surely fall, and possibly be killed by the Fren. She clenched her teeth and moved on.

Nola could hear the banging sounds now, as if they were beyond a few inches of tunnel wall. She could hear the rough and booming voices of the Fren, shouting directions.

The tunnel they walked in was lined on both sides by windowless doors made of wood. The Fren escorting her gestured for her to stop beside one of them.

"I am going to give you some good advice, because I like you," he said, giving her a poke with his jag, forcing her toward the door. "If you do not behave, and do not work to your last breath, you will end up in this cell sooner than we planned." He laughed and opened the door a crack so that Nola could see inside.

Nola saw a vision from her dream. There was a tiny fairy being taunted by several Fren. The fairy was quickly reduced to tears and curled up on the floor trying to hide her face from the cruel Fren. Nola had trouble seeing the poor thing because the Fren had closed in on her. When they finally backed away, the fairy was gone, replaced by a Fren as hideous as any other in the cell. The Fren was much larger than the fairy had been, which surprised her until she remembered that such transformations were independent of size.

Nola couldn't stand it; she turned away. The Fren shut the door and laughed a little. "Beautiful, isn't it?"

"It's barbaric!"

"Barbaric?" The guard seemed to relish the notion. "Perhaps."

"Why don't you do it to me and my friends now? Why wait?"

"Why wait? The chief needs his amusements! Even he gets bored. Why turn you into a butt-kissing servant, when you can be tortured and tormented, and have your will to live broken?"

He prodded her and forced her to walk on her bad foot, sending shooting pains once again through her body.

Nola was so angry that she could barely control herself. She wanted to turn around and kick the little bastard back down the tunnel. But no matter how badly she wanted to, she knew it was not wise to do so. She must be patient and keep her wits. As her dear friend Spirit had said, she mustn't lose faith. So she squared her shoulders and limped on down the tunnel, closing her mind to the tortured crying coming from the cells as she passed them.

20

CURBIE

Nola was forced into one of the dirty cells near the end of the tunnel. The door was closed and locked behind her. She pounded furiously at the door with her linked fists. This wasn't very effective, because she had to face away from it to do so.

"It's no use, you see?" said a familiar voice.

Nola turned and saw the orange-spotted Dalmatian, sitting on his haunches in the middle of the tiny cave, one sore paw lifted slightly.

"Your name is Curbie, isn't it?" she asked, slipping her hand free. Obviously the Fren no longer cared about the bonds, one way or another.

"Yes, Curbie the cur. And yours?"

Nola was amazed at the way the dog's mouth moved. Somehow, his chops formed the words perfectly. The effect reminded her of a cartoon character talking.

"Uh, Wilma."

"Well, Uh-Wilma—"

"No, my name is Wilma."

Curbie shrugged his dog shoulders and continued. "It would seem we are to share a cell. You know, we are very lucky. Most of the other cells in this sector are packed with slaves. You see, each cell is delivered the same amount of food. Those like ours will have more to go around, but those with five or six to a cell will soon starve, or else kill one another over the food." His dark eyes glanced around Nola's face.

"You seem to know a lot about this place," Nola said as she took a seat on the floor, stretching out her injured foot as she got her hobble off. "How do you know those things?"

"I am from a family that practices telepathy. My mother and father practiced, but weren't very good at it. Most of my brothers and sisters can communicate with my parents. My sister Curbia and I were very good at communicating with each other, but we couldn't communicate with anyone else. You see, my sister was taken by the Fren. I kept in contact with her. I was coming here to rescue her but was captured myself. She tells me many unspeakable things about this place. I am in fear for her life."

Nola felt a little uneasy. What could she say about the loss of his sister? At least he could maintain mental contact with her, unlike Nola with Spirit. Curbie's powers of telepathy must be strong, at least where his sister was concerned. She wished hers were strong enough to reach Spirit. She was terribly worried and would do anything to know how he was being treated. She could readily identify with Curbie. Even though he could still speak with his sister, the things Curbia told him obviously frightened him. She wondered if it wouldn't be better to be cut off. If she was in contact with Spirit and he was being tortured or something like that, she was sure she would lose control.

She decided to change the subject. "What goes on here?"

"These are the dreamstone mines. Creatures are brought here to dig and to have their spirits broken. That makes us easier to convert, you see?" Curbie stiffened and stared at the door behind Nola, his nose quivering.

The door cracked open and a gnarled hand threw in a metal plate. The plate landed on the floor with a clank and the door was locked once more. The plate contained a sort of slop and a lump of something. When Nola inspected it more closely, she could see the slop looked much like animal entrails. The lump was a big piece of moldy bread.

Curbie approached and took a sniff, his black nose twitching. "It's exactly as Curbia described it," he said. "The creatures in her cave fight mercilessly over every scrap of the stuff, you see."

Nola smiled and drew the plate away. Curbie snarled at her and she covered her mouth in surprise. His fangs were bared. "No, no! You don't understand!" she protested.

"What's to understand?" he growled. "You are trying to take all the food for yourself!" His hackles bristled about his shoulders.

"No, you don't have to eat this stuff, if you don't like it, because I can—"

"I like it just fine!" He snapped the air in front of her and pawed at the plate, scooping out some of the guts onto the floor in front of him.

"Okay," she said, smiling. "But I'm not going to eat that slop! Not when I can have a big juicy steak!" A plate appeared in her hand. The smell of the warm meat quickly overwhelmed the stench of the air.

Curbie's ears perked up and he was drooling, his tongue lolling out. "Illusion?"

Nola looked at him and smiled warmly. "No. See for yourself." She put the steaming meat in front of him.

He did not touch it, though he continued drooling a torrent of saliva. "You are a Creator!" he whispered with force.

Oops! Nola had forgotten not to use her skills. What if someone saw her doing it? They would know who she was and the Fren would surely dispose of her.

Curbie seemed to notice that she was worried. "Do not worry, Wilma," he said, winking at her. "You caught me by surprise. You need not fear me! I am on your side. May I eat that delicious-smelling food?"

Nola thought of correcting him on her name, since he knew the truth anyway. She decided to play it safe and let the name stick. "Of course you may," she said, creating a bowl of fruit for herself.

She conjured luberries and spotted oranges. She wanted to eat the things that she ate on the surface. She felt trapped and alone in the ground, separated from her friends and her love. She felt as if she'd never see the surface or the light of the sun again. The fruit eased a little of that feeling.

Curbie placed his sore paw, gently, on the steak and chewed it as if it were a rare treasure. Nola ate an orange and two fistfuls of the white luberries. When they were finished, Curbie walked around in a tight circle and curled himself on the floor of the cell, his paws tucked neatly under him.

"You had best get some rest. You see, the guard will come soon and take us to the tunnels to dig." With that he closed his eyes and refused to speak further.

Nola cleared the pebbles away from a flat spot near the wall and leaned back. It was terribly uncomfortable, but she knew better than to conjure a bed or a pillow, lest the guard see it when he came. Before closing her eyes to rest, she gestured with a hand, and the extra plate and bowl disappeared. Then she disbelieved the fragments of rope that had hobbled her. She doubted that the guards would miss them.

Her eyes closed, and she tried to rest with her arms crossed over her chest. Her ankle throbbed and the rough wall pained the sores on her back. She was forced to change positions. She stretched out across the floor on her stomach, but this caused her ankle to twist when she started relaxing. She was forced to hold it straight by holding her shoe upright, and she had to remain alert to do so. Thus she got very little rest before the Fren guard returned.

She had no idea if it was night or day, or how long she had been lying there. The light in the tunnels outside the cell was the same as when she first arrived. Curbie trailing her, she followed the guard through a door and into a new tunnel. The din grew to a roar.

The tunnel was short. It opened into a catacomb of incomplete tunnels and passageways. She strained her eyes in the dim light to make out the shapes she saw.

The walls seemed to be lined with a myriad of creatures, fifty or more. Most of them were four-footed or humanoid. There was a bird close to her. It had very short wings, strong-looking feet and blunt talons that seemed to indicate a life spent in burrows. They were all busy digging and banging with tooth and nail. None of them had shovels, or even sticks. Some of them used fallen stones to help them dig.

There were also several Fren. Nola noticed that one of them with a whip was severely lashing a large rodent that had fallen down. It had collapsed in exhaustion. The Fren did not let up until the creature started feebly to scratch at the floor. "That's better!" yelled the Fren.

Then the rodent stopped scratching and lay still, its eyes closed. Nola knew it was not dead; she could see its back rise and fall as it breathed. It was simply unconscious, or beyond exertion. The Fren whipped the poor animal again, and when it no longer responded to the lashing, it was dragged across the cave floor, past Nola and Curbie. The creature looked up at her as it was pulled past on the rough stones. She had never seen such a pained expression, nor had she seen such a look of pure hatred.

"He's off to the room," the guard said with satisfaction, speaking loudly over the noise of digging. "Which is where you will go if you don't obey." He pushed both Curbie and Nola into the short depression made by the rodent.

"Now dig, or else!" shouted the Fren. "I'll be keeping my eyes on you two. Especially you," he said, poking Curbie with his jag. "The chief told me you'd be trouble." He walked away.

Nola looked at Curbie as he started to dig, doggie style. She picked up a stone that looked promising and began to scratch at the soft rock with it. The rock was surprisingly porous, and chipped away slightly with each scrape.

After a moment, she looked around the cave. She noticed that most of the Fren had left and only one or two remained, watching over the throng. It seemed a crazy thing to do, leaving so many oppressed creatures unattended. Any of them could escape. If they all ran at once, there would be no way of getting them all.

"How come the guards left? We can get away now," Nola whispered.

"Speak for yourself," Curbie growled. "Don't you know what we are all looking for?"

Nola hadn't thought of that. It did seem like a lot of trouble just to dig holes. "No. What is it?"

"The magic dreamstone. The twin of the one Reility took from you, Nola. Besides, even if we could escape this sector, we'd never make it out alive."

"How did you know my name?" she asked, alarmed.

"Everyone knows you. That is, that you are the Creator. You are to be our salvation. But I now have my doubts that you will escape. You seem to lack the required strength to deal with our problems, no offense intended."

Nola ignored his doubts, lest they shake her faith. "But I thought there were no more stones like mine."

"There is one more. They tell us that whoever finds that stone will be set free to live in peace. I'm going to find that stone. When I do, I will ask that my sister be released."

"But what's the big deal about finding the stone? I mean, he already has mine. What good is having another? He can't even use them. He's not a Creator."

Curbie did not answer right away, as he was concentrating on a larger fragment that was resisting his efforts. He did not want to attract the attention of the Fren by progressing too slowly.

Nola noticed that her mud was dry and flaking off. She paused a moment to renew it.

Curbie struck something in the rock and dug vigorously, trying to dislodge it. It turned out to be a large hunk of colorless dreamstone, in crystal form. It looked a lot like quartz. He barked loudly and one of the guards shuffled up and took the dreamstone away. He was safe, for a while: he had produced.

He answered her as he resumed digging, occasionally sifting through large chunks of fallen rock. "Two dreamstones of that type are better than one, you see? When the two are brought together and drenched in the River of Thought, they cause the one who holds them to become fully real. An Earthling, like you. He would be a Creator. He would therefore be able to control your world by giving tormenting dreams to all of Earth, once the Fren of this world have been Forgotten."

Nola dropped her digging stone and stared, open-mouthed, at Curbie. Her shock and horror were becoming one and the same. This new information was a knife in her heart.

Curbie continued, oblivious to her expression. "That is what all of these creatures are looking for, you see? We all want to be free. We all want to be the one to be freed, you see?"

Nola noticed that a guard was looking in her direction. He had noticed that she was not digging. She immediately turned back to the deepening hole and dug at the wall.

This was awful! If Reility got hold of the other stone, not only would her friends die, but so would Kafka. So would Earth. Just as she had feared all along. They would have no hope at all, no faith, no reason to live. Earth would be full of killers and suicidal people.

What could she do? She knew. She must find the twin stone and recover her cross. She had to stop Reility. Still there was the question: How?

21

TWIN

Mich's arms were numbing from all the digging he had done. His body ached and he longed to lie down on the cave floor and rest. He was not quite sure how long he had been in this dark tunnel, but he was sure that it was at least five hours. He was very hungry and had not gotten anything when the meal was served. The creatures that shared his cave ate every crumb in a matter of seconds.

His new friend, Curbia, was tiring also. She was very determined to find the twin stone and free her brother. She was digging in a tunnel adjacent to his and he could see that she was slowing. He threw a pebble in her direction, jolting her to keep awake. He was afraid that if she fell that she'd be killed, or worse, converted. She yiped when the pebble hit her and she resumed her digging. It seemed cruel, but she had asked him to do it, because the penalty exacted by the Fren would be worse if she faltered. She had approached him when he arrived, and helped him get adjusted. Her help had been invaluable, and now he was repaying her in what little ways he could.

The Fren began calling names and escorting the slave miners back to their cells. Mich continued to dig until his name was called. He was more than happy to stop. He felt like collapsing where he stood. His hands were beginning to blister from the constant friction of the rock wall rubbing against them.

Curbia and Mich were forced back into their cell, along with four

others, consisting of a sow, a winged badger, a goat with six horns—
one sticking from his chin like a beard—and some sort of creature
that seemed to be all teeth, except for a pair of fairylike wings.

Mich leaned his back against the wall, putting his head between
his knees. His body was so tired that he was instantly taken by a rest-
ful numbness. All except his stomach, which growled continuously.

He was awakened in what seemed like only a moment. Curbia's
red, spotted paw was on his head.

"Mich," she whispered. "You've got to come round! The meal
will be delivered soon."

Mich groaned pitifully and tried, in vain, to brush away her per-
sistent paw.

"Come, you must be aware! You need to eat. You must keep
strong for your love. When she comes for you, you must be prepared
to help her and you cannot if you are weary and starved, you see?"

Mich knew she was right. He fought the temptation of rest, and
rose. He took a position with Curbia near the door to wait, along
with the others. He was hungry enough to eat even the slop that
would be thrown in to them. Everyone was tensing, ready to scram-
ble, as soon as the plate appeared.

"I wonder where she is now," he said, watching the door. "I hope
she is okay. I wish Kafka wasn't treating her this way. This used to be
such a beautiful place. I wish I knew what went wrong."

"If it will help you any, I will ask my brother to keep his eyes
open," Curbia said consolingly. "He asked me to help you, because
you were processed when he was and he knew you would be confused."

At that moment, the door unlocked and swung open. The plate
was heaved in and there was the normal chaos.

Mich was thrown aside and trampled by the toothy-fairy, then the
goat. There were hands reaching and voices screeching. In a flurry

of fur and tails, the food was gone and the plate was being licked clean by the goat.

When he finally looked around, he saw Curbia fighting the badger for half a lump of bread. Mich helped her drive the badger off and she happily shared her moldy prize with him. His stomach calmed down a bit now that it had something to work on other than itself.

"What about your other friend, Tina?" Curbia asked after she had finished her bread. "Is she a Creator also?"

"Yes. But for some reason, only my love can use the magic dreamstone to create magic."

"I see. So she is the only one who can destroy the dam, because it is magic in nature."

"That is true, but Tina is needed also, as are all Creators. The Volant told us that we must bring all the Creators here to help."

Curbia placed a paw on his knee and looked at him with dark gray eyes. "I want you to know, Mich, that I am loyal only to Kafka. Most of these creatures are loyal only to their own hides." She cast an irate glance around the cell. "I promise to help in any way I can, you see? Even give my life."

Mich did not feel right about getting the poor bitch into this mess, but he could say nothing. He was grateful to her. If she weren't here, he would most definitely starve. He hoped she would be reunited with her brother before anything happened to him.

"Now we have a few hours to rest before our next shift begins," she said, closing her eyes.

"Next shift?" Mich asked, chagrined. Curbia did not answer, but simply placed her tail across her muzzle and tucked in her hind legs.

Mich had not expected another shift in the same night (or day, whichever time it was). He shrugged; after all, it was the Fren they were slaving for.

Having taken a spot near the door, he nestled his head into a crook between the door and the wall. His body was ready, and his senses dulled until he was in full repose, which he needed badly.

When it was time for the next shift, Mich still felt he needed rest. His limbs were aching, but the Fren forced him into the mines once again. They were put to work in the same tunnels as before.

He sighed as he picked up a rock. "There must be some way," he mumbled.

He heard the rock to his left crumbling. He looked closely. The rock seemed to be falling away from the wall. He saw a glistening black nose poke through the wall. It was Curbia.

"Listen," she whispered. "While we rested, I spoke with Curbie. He has a friend, a human girl. He believes her to be the one you seek. That is why he had me help you; I did not realize before. Is her name Nola?"

Mich's heart leaped up to his throat. He swallowed hard. "Yes! That's her! She is with your brother? How is she?"

"Stay calm," she whispered. "We do not want to draw unwanted attention. Give me a moment."

He heard her resume digging. Mich did the same, but kept his ears open for her next words.

"He says she is fine. She is tired, worn out, and her ankle is paining her, but she is doing better now that she knows you are okay. She says not to worry and to tell you she loves you."

Mich smiled for the first time since coming to the mines. "Tell her I love her and I'll find some way to get her out of this."

"I think she knows that already." She looked around his tunnel. "Dig in that direction," she said, indicating it with her nose.

"Why?"

"I sniff something interesting. If you find any deep-blue stone, save a piece for me."

"Anything to please a friend."

Mich was happy to learn that Curbia's brother was with Nola and that she still endured. He was worried for her. He hoped he could fulfill his promise to find her a way out. He tried to remain confident that things would work out.

Digging became a little easier now that his attitude had been uplifted. He made great progress and the tunnel began to deepen. Near the end of the next shift, his eyes were straining so much in the darkness that his head ached. He wished he had some healing spice. He suddenly got an idea.

"Curbia, please get a message to Nola," he spoke through the hole.

Curbia's nose appeared. "Yes, of course; what is it?"

"Tell her to create some healing spice for her ankle. It'll take away her aches and pains as well."

She nodded once and her head disappeared again. Then it reappeared. "Have you found any unusual stone?"

Oops—he had forgotten her request. "Yes. I'll get you a piece." He moved back to where he had seen a very faint glow, similar to what they had seen in the deep caves when traveling, but of a different quality, and chipped at it. It came from only one section, so he was able to isolate the glowing fragment. He put it in his pocket, and forgot the matter.

A Fren guard approached his tunnel, whip in hand. Mich followed him back to the cell. Curbia arrived soon after.

Both Mich and Curbia settled down on the rough floor in front of the door, awaiting the plate of slop. This time, Mich managed to snatch the whole piece of bread. It did not even have much mold on it. He tore it in half and gave half to Curbia. She thanked him and offered him some of the guts she had grabbed.

"No, thank you," he said, smiling and crinkling his nose with distaste.

"Nola says, 'Thank you for the advice.' She says it worked perfectly and that she wished she could give some to you."

"Tell her that I don't need any, but perhaps Curbie does."

"She says she gave him some first and that it even put a shine on his coat. But she doesn't wish to burden Curbie further with her messages, which do take effort to transmit. She says to say good night."

Mich's smile did not leave him for a few moments, but when it did, it left him completely. He drew in his knees and scraped the dirt at his feet with a rock.

"You look sad. What is bothering you?" Curbia asked. "Besides this place, I mean."

"It is Nola. I love her so, but I know that even if Kafka is saved, she will want to return home."

"Does she not care for you?"

"Yes, I know she loves me also, but she has had nothing but heartache since she's gotten here. My world must seem an inhospitable place to live."

"But, you see, if she loves you as much as Curbie tells me, she will stay with you."

"It's not just that," he said, as he felt a small chunk of rock in his pocket. It was the one Curbia had asked for. Absentmindedly he brought it out and flipped it toward her. It hit the floor and rolled toward the dog. "It's that she has her own life, on her own world. Why would she want to stay in a place she has only bad memories of, when she could return to a place where there exist magic water showers and fine eating chambers and magic numbers that are much like your telepathy and—"

Curbia had moved close and slapped a paw over his mouth. Her muzzle was in his face, an unusual mannerism for her. He saw the small rock that he had dug out between her front teeth. "What's wrong?" he asked after she removed her paw.

She slowly shook her head. The rock made a rattling sound. She spit the rock out in front of him and leaned in close. "It's the twin stone," she whispered.

Mich jumped a little. "But it's just a rock."

"No, it is encased in light-dreamstone crystals, like the ones that line the walls, only a higher concentration, you see? What you must do is hide the stone, say, in your trouser leg, and carefully break it open. Light will shine from it, so you must hide it. Otherwise, the others will see it and try to take it from you. After you crack the light shell, take the stone out, then take a rock, grind the shell into powder and spread it into the dirt on the floor so that it blends in. Do it quickly now, before the others begin to come round!"

He did so. She was right. When he broke it open, much stronger blue light shone from the inside of the encasement walls, as if it were a minute star. He found the stone inside, just like the one Nola wore. A smooth, half-circle of blue stone. A white star in its center captured the light of the encasement and followed it over the curving face of the stone.

"How did you know?" he asked Curbia, realizing that he had found the stone by no coincidence.

"My telepathy is limited, but does react to some magical things—and that is one of the most magical," she explained. "I knew it was close, very close, but it was out of my digging territory. I could not get it myself without alerting suspicion, you see? But you could get it."

"Then it's yours! You located it, you directed me to it, you recognized it."

"It is not mine or yours. It belongs to Kafka. You must reserve it for the good of Kafka."

She was right. He covered the light crystals in the loose dirt and pounded them with a rock. He uncovered a portion and a slender ray shone into the closed eyes of the goat. He quickly brushed more dirt over it and continued pounding. When he was finished, he brushed his hands through the dirt, so that the now-minute pieces blended in with the surrounding light crystals.

He fingered the blessed stone for a moment, then wedged it in his armor. "What if they search me?"

"They will not, you see? As long as they do not discover who you are, they will assume that you will be more than happy to deliver the stone to them, in exchange for your freedom, you see?"

"Yes, I see. But how can I get the stone to Nola before it is too late?"

"That I cannot tell you. I have informed Curbie. Nola is presently smiling. Perhaps she will come up with the answer."

"Does she have any ideas?"

"She says no. She says there is no way for her to escape her cell without being caught. She is worried that if she makes any strange moves, she will be found out."

This was a problem that seemed to have no solution. But at least there was now a light at the end of the tunnel. A faint blue light. What irony.

22

DRAKE

Tina was glad her shift was over. Her cell seemed like a closet, occupied by several other creatures. She was forced to wait until they were all resting before she dared make her supper.

She could hear the creatures breathing heavily as they rested. One of them, a large dragon, lay curled in a corner. He snored loudly, shooting small flames from his nostrils. He always ate first, and therefore was always first to fall into repose.

Her hands opened and were filled by a plate containing a hamburger and french fries. She smiled to herself. The food reminded her of better days back home. She bit into the delicious hamburger. She spat it back out as she was startled by a growl.

It was the dragon. His head was raised and his red eyes stared at her. His nostrils were opened wide and quivering. He slithered over to her. "Where did you get that?" he growled.

"None of your business," she replied smugly.

"There is no such food in Kafka. I've never smelled it before." He lifted his head and looked down his nose at her. He belched a flame into the air above her head.

"Hey! Watch it!" she yelled. The other creatures in the cave began to stir.

"I know you!" he said. "You are a Creator! If I turn you in, I will get my freedom!"

Tina went stiff with terror as the dragon sauntered over to the door and began butting it with his head. "Stop! Stop! What are you doing?" she yelled.

The dragon ignored her and continued to make as much racket as possible. It was only a moment or so before a Fren poked its hideous head through the door. Tina was distracted for a moment, despite her predicament. There was something about this particular Fren; she had noticed it before, but still had not been able to pin down what it was.

"Whatsch going on here?" he shouted. His eyes went wide when he saw Tina's hamburger lying in the dirt. He shoved the dragon aside and stormed into the cell, jag waving. The other creatures were up and staring. "You! What have you got there?" he asked Tina.

The dragon bounced up eagerly. "She's a Creator! I saw her making food! I found her; now I will be free!" he said, staring hopefully at the Fren.

"You will be nothing of the short, lizard. Now get back before I render you schexlessch."

The dragon shrank back, tail between its legs.

"Now, you," the Fren said, poking Tina. "You are coming with me, now!"

Tina stood and followed the Fren out of the cell. A thought was worming its way through her panicked mind. Something about this particular Fren was nagging at her. There was something in the way he spoke. She knew she could discover what it was. She racked her brain trying to remember.

"What is going to happen to me?" she asked him.

"You will be dischposched of," he replied nastily.

In a flash, she knew what it was. The accent was not quite the way it should be, but that could be due to a different type of mouth. She knew this creature!

However, they were approaching the main chamber. She must act quickly. She stopped walking and closed her eyes, concentrating with all her might. If this worked . . .

"Get moving, you!" he yelled. "What isch wrong with you?"

Tina heard him make a guttural sound as the image she held in her head began to shimmer, then disappear. She let it go and opened her eyes. There before her was the worm king's concubine, his eyeless head bobbing excitedly. "Oh, oh! My heart feelsch—you don't know what it wasch like!" he said.

"I knew it was you!" she exclaimed exultantly. "There was something about you. I was almost drawn to you, before, but didn't know why. It's because you're really an ally."

"Quickly, come with me," he whispered.

Tina followed him into a small tunnel that led to a dead end. They could not be seen by anyone in the main tunnel. Here they sat and made arrangements to free his brothers and find Nola and Mich. With the help of his brothers, the warrior worms, this just might turn the tide in their favor.

Tina felt a sense of pride. If she could save her friends, she'd finally be able to show her appreciation. Their friendship meant the world to her. She smiled. She could finally feel like something more than a dirty whore. She might not be able to do the things with dreamstone that Nola could, but her sense of affinity was paying off.

"What is your name?" she inquired as they waited.

"I am Drake," the worm confided.

"Glad to know you better, Drake," she said, patting his slimy hide.

Tina and the worm waited until the shifts in sectors nine through twelve were over. The inefficiency of the Fren supervision was evident, because it seemed that neither she nor Drake had been missed.

They began searching tunnels and cells, starting with sector twelve and working their way to sector nine.

Drake had an excellent sense of smell and remembered Tina's friends well. He poked his long tongue beneath the cell doors, sniffing with it, then drawing it back into his mouth to taste the things he smelled. Unfortunately, the occupants of the cells were hostile and hungry. Near the end of the third tunnel, his tongue had been bitten off twice.

"Won't your tongue turn into another worm?" asked Tina.

"No, not if I do not wisch it to. Reproducschion in that way isch very draining on our kind. It isch schafer and much lessch draining to schimply regenerate my body. Besidesch, digeschted portionsch don't regenerate."

Tina shook her head. "I should know these things, shouldn't I?"

"How could you? We are juscht a memory of a schtory that you heard asch a child. It wasch the one who told the schtory, your grandfather, who made usch who we are. He wasch our Creator. He told you about usch to keep usch alive."

"Grandpa? He Created you?"

"He loved you very much. He wanted you to schare in hisch dreamsch."

Tina found that extremely touching and comforting. "And the worm king, Kras—why did he reject me?"

"Becausch he did not want you to perisch. He knew he was loscht, but you might schurvive."

And of course that was the truth. She had been foolishly angry with the king. Foolish anger was the story of her life, in a way.

During their search of sector nine, a Fren guard surprised them from behind. Tina was thrilled when the Fren told her that she'd be "deschtroyed for her inscholence." She wasted no time in converting him. He turned out to be one of King Kras's spiked-collared warriors, one of the ones they lost in the glade. He was grateful to Tina for rescuing him from his imprisonment and pledged his loyalty to her until Kafka was restored.

She realized that it hadn't been such a coincidence that she had found Drake. The Fren tended to make use of whatever was handy, and the newest converts were the handiest to use for prison duty. They would have the lowest rank, so would be assigned to the dullest chores too. There were probably many friends among the prison Fren, ironic as that seemed.

They continued to search together. Drake lost the tip of his tongue once more before they were through. He was searching the last cell when they heard guards approaching to take the prisoners to the mines. They quickly moved on to sector eight.

When they reached the prison tunnel of sector eight, they discovered the cells were empty, which meant that the prisoners were all in the mine tunnels. They proceeded down the tunnel until they could see the rough chamber in which the prisoners slaved.

They were forced to keep close to the tunnel wall, hidden in shadow lest they be seen. The guards were unusually numerous. Perhaps the shift had just begun, which meant some guards would be leaving soon, and would see Tina and the two worms hiding in the tunnel.

Tina scanned the chamber with her eyes. In one corner, at the far end, she saw Mich. At first she did not recognize him, but then she remembered that Nola had sheared his hair and colored his skin. There was no way to get to him. The moment they stepped into the room, they would be sitting ducks.

"I schmell one of your friendsch," Drake said.

"Yes, there," she said, pointing, though knowing this gesture was futile because Drake had no eyes.

"Get on my back."

Tina smiled. She had forgotten about that. Drake could take her through the rock to Mich. She reached up and dug her nails into Drake's back. "Doesn't that hurt when I do that?" she asked.

"Take out your fingersch and look at my schkin."

She did so and saw that there were now perfectly shaped finger holes in his back. No blood or other gooky stuff came out. The skin was smooth down inside the holes, coated with a healthy slime. His body had healed itself, instantly, around her fingers.

She shrugged and hopped aboard. Drake dived into the wall and "wormed" his way through the rock. Tina was electrified by this strange ability to tunnel. She didn't think she could ever grow tired of riding. They almost flew, the rock magically evaporating as it touched her skin. The rock never injured her and she could barely feel it. In fact, it felt almost like a soft breeze. Drake's body stretched out to three times its normal length, then he would anchor his head with his tongue, then pull his nether portion along. He traveled very swiftly, for a worm, and the ride was surprisingly steady. Drake's friend followed at a distance.

Soon Drake announced that he smelled Mich. He poked his head through the tunnel wall in which Mich was working and immediately stuck out his tongue, wrapping it around Mich's head and mouth in order to keep him from screaming in surprise and running out of the tunnel.

Drake brought his entire body through, carrying Tina with it. Mich's look of horror soon eased as he recognized Tina. His face was covered with tongue, except for his eyes, but they crinkled in a way that showed he was grinning from ear to ear.

"My God, Tina, it's you!" he said over the noise of the mining, after Drake released him. "It's so good to see your face. How did you get away?"

"It's good to see you too! I'd like you to meet Drake, again."

Drake bowed his head.

"Again?"

"He's King Kras's lover. You met him before."

"Yes, of course, I remember. Where'd he come from?"

"He was guarding me as a Fren. I recognized his accent. All the worms who turned into Fren kept their accents, so they are easy to recognize. We found one other—he's following behind us—and we are looking for the rest. We figure we can get Nola's cross back and get ourselves out of here."

"Good girl!" he exclaimed. That made her feel great, though there might have been a time, back on Earth, when she would have been insulted. Mich didn't know about Earthly sexism.

Tina noticed a pair of dark eyes staring at them through a hole in the tunnel wall. She advanced on it menacingly.

"No, Drake, wait! That's my friend Curbia. I've got to take her with me."

"Humpf," Tina muttered. "I suppose she can ride the warrior." With that, she could hear the wall crumbling in the adjacent tunnel and a dog's surprised bark. "Curbia's a mutt?"

"I'm not a mutt!" Tina heard someone say in a feminine voice. "I'm a bitch and proud of it!"

Tina laughed out loud. "That's a dog after my own heart!" she said as she mounted Drake's back.

She stretched out a hand to Mich. He jumped into the air and landed in the dirt with a thud. Behind him stood four Fren. One of them had poked him with a razor jag.

Tina immediately opened her mind and closed her eyes. As luck would have it, three of the four were worm warriors. She converted them as the remaining Fren stared in horror. He was gone in a second, in a puff of dust.

The worms, recognizing her power, lavished Tina with praise

and thanks. They promised to stay close and help her in any way they could.

But she couldn't rest on her laurels, such as they were. "I guess it's time to confront Reility and take back Nola's cross. He should be in the main chamber. We had better be quick about it, before Reility learns we are here. Is everyone ready?"

Mich, Curbia and the worms all nodded. Then they were off into the rock. Drake searched ahead with his tongue for a smell of evil. It wasn't long before he found the right direction and picked up speed.

When they reached the main chamber, there was no hesitation. The five worms plunged through the rock and headed toward the small desk where Reility sat, cross ashine in the dim blue light.

Reility looked up and did a double take. The worms advanced on him. The guards in the room attacked.

"Warriors!" Tina yelled. "Do not kill them! Get the cross!"

The worms fought off the Fren. There began to appear more worms as pieces of them were sliced off.

"Drake!" Tina yelled as she dismounted. "Find Nola! Bring her back here! Hurry!"

Drake wormed his way down one of the tunnels, following his tongue.

Suddenly, there was a Fren at Tina's back. He was striking her with a club. She concentrated and a bear trap formed at the Fren's feet. She pushed him and he danced a little, trying to keep his balance, and stepped into the trap. The trap snapped closed on his leg.

But no sooner had she incapacitated the one when another was on her. This one wielded a whip. She created a trapdoor beneath him and he slipped through. She closed the door over him. This was almost fun!

She looked around and saw that, though the worms far outnumbered the Fren, her order not to kill the Fren caused the worms a great handicap. Many of the original worms looked very weak and seemed to weaken further the more they were cut. Even the new worms that formed seemed almost unable to move about well.

As she tried to think of something to help, she was struck from behind with a heavy club, and all went black.

23

INDECISION

Drake had found Nola in a matter of a few minutes. She and her new friend, Curbie, returned with him and witnessed Tina's injury. The girl lay motionless on the cave floor. One of the worms was wrapped around Reility, trying desperately to keep hold of him while being slashed at the same time.

Curbie rushed to help Curbia, who was fending off two Fren with the help of a rather slow worm. Mich was also doing his best to protect himself from two more. Another worm was trying to help him. Actually, it seemed to get in the way.

"What is wrong with the worms, Drake? Why are they so slow?"

"They are dying," Drake said solemnly. "They have repro-dusched scho many timesch that they are draining the very life out of themschelvesch. They are trying to outnumber the Fren."

"Well, tell them to stop!" Nola said.

Drake screeched a command and every worm turned its head and nodded. During that distraction, a Fren approached with a razor jag and quickly slashed Drake's head off. He writhed on the floor for a moment, then was healed. Another worm, looking just like Drake, slithered into the fray.

"I'm afraid we cannot overcome Reility thisch way. We will losche our livesch," Drake said.

"Tell the warrior with Reility to let him go."

"What? That would be inschane!"

"Please!" Nola shouted. "I'll try to handle him myself." She hoped she could.

The worm paused a moment, then screamed another command. The worm that held Reility was already loosening its grip. Reility jumped out of its coils and sped toward the nearest tunnel, running for his life. Nola was heartened somewhat to see his evident discomfort; Reility must think he was losing, despite the damage being done to the worms.

Nola made a throwing motion and a huge steel net sank down over Reility. Tendrils shot from every edge and snaked into the rock around him. He hissed and spit and chewed the cords. The cords began to pop loose. Nola knew that she could not hold him long without the cross; Creation alone was not enough.

She looked around for help, but all of her friends were busy fighting the other Fren. She would have to risk losing her cross by taking care of the matter herself. She had to have faith in herself for once, even though she was never more afraid of anyone in her life. Reility struck fear in her like no other person.

She ground her teeth and strode forward, throwing another net atop him as the hole he made in the net was growing larger. He cursed at her and threatened her, but still she approached, tears of terror streaming down her face.

Her cross dangled around his neck, begging to be rescued from him. But somehow, she couldn't reach out to take it. It was her own fear holding her back. She knew it, and cursed it, but couldn't overcome it.

Do not fear, my friend came Spirit's voice in her mind.

"Esprit! Where are you?" she cried, looking around.

I am here, he said, sounding closer.

She turned and Spirit stood behind her, as huge and black as ever. His horn shone bright with pride. He had a Fren pinned by the arms under his hooves. Heat was there as well, standing guard over Tina where she lay.

You cannot be afraid now, Nola. You must do what is meant for you to do. Take the cross.

Nola's joy at seeing her dear friend disappeared when she turned back to face Reility. He had broken through the net and was climbing out. The cross hung within her reach.

She stretched out her quivering hand. When she did so, Reility looked up at her with all the evil of the world in his black eyes. She let her hand drop away in another surge of fear.

"You should have killed yourself," Reality growled. "You know as well as I do that your mission will fail. You will *always fail!*" He showed his nasty pointed teeth. "Your dreams will be destroyed."

He kept saying that, yet he was trying to escape. She realized that he was attempting to terrify her, because he wasn't sure he could beat her if she didn't beat herself. That started a countercurrent in her that stirred her emotions and stiffened her dissolving spine.

Nola's expression changed from one of trepidation to one of anger. "Yes," she said, "I may fail. You may strike fear in my heart. But the fear you bring me can never match the fear of losing my dreams." She was speaking the truth, and her own words were shoring up her courage. Now she could do what had to be done!

She wrapped her fingers tightly around the cross. Reility's head came down on her fist, teeth threatening. In the same instant, he bit down on a Created gauntlet, covering her wrist and hand. He yowled with pain as she snatched the cross from his neck.

You see, you can fight him, Spirit thought approvingly. *All you need is confidence to use your power.*

True. But how hard she had had to struggle to believe that deep down, where it counted. To believe in herself.

She promptly Created a magical net and encased Reility. She

turned to the melee and began throwing nets. In moments, she had it all under control. Every Fren was safely contained.

She approached Tina and knelt by her side. She gently lifted her and tapped her cheeks until she came around enough to consume some healing spice. After treating Tina, she passed healing spice to Mich, Curbie and Curbia, and all of the weary worms.

When everyone was well, she took a moment to throw her arms around Spirit's neck and kiss his cheek warmly. She saw, in a flash of thought in his mind, how he had escaped. He had simply burst his bonds and come galloping through the tunnels to find her the moment he knew that she was free and the Fren were attacking. He couldn't risk it as long as she was captive, because the Fren might have killed her rather than let him join her.

"Thank you, friend, I love you dearly," she whispered.

No, the thanks are all for you, he replied, nuzzling her face.

She turned as she felt a familiar hand on her shoulder. She threw herself into Mich's arms, and he hugged her closely. They kissed passionately.

"You have your cross back," he said as he released her.

"Yes, and now it's time to call on some help," she said, "Drake, I need you and your warriors to stay here. Make sure all of the Fren are contained." She threw some more nets in front of him. "I'm sure there are many more of them roaming Kafka, but at least half are here, in the cliffs. The nets should work when you throw them. That way, you won't have to be concerned about being cut up anymore, and you'll be able to recover your strength."

"Yesch," he replied. "When will you be returning?"

"Soon, Drake. I will bring you to me when I need you. Please send a few worms out, give them a net each and have them release the Kafkians in the cells."

Drake bowed to her and picked up a net in his tubular mouth.

"Oh, and Drake—thank you. You made it all possible." She had learned the value of a compliment, and was pleased to see the great worm turning another shade of color. This said, she mounted Esprit, holding Curbie in her lap.

Mich and Tina mounted Heat, holding Curbia between them. Mich reached out to take Nola's hand, and she closed her eyes.

She conjured them to the top of Mangor.

They landed directly in a group of startled Fren. "What next?" Tina yelled as a Fren jumped her.

Nola threw a net over it and continued to throw nets over the rest until they were secure. When they were all contained, she tried to "see" them, but could not.

"Can you figure out who they are?" Nola asked Tina.

Tina tried. "No. I can't."

Mich touched Nola's arm. "It's time. You'd better do it now. It may take some time for them to arrive."

"Yes, I hope this will work!" She sighed, unsure of how to go about finding the Creators.

She took off her cross and held it in her hand. If this dreamstone could make any magic spell at all, it would be simple to find the Creators. All she had to do was spell each one so that it could be appreciated only by a Creator. The next question was how could she make sure that the spell would be used. That was simple, maybe: just attach a note.

A bed spell formed in her free hand. A translucent globe of spinning lightning. She considered it.

That would not do. She had to make it something a little more ordinary.

The globe shrank and became hard. It was the size of a marble and the lightning inside looked like glitter. She was sure this would not startle anyone too much, but was just pretty enough to inspire wonder and curiosity. She put the spell into a box with a note saying, "Please make a wish and dream a little dream."

She closed the box and held it in her hand. She concentrated and the box was now spelled so that it would go only to a true Creator. Then, the box disappeared from her hand.

"I hope it gets there! I've never done this before," she said, worried.

"It's all right," Mich said.

Yes, Spirit agreed. *Trust in your ability.*

Another marble appeared in her hand. She put a note with it and placed it in the box. The Volant had said there were only ten or so other Creators left in the world. She made twenty boxes, just in case. The ones left over would never be found, so it was safe to do so. She made sure to fine-tune each spell so that it would bring the Creators to the mountaintop in slightly different spots. She didn't want Creators landing on one anothers' heads, or, worse, all jamming onto the very same square foot of ground.

When she was finished sending the spells to Earth, it was time to wait. She had no idea what to expect. Would there be several Creators in the next minute, or would it take hours? Or would they misunderstand the spells, and not come at all?

There are many Fren left out there, Heat thought. *They will soon be coming for us. They are quick and will probably have searched all of Kafka in an hour. They will find us.*

"No, they won't!" Nola said. She waved her hand over her head and a tall wall was formed around her group and the captured Fren, with enough room left over to hold the Creators who would be coming. The wall was made of the same material as the dam across the river: dreamstone. They would not be seen.

Curbie sat down beside her. "I'm sorry I mistrusted your strength, Nola. You truly will be Kafka's hero."

Nola was as unsure as ever of her ability, but she had to show confidence. "Thank you, Curbie. I'm glad you and your sister are together again. I never had a brother or sister, but I can imagine what it would be like to lose a loved one. I came close to losing my friends. I thought I would die."

Curbia trotted over to Mich. "Mich, show Nola what you found."

Mich looked confused for a moment. "Oh, yeah!" he said as he fished in his armor. He pulled out a pallid blue stone, about the size of a pea, cut in half.

Nola's eyes went wide. "You found it?" she asked as she reached for it. "The twin stone?"

"Sure did!" he laughed, handing it to her. "It was right in the section I had to mine. Curbia sniffed it out for me, telepathically. It was there all along, but the Fren didn't know how to find it."

"I knew there was something important," the Dalmatian said. "I just didn't know how to get it, until Mich came."

Nola looked it over. It was the same size and shape as the one she wore. She felt a great relief at having both of them. She would do anything she had to, to keep Reility from gaining possession of either of them. She wondered whether he knew that she had the twin. If so, he would surely try to take it from her. Of course, he couldn't do anything as long as the worms kept him captive in the nets, but Nola didn't have a lot of confidence that that would last. Probably the best that could be hoped for was that by the time the Fren king escaped, his minions would have been defeated, so he would have no real power to draw on.

The group of travelers feasted on Nola and Tina's Created food. When they were finished there was a chill in the air and silence settled. Everyone felt tense and nervous. What if none of the Creators caught on to the nature of the bed spells? What if only some of them did? That would leave many Fren unconverted and free to molest the peaceful Kafkians. If Reility got away, the whole mess could start over.

As Nola sat in the growing darkness, she could hear nothing but the scratching and chewing of the captured Fren. Mich sat next to her, smoothing her hair and holding her.

When the others were resting, he whispered to her, "What are you going to do when this is over? Will you stay with me?"

Nola noticed some apprehension in his voice. "I have thought about this. I know I cannot stay here."

That was not the answer that Mich was hoping for and it hurt deeply to hear it. "Why not? I love you and I need to be with you. Now that I know you will be alive and well, on the other side of my world, my life will be empty if you leave. Though I didn't know it, I had an empty life before you came, and I fear going back to it."

Nola stared into his eyes as hers began to fill with tears. "I love you, so much, but I just can't stay here. It took me a while to realize it, but I love my home, I love my mother and my cat. I suppose I love my life. I now have the strength I need to get away from someone back there who was hurting me. Your love makes it easy. This place is so beautiful, but Earth needs dreamers. If we all stayed here, where would that leave Earth? Where would that leave my home and my friends? I have to set an example and maybe get others on my world to believe. The more people believe, the better a place Kafka will be."

Mich looked away from her and she could see the hurt on his handsome face.

"But that does not mean that I can't visit," she added quickly. "I'll come back if you need me. I'll be here for you, the way you are here for me now."

Mich continued to look away and Nola longed to see his face, but she knew it would only show pain. "I can go with you," he said.

"Not for very long. You would die there."

"No," he said gently. "You have the stones. You can make me real, make me be like you."

Nola had forgotten about the twin stones' power. She thought about it for a moment. "I don't know if that would be such a good idea. Kafka needs you. But I do want to be with you. Please give me some time."

"Of course, Nola." Mich leaned back on the ground and closed his eyes. "I love you, whatever you decide."

Nola lay beside him. Just when she was sure she would get some rest, Esprit's gentle thoughts surged into her open mind.

I'm sorry to disturb your rest, he thought.

"You could never disturb me," she thought back.

I hope you don't mind my always reading your thoughts. I suppose it can become quite a burden. However, I must discuss something with you.

"Yes?" She waited, feeling the tension and excitement in his thoughts.

You know, I have known of you ever since I was created. We share one soul. I know of Mich's request, yet I too have always longed to share in your human life. Though I cannot become a real human, I can become a real horse.

"Horses are stupid and beasts of burden. I could never do that to you!"

I would not be an ordinary horse. I would retain my intelligence, as well as my magical ability, but I would be real. I would lose my distinguishing characteristics, such as my ability to fly, my horn and my eye color. This would be necessary to blend in. I would gladly give up those things to live with you on Earth.

She knew that Esprit immediately felt her dismay and confusion. She wanted both him and Mich to go with her, but Esprit had warned her the stones could be used only once in this way. When used to make an unreal creature into a real one the stones disappeared, having spent all the magic within on such a large spell. If she used them to take either of them to Earth, not only would she leave one of them hurt and rejected, but she would lose her ability to ever visit Kafka again. Once the stones had been used, they would be gone forever. *I know I must let you decide and I don't mean to hurt you or your true love, but it is my fondest wish to be real, as I'm sure it is his as well. The decision will be yours. Do not let either of us influence your choice, or you will be unhappy with it.*

He gave her mind a loving touch, then departed from it, leaving her to wallow in her confusion and sadness. She had to decide between her true love and her best friend. She would rather die than ever have to desert either one of them. How could she turn them both down without hurting them? Right now, she was faced with a different problem. Should she hurt both of them by not choosing, or hurt one of them by choosing? Then, if she did choose, whom would she choose? *How* could she choose?

24

CREATORS

Sometime deep in the night, the group was shaken by a man's shriek. Nola created torches all around the inside wall of the enclosure, so that no creature could escape the light.

Between the unisi and the netted Fren stood an older man. He was wearing a loose white shirt and a pair of rumpled pants. He looked as if he had just gotten up from bed. He was holding his knee; he'd apparently wandered too close to the Fren and gotten himself cut.

"Who are you? What are you doing here?" Mich demanded.

The man looked up with a pained expression. "My name's Newton, and I don't know what I'm doing here."

He's a Creator, Heat thought.

"Oh, cool!" Tina chimed in.

"What's going on here?" the man demanded. "The last thing I remember is playing with a marble that I found on the ground. What is this place?"

Nola approached him. "Hello, Newton. My name's Nola. These are Mich, Tina, Heat, Spirit, Curbie and Curbia. All you need to know about them right now is that they are friends. Elsewhere there are the worm warriors, led by Drake, who may look horrendously ugly, but are also friends. Lastly, those things over there are the Fren."

"One of those things cut me!" He glanced around. "And what the hell are those?" he asked, pointing to the unisi.

"I just told you—" Nola began.

All questions will be answered now, thought Spirit to his mind.

Nola stared at Newton. His eyes went blank as Spirit's mind filled his mind with answers to his questions. His eyes went from confused to surprised, to happy to angry to sad, then to angry again: Spirit had filled him in, in a matter of a few moments.

"Wow" was all he could say.

Spirit informed the rest of the group that Newton was an abused patient at a mental hospital. He had made the mistake of making his belief in his dreams known to everyone around him, insisting that hippocampus and other bizarre monsters were real. His wife had committed him. He continued to believe, and resisted counseling. Therefore he was subjected to painful experiments, at his cost.

While Spirit sent Newton's thoughts to everyone, there was another arrival. Another man. This one looked to be about twenty-five years old. He wore a sweater and a pair of jeans and sneakers. He looked just as bewildered as Newton had. This time, Heat filled him in.

His name turned out to be Joseph. He was a grown-up child who had nothing but his dreams and cocaine. His family had all been killed when he was young, and he had grown up in several foster homes. He had hidden himself from the world with his drugs. The drugs brought him closer to his dreams, his escape of reality.

The next to come was a young girl. She was eight years old and her name was Lucina. Tina identified with her. She had come from a broken home and her mother was extremely abusive to her.

A woman, named Joelle, lived with an abusive and alcoholic husband. She and Nola hit it off right away.

By the sixth arrival, Nola began to realize that everyone who had arrived so far seemed to be a lot like her. Many of them were suicidal and all of them had very difficult lives. They all complained that the real world had been dragging them down. Many expressed an interest in staying in Kafka, when they learned that everything that ever meant anything to them was here. Nola stressed to them that Earth needed them and they all eventually agreed, saying how much better they felt knowing that Kafka existed.

The Creators stopped coming early the next morning. Nola took count. There were six women, four men and two children. One of the children was confined to a wheelchair. They seemed to come from all walks of life and were of different races. Some of them did not speak English, but Nola easily took care of that by spelling them.

Nola wondered why there weren't more children here. Children surely had the greatest imaginations. Perhaps it was because the longer one lived, the more pain was endured, and the more the person needed his or her dreams. This thought put in perspective the amount of abuse the two children must have suffered to cling so tightly to their dreams.

When things seemed to be taking shape, Nola transported Drake and his warriors to the enclosure. Drake was happy to be back by her side. He informed her that almost every Fren left in the cliffs was now netted and there had been no escapes.

Mich and Tina worked with Drake and his warriors on a plan while Nola tended to their guests, making them comfortable and answering questions, which were now increasingly practical rather than perplexed. The new Creators were taking hold of the situation, and however crazy or hopeless they had been on Earth, they were emerging as the powerful figures they were in this realm. Some were practicing small acts of Creation, getting the technique straight. But there were so many miscues that it was clear that some instruction would be needed.

"We must put the barrier down in order to deal with the Fren,"

Mich said. "You can be sure that they are in the vicinity. As soon as we put it down, they will try to attack us."

"That ain't good," Tina said. "I know, from experience, that it's hard to focus on anything else while you're tryin' to convert a Fren. I prob'ly wouldn't be able to fight 'em and convert 'em at the same time. We can't net 'em all. If we tried, they'd keep us busy throwing nets, while one of 'em snuck up behind."

"I will have my wormsch guard you," Drake suggested.

"But there are only fifteen of you. Some of you are still weak from our last encounter with the Fren, and the new worms are still very slow. We'll need some help."

It was then that heads turned in the direction of the netted Fren. They were Fren no longer. They had snapped the net, not by strength, but by growth.

The Creators crowded into one corner, pressed there by the huge dragons that thrashed about. One was red and gold, one green and gold, and three more were blue and silver. Each one had a set of eight transparent wings, six armored legs and huge multifaceted eyes, much like the dragonflies of Earth. They seemed to be Kafka's literal translation.

They growled and hissed at one another in the confusion because of the sudden lack of room. One dragon's foot was on another's tail and yet another's slender nose poked another's eye. Scales rasped against scales, wings buzzed and nostrils gurgled forth slender flames.

"Who converted them?" yelled Mich.

"It was the children! They wanted to practice!" Nola yelled.

One of the dragons laid its heavy, claw-covered foot too close to them and they screamed in terror. It was then that a dragon took notice of them. It lifted its head high and gave a strange honk. The other dragons immediately took note of the morsels at their feet.

Both Nola and Tina went into action. Nola expanded the enclosure to give the inexperienced Creators more room to get out of the way while Tina threw up a wall in front of the them. But that wasn't enough. Though there now was more room, Tina's walls were not magical and the dragons simply knocked them over.

One of the dragons opened its mouth to pick up a child. The little girl screamed and ducked as the dragon's yellow tooth caught in her belt loop. It lifted her high into the air and was about to crunch her to bits.

A bolt of lightning shot down from the sky and landed at the dragon's feet with a loud crack. Everyone paused, staring—dragons, worms and people alike.

A dark-skinned woman with silver-gray wings descended gently into the enclosure. Nola recognized her as the Volant.

"Listen to me, creatures of air, your lives are in danger unless you help the ones you seek to eat."

"Why should we help them? Do you ever help us?" asked the dragon. "Why do we turn into such vile creatures and you not help us, our mother? Tell me why I should not avenge myself, and do tell why I should listen to you? Tell me."

Ventus stifled her ire. She was well aware how rude dragons were. "Behold, the Kahh."

She raised the crescent-shaped iron object high so that all could see it. The effect was immediate. All the dragons froze, staring as if hypnotized. "The medal of honor," the spokes-dragon breathed. "We are yours, O great goddess!"

"You know what to do," the Volant replied.

The dragons set the girl free, apologized and vowed to help. They and the worms would do their best to guard the Creators while they captured and converted Fren. All of the Fren would not be there, but the ones that came would be going for blood. Nola, meanwhile, would need special attention, as it was up to her to destroy the dam.

The Volant departed with best wishes to the Creators. She wanted nothing to do with the ensuing war.

After she had gone, the red and gold dragon that had spoken earlier introduced himself as Z. His proper name was too difficult to pronounce. "Please, human sister, when shall we ignite our fires on the backsides of the Fren?"

"There will be no injury to the Fren," Nola replied.

Z curled his lips with displeasure. "Why not? Do they not deserve it for what they have done? Please explain."

"Of course, Z. Spirit will fill you in on the details. While he does that, a feast will be prepared and healing spice distributed. All of us must be fully charged for tomorrow morning. That is when I will conjure us to the dam. The Fren will be waiting, no doubt, and we will need all of your best efforts. I would like to request that you stay by my side, Z."

"Yes, human sister. It would be my humble honor."

While Spirit filled in the dragon, Nola began creating meals for the huge creatures. They couldn't be expected to perform well on empty stomachs, and it was best to provide no temptation.

Tina worked with the twelve Creators, helping them practice. Most of them were amazed by what they could do. Joelle fainted. The only ones who acted as if this Creation business were routine, at first, were the children and Newton. Newton seemed quite at home and in fact was doing very well. "Why can't we just Create a bunch more dragonflies or something?" he asked Tina. "That way we don't have to worry about it."

"That's a good question, but the answer's not so simple," Tina replied. "The dream creatures that become real here don't last too long. It's easy to create things that aren't living, like food and houses and stuff, 'cause they don't got no feelings, no lives to live. People and creatures have to be believed in for a long time in order to make 'em real."

Newton still looked confused.

"Take Nola and Mich, for example. Nola knows everything there is to know about Mich, because she made him. She believed in him for lots of years, makin' him real. She gave him a sense of humor, and a sense of loyalty, and a big dollop of naivete, and she gave him her love. Only then did he become real. See, if you created a creature in one day, it would die. It wouldn't have a soul, no life. Even though Kafka is a dreamland, these people have souls. I know." She smiled.

"I understand. So we are forced to use the resources that we have left, which aren't many. But how is it there are demons and such? Why would a person want to create a horror like that?"

"Sometimes people can make their darkest fears real, when they don't face 'em. The more you hide from 'em, the more you get to know about 'em and the more they bug you. I never learned to face my demons. But they all have a place here, good or bad. You understand now?"

"Yup." Newton nodded his head.

"Well, keep practicing." She addressed the rest of the group. "I'm sorry you all don't have Fren to practice on, but it'd be too dangerous to find any. I think when it comes time to convert them, you all will do fine."

The new Creators practiced until noon, when they snacked on lu-cream pastries. They practiced even more when they finished and by the time Nola's feast was ready, all of them felt confident that Kafka would be saved. The morale was high and things finally seemed to be turning in their favor, though they would have much work to do. The possibility was great that lives would be lost.

They feasted on roast beef, mashed potatoes, parsnips, corn-bread, sweet peas and soda pop. Everything was sprinkled with heal-ing spice and everyone loved it. They gobbled the steaming food with relish, savoring each bite.

When the meal was over, everyone felt very healthy and very full. When darkness fell, they discussed the next day among themselves, and the new Creators had their first experience with sleepless sleep. Eventually, everyone fell silent.

Nola stared up into the midnight, her eyes reflecting the stars as the clouds drifted between them. Her heart was sad. She knew it was best to put aside her worries until it was time for them, yet she could not. She wondered what she would do with the stones. Should she use them and lose her chance to return here? If she did use them, whom would she choose to take back? She wished desperately that she could take both Mich and Spirit with her.

She shook her head in the darkness, as the looming war filled her mind and mingled with her other thoughts. The stars in her view began to blur. She blinked away her tears, turned over and closed her eyes. She was worried.

She felt Mich's consoling hand on her shoulder, squeezing gently. Somehow, this night, it did not comfort her. She pulled her knees in close to her chin and forced herself into repose.

25

DAM

That night, as Nola's mind wandered aimlessly, something strange happened. An idea came to her, and she suddenly knew exactly what to do. She cracked a smile as the sun began to rise.

Breakfast was nervous and rushed. Joseph could not even hold his meal down. Perhaps that had something to do with the fact that he had not brought any drugs with him, and he was going through withdrawal symptoms.

"Create some," Tina suggested wryly.

He was astonished. "Would that work?" Without waiting for an answer, he tried it, and soon was back on an even keel.

"But don't overdo it," Tina said. "I don't care how you come by that stuff, it's bad for you."

"For sure," he agreed. "I'll see what I can do about it when the crisis is over and I have time to sort things out. Maybe I can Create things for treatment."

Nola, overhearing the dialogue, wished she could do the same to solve her own problem. But she didn't see how.

Then Nola gathered everyone close and held her cross in her hand. Her mind felt strained. She concentrated, but it was as if she were trying to take a picture of the group and could not fit them all in. If she backed up too far, the picture would not focus.

"I can't do it," she announced. "Not all of us."

It seems in our best interest that some of us should find another way to get to the dam, Spirit thought.

"I agree." She turned to the dragons. "Z, do you think your entourage could fly there?"

"Yes, they can fly. I shall stay near you here, human sister."

"All right, then. Please have your dragons back off while I conjure us. When we get there, I will build another enclosure and wait for them to arrive."

Z honked and the dragons moved away. Nola closed her eyes. This time, everyone fit into the picture, and after the flash went off they were gone. She opened her eyes.

The dam was before them. So were thousands of Fren. They were everywhere, like a black swarm of killer spiders. Each one of them carried a lightning-jag razor that glinted red in the morning sun. Some of them stood or sat on top of the dam. A thick cloud of them surrounded it. Most of them were scattered about, but began to concentrate more when they realized that the Creators had arrived.

From somewhere amid the writhing throng came a grating voice. It was Reility's. Apparently he had escaped the nets, which really was not surprising. "I told you, you would fail, and you will!" He turned to his minions. "Kill them!"

Z wrapped his armored body around Nola while she began to clothe herself in armor. Why hadn't she thought of this detail before coming here? They should have arrived ready for action, instead of giving the Fren time to organize. The other Creators stood scattered and did the same, encasing themselves in metal.

The Fren wasted no time in attacking. All of them came at once. Nola's heart sank. The masses of Fren were just too much! She knew that it would take only a few moments until the Creators were washed away in a wave of evil, shattered dreams.

The Creators were busy throwing nets and building walls. This seemed to slow the Fren a little, yet it was ineffective in stopping them. Nola realized, belatedly, that she was no general; she hadn't planned for this battle at all. She had figured she just needed to get here and do the job. She would know better next time, if there was ever a next time, if she survived this mess.

Here and there, a Fren would drop to its knees as a Creator recognized and converted it. The Fren would ignore the newly recovered Kafkians, as if they were not alive, and focused on killing the humans. Until the converts joined forces with Nola; then all were fair game.

The worms fought bravely. Their bodies were being cut to ribbons. There were now almost fifty of them and they were weakening rapidly.

Nola screamed when she saw the boy in the wheelchair lose his arm to a Fren that had sneaked up on him.

"Z! Let go of me!" she screamed, struggling.

Z loosened his coils and she clambered over his back, landing with a thud on the ashy ground. She ran over to the boy. He was screaming hysterically and his blood was pouring from his severed shoulder.

She tried not to lose her head. The sight of the blood made her wretch, while all around her there were screams of terror and the sounds of evil beginning to overcome good. Soon, if something was not done, they would lose.

In a moment, Z was beside her. He nudged away a Fren who struck at Nola. The Fren tried to cut Z, but the razor did no good on his scales.

Nola held back another wretch as she picked up the boy's arm and held it to his shoulder. The boy screamed again and Nola put some healing spice on his tongue. He swallowed, and his arm healed instantly. The boy stared, astonished, as his pain faded. He flexed the arm, wiggling the fingers. "Gee. That's neat!"

Nola looked around again. Two Creators were now fleeing in

panic. They were hemmed in by Fren who were chasing them with clubs and razors. The razors did not do much damage, but the clubs tended to dent the armor and even break pieces off.

Nola knew that they could not go on this way. Something had to be done right now, or they would all be overcome.

She felt her anger surging forth. Her sadness, happiness, confusion and fright were slowly being eaten by her anger until she was filled with it. She used it as a tool to help energize her next creation. Z stood by her, protecting her while she concentrated.

She threw her arms into the air, concentrating on her hands and forcing the anger and energy outward and upward. She used every emotion she could find, and when she felt drained, she dropped her hands.

For a moment, nothing happened. Then, she looked up, because the sky was momentarily darkening. A gigantic net was floating down.

"Look above!" Z roared. *"Get out of the way!"*

The Creators looked up. So did some of the Fren. Both Fren and Creators ran, scattering like drops of rain in a calm pond, spreading out.

The metal net began shooting out cables as it neared the ground. It covered at least half of the mobbing Fren. But it covered some of the Creators too. Now, again way too late, she remembered how she had promised to build an enclosure around their group so that the Fren couldn't reach them. She had forgotten, being absorbed by the immediate challenge of so many Fren.

"Face it, Nola," she muttered to herself. "You're much better at being a fouled-up, suicidal girl than a general."

Her energy spent, Nola collapsed, exhausted. With only a thousand or so Fren captured, there still were a great number. Still far too many to deal with. She cried as she watched her friends fight a losing battle. This time, she was completely useless. She couldn't even stand up. If her friends were overwhelmed, she could not conjure them away. She shouldn't have let anger take her like that.

Z's dragons appeared in the sky above, neither landing nor flying away. They stared down, unsure what to do. It was quite obvious that the humans were being overtaken. They could not fire on the Fren and knew that they could do nothing to help. After a few minutes of hovering, the dragons flew off, not looking back.

"Cowards!" called Z.

Z coiled around Nola again, realizing that she was helpless. Even her imagination seemed to have run out. She had no more good ploys to suggest.

It was Tina who finally came up with the solution. "Everyone!" she shouted. "Balloons! Make balloons!"

Many of the Creators looked confused, until Joelle created a huge hot-air balloon. It was red and yellow and was powered by a propane furnace. She helped the chairbound boy into it and climbed in after. She released a couple of sand bags and lifted into the air. A few Fren clung to the basket. The boy leaned out over the side and used a confiscated club to bash them off before they got too high.

By this time, the others were getting into their own. Newton took along Curbie and Curbia, while Lucina took Drake. The other Creators were saving themselves from the disaster Nola's folly had made. All they had to do was discover how to use their power effectively.

A balloon appeared before Nola, though not one of her own making. Someone had made it for her. Nola tried to find the strength to climb in, but could not.

Mich saw her failing effort. He pushed the Fren off his legs with the hilt of his sword and ran over. He picked her up gently and placed her inside the basket. He climbed in after her and fired up the balloon. Z took to the sky as well.

Nola was relieved that not only were they now safe, the Fren did not retreat. The Fren became angrier and began shouting and jumping up and down. Nola had to smile: the Fren were in a frenzy, appropriately. The Fren were frenetic. So they were being stupid, just as Nola had been before.

The Creators wasted not a second in containing the rest of the Fren. The nets that fell could hold only nine or ten at the most, so work was slow.

Nola lay back in the basket, knowing that the best way to recharge her mental energy was to rest. Mich promised to rouse her when the work was done.

She appreciated him being there. He stayed close, humming a strange yet lulling tune.

The other Creators, feeling bad for her, let her rest. The Fren would escape after a while, but the Creators would simply drop more nets, keeping them under control and contained until she had rested. The huge net that Nola had dropped remained intact, being of a magical nature.

It was four hours later, the sun high in the ksy, before Nola rose and had a look around. The other balloons floated near, each of them holding a smiling person. It made her feel better, knowing that she had so many people rooting for her.

Spirit's thought came to her. *You have been preparing for this. Are you ready to begin?*

"Yes. I hope everyone else is." She sighed. Then, to the Creators: "Let's land the balloons and start the conversions."

The colorful balloons began floating downward, their baskets touching ground one by one. Finally, everyone was down and the work began.

Newton went first, being the most eager. As the first Fren was converted, the others joined in. Their minds searched over the hordes of Fren, looking for something familiar.

Nola reached out and took Joseph's hand. She found herself sharing his mind. He was seeing something that he did not recognize, but Nola did. She in turn saw something that he recognized. As each Fren was recognized, it was separated from the horde and re-netted. They traded their mind's images and a happy nymph and a griffin emerged from the nets, as Nola released them.

"Join hands!" Nola said. "It helps you see!"

Mich stood out of the way with the worms, dragon and Dalmatians. The Creators moved close, standing in a tight circle, eyes shut, hands clasped. The group of them seemed almost to radiate with the power of thought.

Fren began disappearing from the horde and reappearing under nets all around the group. Creatures were appearing; they seemed as if they were waking from a nightmare. They all were very happy when freed and many of them stood near the Creators, admiring them as if they were movie stars.

The Creators continued casting their minds across the land before them. The tide of Fren had been turned. Now there were more Kafkians than Fren.

Mich called out when he recognized someone. The old woman he called Madrid had a funny red Afro and really long fingernails.

Lucina found the Centicores. They stood beside her, pawing the black ground.

There were very few Fren left when Nola saw someone she recognized, vaguely. He was older and had graying brown hair. He came more into focus and then was gone. She opened her eyes. The man stood before her. He was wearing lavish robes of red, yellow and gold. He wore a crown slightly askew on his brow.

"Father!" Mich shouted from behind her.

She turned and saw Mich heading toward the man. He reached out, and the two embraced warmly. When they broke, Nola could see that this man was indeed Mich's father, and Kafka's king. He looked exactly as she remembered him. Noble, yet warm and friendly.

She had Created him to help Mich seem more real to her. He had needed a family. She and her own father had never had a real relationship. So she had Created the king in the image of the father she wished she had.

She turned her attention back to the hundred or so remaining Fren. The other Creators seemed entirely comfortable with the conversions and were working much faster, though some of them were showing signs of exhaustion. Nola herself had converted only a hundred or so, while the others converted two, three or four hundred apiece.

The fields surrounding the River of Thought began to clear out as creatures went in search of their homes.

She could only "see" two more Kafkians, consisting of a mermaid and a small dapple-brown unicorn.

The work was tiring. It took a lot of concentration and a lot of faith to restore her belief in her crushed dreams.

A few more moments and all of the Fren had been converted. Everyone was beyond relief, and many stood with their Creations, talking, hugging and regaining lost memories. Nola thought the scene was very touching.

Tina was talking with King Kras and Drake. Newton was petting a creature that was half bear and half cat. Lucina was hugging a beautiful woman who acted very motherly toward her. Joelle was sitting with a magnificent white wolf with big gray eyes.

Nola was glad to see all of her friends so happy. Especially Mich, whom she loved so much. But that thought reminded her that she had not yet decided what to do about that situation. She still saw no way through that would not leave her and either Mich or Spirit miserable in some way.

Spirit approached Nola as she watched Mich and the king. Mich looked up a moment, said something to his father and walked over to them. He enfolded her in his arms.

"Thank you, Nola. Kafka would have died, and my father too. I love you."

Nola touched his chin with a finger. "I love you too," she said, smiling, feeling the words in her soul as she spoke them. She turned to Spirit. "This is so wonderful," she said to him.

Yes, he thought, nuzzling her outstretched hand. *I knew you had the strength.* He paused. *Now, it is time for you to decide.*

Nola flinched visibly. So soon! She must decide between her true love and her heart-friend. How could she do that? She loved them both.

She took off her cross and pried the stone from its setting. She held the twin stones in her palm, watching the stars move across their surface, praying for a solution. Then she remembered something else, almost with relief. "The dam! I still have to destroy the dam." Until that was done, her mission here wasn't over, and she didn't have to make her choice.

Curbie trotted up to them, urgency in his voice. "There is something amiss, you see? Something's not right."

"What could be wrong?" Mich asked. "Every Fren is back to normal and everyone's happy. Nola is about to destroy the dam, so that the River of Thought will flow freely once more, and never again will Kafka suffer."

Not so, Heat broke in. *I smell something too. It smells like anger.*

Spirit lifted his nose to the breeze. He nodded agreement and began stepping nervously backward. His eyes fixed on a point behind Nola. She instinctively turned.

Reility was striding toward her. The one Fren they hadn't accounted for—the worst one. Possibly worse than all the others together. How could she have forgotten about him? "Idiot!" she cursed herself.

The Fren king was some distance away and seemed to be moving very slowly, as if weak. He carried a crooked stick in his fist. His dead eyes fixed on Nola's. "I want those stones, you whore!"

"You got it wrong!" Tina yelled. "She's not the whore. *You* are!"

"Tina!" Nola said. "This is between him and me. Have faith in me." But she sounded unsure, even to herself.

She was indeed unsure. But she had to do something. She threw a net over him. He waved the stick over his head and it caught the net, pushing it away. He didn't even lose step. His evident confidence rattled her further.

He was getting a little too close. She backed up a few steps and threw a bigger net. He brushed it aside again and left it lying on the ground.

Mich drew his sword and stepped in front of her.

"No, Mich," she said pleadingly. "You will get hurt!"

"But he's going to kill you!"

"No, no. It's okay. Please, Mich—please let me handle this!" Mich grudgingly sheathed his sword and stepped out of the way.

She combed her brain, trying to think of a solution, and at the same time trying to fathom how Reility was able to brush her nets away. He shouldn't be able to affect their magic.

She tried once more. This time, she threw a load of cement blocks. They fell on top of him. She waited a moment for something to happen. She had seen too many horror movies. This was the part where she would turn her back and he would jump up from the pile of bricks and cut her throat. But nothing happened.

She approached the pile of rubble. The crumbled bricks did not move, or give any indication that he still lived. She stared a moment. Slowly, she stretched out a hand and touched one of the bricks. Still nothing happened. She flipped one of the bricks off the pile. Nothing. She reached down with both hands.

A nasty, clawed hand reached up and grasped one of hers. "You see, you inferior creature, I have absorbed your worst without resistance, and been unfazed," he said. "Now you know you can't hurt me. But I can hurt you."

Nola screamed with terror and tried to pull away. She could not. She tried to pry the dark fingers off her wrist, only to have her free hand captured as well. Reility's ugly head burst through the shattered pieces of cement and he stared right into her eyes.

Something in the way he looked at her chilled her to the marrow. Something was so familiar about the way he stared right through her, as if she were nothing more than a bug to be squashed. There was a quality she couldn't quite grasp. What was it? There was so much evil in that face!

He squeezed her wrists until she was forced to open her hands. When he saw the shining stones, his eyes got blacker (if that was possible) and he snatched the stones from her flaccid hands.

Nola was still staring at his eyes. There was something there that she knew and had known for a long time. Her eyes were locked, unblinking, on his, unable to look elsewhere and unable to make a move. For some reason, she was frozen with fear, like a bird before a python.

He released her and laughed, half to himself. One of the worm warriors approached and attempted to swallow Reility. Dumb move. Reility chopped the creature into a thousand bits before it could engulf him. The tiny pieces lay quivering, unable to reconstruct.

"Don't just stand there, Nola! Do something!" Tina shouted. Her voice seemed very distant, and not worth noticing. Nola just stood and stared, frozen.

Reility stepped closer to the trickle of water that was the River of Thought. He kneeled by the bank. He pressed the twin stones together, back to back. The stars on the stones' surfaces glowed brightly, then dimmed again, and disappeared completely. The stones became one. It looked very much like a bed spell, with lightning swirling and cracking in its center.

"You see, you've failed, Nola. You'll always fail! I know! I know you. You know me as well!" he cried as he drowned the stone in the River of Thought.

There was a loud boom and rays of fine light were shooting up from the water. Reility's face was covered with a crooked smile and his dark skin was afire with beams of white light. When he lifted out the stone, all that Nola could see was a ball of light, as if he were holding a star in his palm. The ball of light slowly dimmed. However, its light was diffusing into Reility's body, traveling up his arm, across his evil face, down his legs to his gnarled toes. The light engulfed him, making his body invisible inside a brilliant shell. The light quickly flashed, making the whole area seem as if there were four suns lighting the day. Then the light was gone and everyone stood in awe, mouths agape.

Nola stared in disbelief at Reality. He was now a human man, taller than she. Worse, he was a human whom she recognized. His stocky body radiated malice; his dark hair, eyes and mustache added to the effect.

Nola stood frozen as before, her hand over her mouth. She felt Mich begin shaking her shoulders. He had been speaking to her, but she had not heard.

"Nola! What's wrong with you?"

Nola started shaking. "It's *him*. It's John," she said with a quivering voice. "My nemesis on Earth."

Mich had no idea who he was, but obviously, she knew him well and feared him.

Tina strode up to John. "How in hell did you get here?"

"I came for Nola."

"What do you want with her?"

"I want her dreams."

"Why?" she demanded.

"She left me to come here. She left me for someone else. Now she's going to be really sorry."

Mich now realized who the man was. He was furious and a desire to do him in overwhelmed him.

Nola created a sword and pointed it at John. "Not if I can help it," she said, still trembling. "You're real now. I can hurt you."

He looked in her direction and paid no attention to the sword that was shakingly pointed at his heart. "Hurt me, Nola? Ha! You're the most spineless bitch I've ever known."

He pushed away the sword with a wave of his arm. He took a few steps toward her. She took a few steps back.

Mich placed himself between Nola and John.

"No!" Nola said. "This is between him and me. He'll kill you! Please, don't get in the way!"

Mich did not move back, but instead stepped forward aggressively. John drew back and his right fist shot out and hit Mich squarely on the cheek. The blow made a sickening crack and Mich fell to the ground.

"Oh, no, Mich!" Nola cried. She looked back at John. Her eyes reflected more terror than she'd ever felt and they filled with tears. John was the only person or thing that she truly feared. She feared him more than death itself.

John grinned. He seemed satisfied with Nola's tears. She knew he was pleased. He was always pleased when she was in pain. She wondered how he got here.

Nola was not the only one whom he hurt by hurting Mich. Heat felt the sting of the blow in his own face. He galloped up and reared, his chrome hooves slashing at the man. John waved his hand and Heat was gone. A Fren was in his place.

"Oh, Lord, no!" Tina cried. "Heat!"

John laughed again. "Failure," he said, advancing on Nola. She retreated.

Soon her back was pressed against the dam and she could go no farther.

John came close and stopped. "Don't you see, Nola? You are nothing. You thought you had found your true love? You didn't. You thought you could hide in your dreams? You can't. I'm the only one who ever cared about you. I knew you were a failure, but I thought you had potential. I was wrong. You are nothing."

He turned his back on her and took a few steps, then turned back. "You get it? Now I am going to torture your dreams, just as I did your life. You know what I'm going to do first? I'm going to convert your friend Spirit. Once I convert him, you won't be able to change him back!"

Nola sank down, closing her eyes. Her tears fell in her lap. "Please, no," she mumbled. "Please don't do that."

She felt Spirit's thoughts in her mind. With them came a warm feeling, unlike any other she'd felt from him. There were no words forming in her mind, only a spot of heat. It was the heat of anger. It gave her strength.

She felt a hand grasp hers. She dared not open her eyes. It was not John's hand; it was soft and firm. She squeezed it and she felt another mind enter hers, bringing with it another warm spot. This time she not only felt anger, but she began to lose fear and to gain strength.

Another mind joined hers, then another, and another. She felt the minds of the Creators in tune with hers. She felt their powers and she knew what she had to do. She had to destroy the dam. Right now. That would keep John from converting Kafka.

She gathered as much strength as she could before it began to overwhelm her. She concentrated, and an image of the dam came into her mind, its invisible wall made visible in her mind's eye. The strength she gathered appeared before it in the form of a hammer.

She took hold of the handle. She could feel the hands of the Creators, in her mind, also grasping the hammer. They lifted it, and swung it forward.

As one, they began smashing the death mirror with all their might. They pounded relentlessly, Nola guiding them.

The mirror first showed cracks. Colored water began seeping through. The hammer still pounded. Then as the effort increased, the dam shattered and crumbled. Beyond it, Nola could see what looked like a sewer pipe with bars blocking it. She could look only for a second.

Every Creator was jolted out of the trance as a roar filled the air. The roar of rushing water.

"No!" John shouted, suddenly aware of what had been going on in their linked minds. *"No! You will fail, fail!"*

Nola opened her eyes. "I have already succeeded," she informed him. "Listen to the flow."

Now he heard what he least wished to. The freed rushing water of the River of Thought. "AAAAAH!" he screamed.

The torrent of human dreams came flowing across the broken dam. The first surge of water captured John and he screamed again, as if the water were acid. He was swept away.

Nola suddenly felt herself choking. There was a tightness at her shirt collar. She was being lifted off the ground, her feet dangling high in the air. The ground moved beneath her as she was carried away.

26
DECISION

Moments later she was put down on a rise. Tina and Mich were there.

It was Spirit who had carried her by her shirt to the hilltop. She looked at the swollen torrent of dreams and could see no sign of John. Neither could she see the other Creators.

They were washed away in the initial break, Spirit informed her.

Nola gasped, horrified.

No, do not worry, my dear friend, they will only be sent home. They will be fine. A spell protects them from arriving in any dangerous situation, such as deep nonmagical water.

She watched the river rise above its old banks, carrying sticks and ash along in the current. Around the edges of the water, she thought she could see grass beginning to sprout.

The relief, when it came, was total and complete. She sighed aloud and held Mich's hand.

"Do you think it's over?" he asked.

"I'm certain it is. For now, anyway. I wish I knew how John got here."

"Do you think he's a Creator?" Tina asked. "Maybe he found a bed spell."

Nola thought about that. "I guess it could be. Where is there a rule that says a Creator has to be good? He did disappear before I came here, and I could not find him. I didn't place the bed spells until after he got here. How do you explain that?"

I believe, Spirit thought, *that he was indeed a Creator. Perhaps he is the source of the crushed dreams. He may have destroyed so many in his lifetime that he became the exact opposite of a Creator: A Destroyer. I believe that Reility simply chose to take the form of John. Now he is* John. *The John you knew has been taken over. I assume it was not a difficult task for Reility. Perhaps he knew your biggest fear. Reility took over John's body, knowing your fears.*

Nola shook her head. "I don't think he is dead. If he comes across another bed spell, who knows what might happen? I've got to go home and see if I can find the rest."

"First," Mich said, with a note of sadness in his voice, "will you come to the castle for dinner?"

Nola smiled weakly at him. "Of course." She squeezed his hand. "I wish I had a dreamstone to help me conjure us there. It'll be quite a long walk. Say, what happened to Heat?" she asked, looking around.

"He was converted, then washed away in the river," Mich said. "I thought you knew that. He's dead."

"That's awful!" Then her expression turned to a sly smile. "I know John doesn't think he'd get away with that! It doesn't matter if he was washed away. He can't take away my dreams, no matter how hard he tries! I still believe in Heat."

With her words, the river, at the foot of the hill, boiled and sputtered as if there were a spring beneath it about to erupt. A splendid white unisus plunged into the sky from the surging waters. It was Heat, reborn.

He flew directly to the hilltop and stood next to Mich. Mich embraced him. "I thought you had died in that river!"

As long as Nola believes in us, we can never die, Heat replied, winking his silver orb at Nola.

Tina startled Heat by grabbing a handful of his mane. She climbed aboard. "I missed you too, horsey!"

He stomped his foot, but he took the insult in stride. He knew she liked him.

Mich mounted up and so did Nola.

They reached the castle in four days. They were greeted at the gate by the king and a jumping-for-joy basilisk named Snort.

When night matured into midnight, dinner was served by a roaring fire and the joyful, reuniting conversations were changed to one that was more solemn.

"So, I suppose you must return home?" King Edward asked.

"Yes, Your Highness," said Nola, "I have to find the other spells before he does."

"I'll help you," Tina said.

Nola looked at her. "You want to return to Earth?"

"It does make sense, unfortunately. But I wish I could visit here, often and long. Maybe there's a dream man here for me too." Her crude language seemed to have faded.

The king looked at her appraisingly. The rigors of the campaign were over, and she was now garbed almost in the manner of a princess, her figure showing to full advantage. Dreamstones sparkled in her hair. "I suspect that your chances are good." Then he turned to Nola. "You will be greatly missed here. I am indebted to you, for everything. Is there anything you need from me?"

"Thank you, no." She inclined her head.

Nola suddenly remembered something. She recalled several nights before, and how she had puzzled over her decision to take Mich or Spirit to Earth and make one of them real. She suddenly remembered the thought that had made her smile that night, before she drifted away.

She stood and curtsied to the king. "We must be leaving," she said. "If you don't mind, I'd like to have a few moments with my friends, to say good-bye." She smiled warmly.

This was the moment Mich and Spirit had been dreading. The two wanted to stay with her. How could they say good-bye?

Mich didn't want to deal with her leaving. It hurt to even think of living without her. He wanted to share his life with her and share in hers. They had both been dreaming of finding each other. Now they had, yet their love was in jeopardy. He supposed he had no choice in the matter. Nola had to go home and keep John from finding the bed spells. Yet without her dreamstone, she could never return to Kafka. Neither could her pretty friend, Tina, despite her talk of frequent visits.

Spirit was feeling the same way. He knew that he could always see her when she dreamed, yet that was not to be compared with the joy of physical contact and of real being.

The king offered Tina his arm, and they departed the dining room, leaving the three of them alone. Nola sat down in a chair near the glowing fire, smiling all the while.

"I guess it's time to say good-bye," Mich began. "I don't know what to say. I want to get on my knees and beg you to stay, yet I respect the fact that you must return home. I wish you well, Nola. You will be taking my heart and soul with you. I hope you can return them to me one day. I wish I could say I love you and have you know how I feel right now. To say I love you is nothing compared to what I feel. Good-bye, my love."

Mich touched her cheek and wiped a tear away from his own. Nola still smiled. He wondered why.

"Is there anything you would like to tell me, Esprit?" Nola asked of Spirit.

I must say only this: I will always be here for you, and remember, we share pain as well as joy, so keep yourself happy. Good-bye, my heart-friend.

Nola still smiled. "So, that was very nice."

Mich began to get a little annoyed. She wasn't acting as if she would miss them at all. Had a demon gotten into her hair again? "What's going on, Nola? Why are you smiling like that?"

"I've got a going-away gift for both of you that I think will ease the pain." She paused and cleared her throat. "I found something out one night. The stones that Reility used to make himself real could perform magic, yet they were not magic themselves."

May I ask what is your point?

"Only this. I found I could do a small additional Creation that I thought you would like."

We would like—in your absence? Spirit inquired dubiously.

Nola looked down into her lap. Her hands rested there, clenched tightly shut. Slowly she uncurled her fingers. Inside each hand was a pair of light blue stones with stars of light on their surfaces. Just like the pair that Reility had used to become real.

AUTHORS' NOTES

PIERS ANTHONY

You may have read before about the collection of young folk, mostly female, I named Ligeia. They have inhabited my Author's Notes since the first Ligeia in 1986, in *Wielding a Red Sword*. As I heard from more of them, typically (but by no means limited to) fourteen-year-old girls, I made a composite character for the Mode series, calling her Colene. I have not knowingly met any of the ones I corresponded with, but I feel I know them. I am not of that persuasion myself, but that gives me a notion of what they suffer. As I like to put it, it is as if I stand at the verge of Hell, while they stand somewhat closer to the fire, and there is so little I can do.

Now one of those Ligeias is speaking for herself, in the form of this novel: Julie. She was mentioned by name in the Author's Note for *If I Pay Thee Not in Gold*, and her decoration of the envelope for a letter inspired the three mermaids in *Harpy Thyme*. Now you have seen her fantasy, *Dream a Little Dream*. She sent me her emotionally precious Clechée cross, and I kept it as long as I was in doubt about her condition, but by the time this novel is published she should be wearing it again. An aspect of her mundane existence is in Nola, just as her dream existence is in Kafka.

Julie has the talent of lucid dreaming—that is, knowing and controlling one's dreams. This story took form gradually as she recorded those dreams. When it was ready, I took it over and reworked it into a formal novel. As with all of these collaborations, the story is the collaborator's; I merely do what is necessary to make it presentable, somewhat in the manner a stonecutter facets and polishes a raw gemstone.

But one thing is all hers: the illustration on the facing page that she drew for this volume. Seldom is the author allowed to show directly what the main characters look like: Nola and Spirit.

Now Julie's dreams are yours.

JULIE BRADY

This being my first author's note, I'm unsure what to say. I suppose I should start out saying something about myself. I'm twenty-seven years old at the time of this page being typed. I was born in Fort Ord, California, into a military family and spent most of my life moving from one place to another. Currently, I live in Maryland in a rural area, surrounded by cows and open fields—a big change from being surrounded by drug addicts and rapists in cities.

I'm sure that many of you loyal Piers Anthony fans saw this book and wondered who I was. Well, I'm no one of consequence, just a newcomer to the writer's world. I enjoyed writing this book, which, incidentally, was taken from a serial dream of mine over the course of a year or so. I used the serial dreams I had to escape the horrors of my life. In the middle of this book's making, Piers interrupted my normal dream pattern to inform me that I was going about writing the book the wrong way. In the dream he pointed out my mistakes and told me how to correct them. I sent the corrected version to him and was surprised to hear that it agreed with his dream-self!

At first, the idea of publishing my journal seemed crazy. I don't consider myself a writer nor could I ever hope to achieve what Piers has.

The main thing that appealed to me was to share what I had seen in my sleep with you. The idea of my dreams living in print thrills me no end and is as close as I may ever get to an achievement I could be proud of.

Since this is my first book and I lack a large amount of friends, I didn't get much help or advice. I don't have a long list of people to thank (unlike the lists you often see at the end of Piers's *Xanth* novels), but I do have a few.

First and most important, I'd like to thank Piers for his unconditional support and encouragement, without which I would not have been here to dream anything worth writing about. I'd also like to thank a friend who taught me most of what I needed to know to become a good person inside: thanks Mike Norvelle—I wish you the best in life! Next, I'd like to thank a coworker, Alfreda Jenkins, who came up with the name "Curbie" when I was stuck for a character's name. I should also give credit to the real people from whom I borrowed names or part-names for use in this novel: Wilma Roberts, Leona Joy Cooper and Lori Fox.

I'd like to thank my parents for constantly trying to get me to stop daydreaming and doodling during school. (Thankfully, reverse psychology was working against them!) Though I didn't have the best upbringing, I love them both very much. We all make mistakes that need forgiving.

Lastly, I'd like to thank everyone who bought a copy of this book. Hopefully, if you didn't love it, you at least hated it. In either case I feel proud to have raised an emotion in you, good or bad.

Dream a little dream /
FIC ANTHO   780977

Anthony, Piers.
WEST GEORGIA REGIONAL LIBRARY